Little Vanities

'A riveting tale of emotional infidelity, in which the reader's loyalty is constantly shifting. It had me hooked from the first page to the last. Gilmartin's wry observations on human behaviour are a joy. She understands that lust and betrayal are thrilling—when they happen to other people. I devoured this book'

Aingeala Flannery, author of _The Amusements_

'Wonderfully authentic, electrifying—there are dramas within dramas here and the unravelling is exhilarating when it comes'

Clare Chambers, author of _Small Pleasures_

'Messy, complicated, compelling, you will not be able to stop reading this story of the deepest of betrayals'

Emilie Pine, author of _Ruth & Pen_

'Gilmartin writes about relationships with great precision and insight. Her characters find themselves trapped by their life choices and reckoning with the cost of overturning them. This is a scrupulous and elegant novel about the realities of adulthood'

Kathleen MacMahon, author of _Nothing But Blue Sky_

'Acutely observed, beautifully written, compellingly readable, fizzing with insight and truthfulness, this is a wonderful novel'

Joseph O'Connor, author of _Star of the Sea_

Author Photo © Seamus Travers

SARAH GILMARTIN is an Irish writer and arts journalist. Her bestselling debut novel, *Dinner Party*, was shortlisted for an Irish Book Award and the Kate O'Brien Award. Her second novel, *Service*, was a *Washington Post* top books of summer and included in the *Irish Times* list of the best Irish fiction of the 21st century.

Little Vanities

Sarah Gilmartin

AN IMPRINT OF PUSHKIN PRESS

ONE
An imprint of Pushkin Press
Somerset House, Strand
London WC2R 1LA

First published by Pushkin Press in 2026

Hardback ISBN 13: 978-1-80533-803-1
Trade Paperback ISBN 13: 978-1-80533-809-3

A CIP catalogue record for this title is available from the British Library

The authorised representative in the EEA is eucomply OÜ,
Pärnu mnt. 139b-14, 11317, Tallinn, Estonia,
hello@eucompliancepartner.com, +33757690241

Designed and typeset by Tetragon, London
Printed and bound in the United Kingdom by Clays Ltd, Elcograf S.p.A.

Pushkin Press is committed to a sustainable future for our
business, our readers and our planet. This book is made from
paper from forests that support responsible forestry.

www.pushkinpress.com

1 3 5 7 9 8 6 4 2

Little Vanities

To Sunil

The old, old story—deceived by life

PHILIP ROTH

Contents

APRIL

ON A COOL WEEKEND MORNING thin fog lifted off the grand canal in Dublin to a fresh stain of blue pushing out across the sky. Still wet with dew, the yellowy bankside reeds held within them the movements of secret animals already at work. A lone swan glided eastwards, leaving in its wake a wide, triangular trail that disturbed the steady surface of the water, beneath which, barely a foot below, the canal bed was littered with bottles green and brown, broken and whole, glass and plastic, the unnatural, man-made artefacts from the long seasonless years of outdoor living in desperate times.

Dylan Turner strolled down the towpath to a nearby bench, took a seat on the damp wood to finish his coffee and wait for the off-licence to open. He had managed to walk all the way from his home in Terenure, just over half an hour, and was tiring. The bitter drink worked to revive him as pale sunlight wrinkled on and off in the shallow water. After a while he roused himself, made his way to the crossroads, then up South Circular Road. He felt full of the jaunting happiness of the night to come, the pleasure of having his two best friends over to the house for a game of cards.

In the offie he stocked up on Dutch Gold, a joke of sorts, but he knew they'd end up drinking it when everything else ran out. With effort he carried twelve cans to the counter, tried to engage the woman on the till, made some crack about how he couldn't believe they still manufactured the stuff, that he used to drink it in college—back in the noughties, like. She looked at him as if he was speaking in tongues, and perhaps he was, it felt that long since he'd been out in the world without assistance. He couldn't remember the rules of small talk, maybe it wasn't even called small talk unless you sort of knew the other person, which—he glanced at the woman again—he emphatically did not.

'Cash or card?' she said.

Dylan fumbled at the pocket of his tracksuit, straining to get the zip down his thigh. Eventually he produced a creased fifty and left it on the counter. She took the note reluctantly, smoothed it, gave him the change. Thanking her, he folded the twenty carefully in case she thought he was a rich douche with no regard for money. There had been a point in his life when he was undeniably wealthy, a magnificent moment, but he'd never felt comfortable flashing his cash, not like the Dublin lads who seemed born to sponsorship deals and luxury.

Something in the assistant's demeanour softened as she sat down on the stool, back to her magazine. Dylan put one four-pack in his rucksack and decided to carry the remaining two pannier-style. He was balanced. He felt able, free. With a cheerful goodbye to the woman he turned to leave. The automatic glass doors parted with an energetic whoosh.

Halfway up Harold's Cross Road his arms began to tense, a prickly twitch in his biceps that went from tightness to cramp just as the narrow triangular park came into view. In the distance the Dublin Mountains tinged purple against the edge of morning sky, distant and forbidding, the gentle peak of Kippure listing south. He tried to think through the pain. The park was only across the way and if he could make it there he could take a break on one of the benches near the entrance. Even as he had the thought, his legs began to shake. He stopped at a low wall beside a barber's and put the cans down. The weight of the rucksack was still too much. On the ground before he knew it, plonked on his behind, which was cold now, and possibly wet, something creeping across his tracksuit.

A woman getting out of a white Beamer locked her car and went quickly up the street. By the gates to the park young lads with matching haircuts were smoking. If he called to them they might help him. They might not. His mind was busy with disappointment. All week he'd been doing his strength routine at home, feeling confident as the days passed and his body didn't give out, certain he would manage a round trip to the offie. He thought forward to this evening, wondered if he'd be able for it. As the first drops of an imminently heavy rain landed in thick specks on his face, he slipped the rucksack off his shoulders then pushed himself up to sit on the wall.

Taking out his phone to call Rachel, he hesitated before pressing her name, as if the memory of last night's fight had ingrained itself in his fingertips. A fat splotch of water hit the screen, another landing on his head. After a few breaths he was able to quash the small bit of manhood that was still persistently alive within him, that clung on when so much else had been stripped away, and make the call.

His wife answered on the third ring. 'What's happened?'

'Nothing. Can you pick me up?' He told her where he was.

'I knew it was too much. Why didn't you go to the near one? Or why didn't you let—'

'Rachel,' he said. 'Please.'

A short while later she pulled up across the road in the Citroën, a boxy purple minivan she'd managed to talk him into back when she was pregnant, when he wanted to give her everything she asked for, and more. Now it seemed to represent all the things that had gone wrong in his life, that everywhere he looked there were people driving around in their delightfully dull vehicles, when he was saddled with—no, when he had chosen for himself—a car the colour of a television dinosaur. An extra grand for the pleasure of it, he remembered the smirk on the salesguy's face.

Rachel put on the hazards, rolled down the window and waved. She went to get out, but he shook his head. He already had the rucksack on, picked up the remaining cans, walked easily to the car. That was the brutal thing about the state he was in, the way it constantly tricked him, undermining whatever reality he thought he was in, undermining the very idea of reality compared to the life he had before. But Rachel was watching him. He shifted to one leg, moved a little slower for the final steps.

Leah was in the back, strapped into a booster. She palmed the rain-streaked window and shouted his name.

'Eggs!' she said, when he opened the door. 'I hate slimy eggs, Daddy.'

He got into the passenger seat and looked at his wife.

'Don't ask,' she said.

Turning to slot the rucksack behind the driver's seat, he balanced the remaining beer on his lap.

'Put on your belt,' Rachel said.

He sighed.

'What?'

'I'm not a child.' He snapped the cold metal into the socket.

Rachel kept her eyes on the road, her face didn't change, pale and expressionless, the perfect martyr. She would make a wonderful saint. He could see her in the shroud of the famous missionary nun, her blonde hair covered, her narrow face rimmed in thin stripes of blue and white, the uneven patches of freckles—no, he stopped himself. He was doing it again. Letting all his rage at the great unfairness of his current situation leach into his marriage. Rachel had done nothing wrong. She had, in fact, dropped whatever she was doing to come to his aid. She'd become an expert in putting him first. As if reading his mind, she now said brightly and with conviction, 'Tonight will be fun. What time are Ben and Stevie due?'

'I told them seven.'

'It will be eight with Stevie. You know what she's like.'

Dylan didn't feel in the mood to comment on what Stevie might or might not be like, so he said nothing, just looked down at his middle, the ever-expanding mass of fat. Who would have thought a few years could reverse decades of training? He found it hard to credit, though the proof was there for him to see any time he wanted, he couldn't get away from it, his body, in all its phenomenal failure. Closing his eyes, he tried to calm down. It could be worse. At least he could always say he'd played for Ireland—five caps, before it all fell apart with one horrendous wrong turn. He eventually got back playing for Leinster but never fully regained his speed, his position lost to a younger, faster wing. In the years since, he'd had a solid if unspectacular career, part of the starting fifteen when the frontliners were on international duty, otherwise a reliable substitute whose name still held some promise or memory of glory.

Before the pandemic, Dylan had already been winding down, or more truthfully, management had indicated that he was, at the warhorse age of thirty-five, nearing his end. The pace of the young lads was the issue. He knew that, he understood.

One of the hardest things to get his head around now was that
he'd actually felt OK about retiring. Rachel and he had made
plans. The European Cup was to be his last hurrah, followed by
a family holiday in America, three weeks of relaxation and fun
and travel that would ease the transition between life as a player
and his plan to go into coaching. But that was back before The
Bomb, as he liked to think of it, the definitive blast that ended
his career, his ability to enjoy life, no, his ability to live. If ath-
letes are said to die twice, Dylan was already on his third go. He
was acutely aware of the passage of time, all the chronic, wasted
minutes of his days.

His seat reverberated, sudden pain in his lower back.

'Leah!' he said, as she kicked again. 'Stop.'

'She's been trying to get your attention,' Rachel said.

'Sorry.'

'Are you hurt?'

'No,' he said, ignoring the darting sensation down his side.
Real and certain, the pain, yet the more he mentioned it the less
she was inclined to believe him. He turned to face his daughter.
'What is it, baby?'

'Daddy!' she said. 'Eggs are yucky.'

'Really?'

'Yesh.'

'You sure?'

'Yucky.'

'All eggs?'

'All. Eggs.'

'No more Easter Eggs?'

This stymied her. She kicked the seat once more and burst
into tears.

'Thanks,' said Rachel. 'Thanks a lot.'

They didn't talk again for the remainder of the journey home, just listened to the sharp little cries of their daughter, their only child, who was behaving, according to the woman at the crèche, exactly like an only child, by which she meant entitled, lonely and, at four years of age, already preoccupied with the greatest of all human quests, the hunt for more and better love.

*   *   *

Emerging from the swimming pool in Trinity, Stevie felt refreshed, reborn, ready for the night ahead. She knew it would be a late one, they always were at Dylan's, some remnant of their college selves dormant within them, effortlessly summoned by a look, an old joke, a nostalgic anecdote or nudge, anything at all, really, which often left her thinking in the days that followed such occasions that too much of her adult life was spent yearning for the past.

She slipped on her faded turquoise flip-flops, wrung her swim hat over the pool drain. The past, *that* past, shouldn't be so easy to access. Thirty-eight now, she had lived almost as many years after college as she had before. Somehow this calculation made her want to get back into the water and do another set, but she knew she'd done enough, there was no point punishing her body for being the age it was, nothing a person could do about that.

Stevie was famously practical. Her older sister Laura was a writer who could do nothing except put words on a page, the younger one, Elise, a violinist currently busking her way across America with a blues singer she'd met in a bar, making Stevie, with her steady physio job and long-term relationship and small apartment in the docklands, the stable one of the family, a reputation she felt she'd never quite earned, rather had been branded with years earlier, possibly the moment Elise was born, when Stevie, through no fault of her own, became the sensible middle child who would one day know how to cook, clean, care for other people, care for herself. She did know how to do all those things; except maybe the last one, which seemed a bit lofty and abstract, like knowing how to pray or wish upon a star. Like knowing her heart's desires, which a doctor had recently said to her, as if the heart had feelings and was not just a vital organ that pumped blood around the body to keep a person alive.

Making her way down the deck to the sauna, she looked through the glass door and saw four or five muscular young men draped across the wooden benches. They had been swimming in rotation in the lane beside her and she'd already had enough of their overenthusiastic, endorphin-fuelled declarations on the benefits of morning sprints. Instead she tried the steam room, which was mercifully free, a cavernous space covered on all sides in characterless white tiles. Stevie lay on a bench, lifted her feet to the wall to stretch her calves, wondering how long she would get before the boys next door wanted to move from dry heat to wet. To call them boys wasn't quite accurate. They were college students and the pool belonged to them more than it did to her, an alumna so many years gone. The pool hadn't even existed when she was in college. They'd only had the sports hall, the testosterone smack of the squash courts, gym mats that smelled of feet. Back then the place was always half empty. There were no philosophy majors on the rowing machines. No classics students doing spin. There were no high-ponytailed girls with full faces of make-up jogging on treadmills with study notes propped on a ledge, a sight Stevie had witnessed earlier warming up before her swim. She'd wondered if she should go over as a physio and advise against it, but then she'd remembered what Ben had recently said to her, that it wasn't her job to look after everyone, sometimes people were more than capable of figuring things out for themselves. He had said that to her this week, or maybe the week before, it was hard to timestamp these things, the insults couched as compliments, the parts of her personality he'd loved initially, and still purported to love when pressed.

Her watch flashed on the hour. She had lingered in the steam room for twenty minutes. Perhaps she was waiting for the group of students, the swim team or whoever they were, those irritatingly happy men-children who through some trick of the hot room, the relaxing hiss of the steam, were turning alarmingly into fantasy figures. Stevie laughed out loud, the tenseness in her groin dissipating, not able to be wished back, she knew from experience. There was always the purple bullet in her bedside cabinet at home. There was always Ben.

The door to the steam room opened. A pool attendant looked in, asked if it was hot enough. The reality of the man's face embarrassed her. She said the temperature was fine, she was just leaving. He held the door for her and she didn't look him in the eye as she mumbled a thank you, rushed off to the shower.

After breakfast in a busy bakery on Pearse Street, Stevie bought the paper and walked down the quays. Among the dazzling glass shapes of the grand offices, there were one or two derelict buildings—an old redbrick she was passing now, from which a sapling sprouted riverward out of the rotten wall. Most people wanted the buildings gone, but she found them cheering, the way they hung on in their old, flawed state amid all the transforming perfection. In the distance, beyond the white fin of the Beckett Bridge, the sky was turning dark, heavy, about to drop into the oily waters of the Liffey. She hurried in the direction of the apartment, keen to get home now, even if she knew it wasn't safe to go back there, that the pills were exactly where she'd left them, in the zipped inside pocket of an old bag under a pile of other bags in the corner of a wardrobe, because of course they were, no one but Stevie knew they were there.

Soon her building came into view, a hulking block of forty apartments whose windows didn't open beyond the regulatory few inches. On sunny days their bedroom was a greenhouse. Ben was always telling people they could live without heating year round, which wasn't true—the living room only got the sun for a brief period in the morning—but she knew it made him feel better about the times he couldn't afford to contribute to the utility bills, that the impassioned environmental speeches he liked to give when drunk were largely borne of his economic circumstances and his perception of himself as a person who could withstand extreme hardship when it came to matters of survival. To be fair, it was an accurate perception. She thought of the flat in Rathmines where Ben had lived for most of college. In first year he'd shared the place with a fellow drama student who slept sixteen hours a day because the heating only came on for an hour in the evenings. There was never any fresh milk. Never enough toilet paper or soap. They seemed to exist on nothing. Compared to the keen, orderly, health-conscious friends she had made through her physio course, it was exciting—even exotic. Canned meat, baked beans, an oven pizza at weekends. She'd call round after lectures and find them stoned on the faux leather sofas, watching the same old comedies and box sets whose overdue fines at the rental shop were so enormous as to make them obsolete. Ben used to call it studying, and who knows, maybe it was. All she could say for sure was that the place had been a haven for skivers until Dylan moved in at the start of second year and took charge.

Smiling at the memory, Stevie knew she'd have to snap out of the recollections before this evening. Rachel hated when the three of them started on the college stories, she didn't seem to get how much easier it was for people to talk about the good old days than the borderless blob of the present. Stevie pictured her prim smile, the deliberate jut of her dainty face, the way Dylan would choose to pick up on her signal or not, depending on his mood. She felt bad then, for the observation, or for Rachel herself. Rachel Turner was not an easy person to feel sorry for. A rigidity to her that Stevie found hard to negotiate, the stiffness of people meeting for the first time, which invariably resolves with time but in this instance had remained. Every time she met Rachel it was like starting over. Her disposition didn't yield, at least not to Stevie. It yielded perfectly well to Dylan and Ben. At the thought of her perky blonde ponytail and amenable smile, the anecdotes that had a rehearsed quality designed to pander to men, Stevie felt the zippy aftereffects of the swim leave her. There was something draining about Rachel. Even the most rudimentary enquiries seemed like work.

Inside the apartment block she checked the mailbox, hit the button for the lift, before deciding to take the stairs, four flights up, delaying the inevitable, the long hours of the day where she would be sharing the same space with those small yellow circles of serenity, consciously not thinking about them, which is to say, thinking about them all the time. It wasn't that she suffered from anxiety, the doctor said, rather she seemed to feel the world's problems a little more acutely than most. This was anxiety-inducing, he decided, which was not the same as anxiety. All

Stevie had to do was care less. She put her key in the door, thankful Ben had nothing on today. She needed his presence, his vitality. He might be stuck for the occasional heating bill, but he did not scrimp on life. His constant yearning to make something of himself filled up the dead moments of their days. Remarkable, his bottomless desire. The energy and glow. Coned spotlight through the mist of time.

*   *   *

Ben had known for years that the odds were against him, his age ticking up like a speedometer pushing red, making him less suitable for even more roles than he'd been unsuitable for the previous year, even if he looked much the same, even if his agent assured him he was still *atypically attractive*, with the type of broad, senatorial face that commanded attention, that was able, on a good day, to project onto its sallow canvas a laborious range of convincing emotions desperate to be tested in the big leagues of the theatrical world.

So, he persisted. For nearly two decades he kept going. Countless auditions, understudy readings, stagehand work, minor roles in major productions, small snippets of almost greatness he had replayed in his head so many times they were close to losing their lustre. And they didn't do much to offset the rest of it, not really, the tedious extra gigs, near misses and final callbacks, advertisement parts which included a novice driver, angry milkman, new dad and a creepy sexual predator in a public service campaign about consent. Yes, in twenty years of *trying to be an actor*, which was what his friends and family called his profession, Ben Brosnahan had endured enough rejection to last a lifetime.

But things were about to change. Ben had been lying awake for hours, long before Stevie rose for her penitential exercise regime he had been wide-eyed, the news fizzing in his stomach, too unreal to share yet with the outside world. He wasn't sure he'd ever been to sleep, actually, the text coming through from his agent just as he was switching his phone to airplane mode last night, containing the four life-changing words he had waited an age to hear. *You got the part.* Caroline was pleased for him, he knew, by the uncharacteristic kiss after the message. She understood what it meant to him, how much he needed a win. Ben wanted big roles and stellar reviews. He wanted stardom. He wanted people on the street to lose control of their facial features when they saw him.

As he heard Stevie's key in the door he wondered how he should tell her. For years he'd fantasised about this moment, dreamt up every ludicrous scenario a man could think of, so that a plain delivery of the news seemed anticlimactic, disappointing even, in a way that made him slow to tell her at all. Mostly he felt relieved he would be earning a decent wage for an extended period of time; he resolved to buy her something beautiful and frivolous.

'Hiya,' came from the living room.

'In here,' he said.

Through the thin walls he listened to her clatter around the kitchen, boil the kettle, take out the clothes horse to hang her togs. The entire apartment would be heavy with chlorine soon, medicinal cleanliness ripping through the air.

Stevie appeared in the doorway. 'Still in bed?'

He patted the mattress and she smiled at him, cast her eyes over the laundry basket, before turning back to the kitchen. Hair in a dark top-knot. All go. She'd been like this for nearly a year now and he wondered if she was charging herself at night, if there might be a secret dock somewhere in the building she plugged into while he was sleeping. Because it wasn't normal to have so much energy.

Ben stretched his feet over the end of the bed, which was just about able to contain him. Six-two, not a great height for a queensize, but it was all the room could take. They were looking to move, had viewed this past year countless semi-detached houses in the wider Dublin region, to no avail. The asking prices were a farce, luring prospective buyers out to sea, suddenly plunging them deep and deeper. It was nonsense. Infuriating. A bore. Which didn't really cover it at all, the fact that up to now he'd paid rent to Stevie, when he could, and it was ultimately her apartment that would have to be sold in order for them to afford a house and mortgage. Ben had virtually no savings. (One broker was incredulous, almost in awe, that a man could live thirty-nine years on the planet without saving a cent.) There was such shame in it that Ben preferred to pretend the whole thing was beneath him, the rat race, the ladder, the game so many of his friends were able to play. Dylan, for example, who owned a large redbrick in Terenure on a grand street of prestigious oaks. Dylan made the game look easy, he always had. Ben's best friend had excelled at everything all his life. All their lives. Sports, obviously, but beyond that too, or perhaps because of it, girls, friends, money, any sniff of a competition and Dylan Turner nailed it. The age-old jealousy was still there, somewhere, if Ben sought it out. Having a best friend superior in every way meant a comparison so constant and instinctive it was barely even conscious.

At the moment, though, whose life would he prefer to have? He thought of their most recent meeting, a bare hour in Dylan's local where the poor guy had struggled to do something as basic as sit in a chair without pain. Ben had assured him things would get better—what else could you say?—but now he felt a glimmer, of guilt or exhilaration, that perhaps their luck had been exchanged and it was finally his turn to cash in. He knew then that he would tell Stevie his news this evening, at the game, in front of everyone. He pictured her delight; Rachel's cool, alluring praise; Dylan's unadulterated joy. Dylan was always happy for other people, unlike Ben, who had become so used to losing he automatically felt envious at the successes of friends and family. It was a thing he hated about himself, a defect he was unable to control. The only thing that worked was to get away from the person, to create a physical distance, or, failing that, to switch conversation to another more bearable topic, until the feeling had ebbed away and he could offer a genuine congrats.

He looked at the time on his phone, just gone half ten, a nice, leisurely weekend morning, though the apartment was busy as a weekday: hairdryer, coffee grinder, kettle, smoothie blender, television, kitchen radio, hoover, bigger hoover, dishwasher, and now a ferociously rhythmic banging that seemed, the more it persisted, to be coming from inside his head. With a yawn he got up, threw on a fleece and trudged out to the noisemaker. In the kitchen Stevie had emptied an array of Tupperware containers and was hammering crumbs into the sink.

'Filthy,' she looked up, 'the whole kitchen. I can't wait to be out of here.'

He squinted at her. 'Coffee?'

She pointed to the glass pot on the draining board. 'Lazy bones,' she said.

Ben was about to remark on the distinction between weekday and weekend, but he moved in for a hug instead, felt her body relax against him, her head finding the soft pocket of his chest. They were an odd-looking couple, Stevie nearly a foot shorter than him, yet they seemed to work; their bodies, through habit or necessity, had discovered the right folds and crevices. It was very soothing. He bent down to kiss her—a tang of chlorine.

'What's the plan for the day?' he said.

She pulled away and began a surprisingly thorough list. Spring cleaning, a cycle to Clontarf, walk on Bull Island, an afternoon trip to the supermarket, sex, pizza, taxi to Dylan's for sevenish.

'Sex?'

For some reason she blushed. 'Yes. If you want to, I mean.'

'Always,' he said, which wasn't entirely untrue, because he did today for sure, he was up for it. For anything. If she asked him to do a bungee jump or visit her parents he would probably agree. But also, he would like sex now, not after Bull Island and the supermarket.

'OK,' she smiled. 'Later.'

He left her to the Tupperware and went to lie on the couch. Flicking through the culture magazine he wondered what the paper's famously harsh theatre critic would make of his performance when the time came, whether he would experience the Irish actor's rite of passage of being ripped to shreds in a national forum. Certainly the play would be covered—a joint production by the Royal Court and The Abbey that would open in Dublin and transfer to London later in the year—there might even be interviews along with the reviews, Caroline was clever like that, she had told him often enough: he only needed to get into the spotlight once and let her do the rest. But Ben would not be tempted by television or film, he favoured theatre, the reason he wanted to act, the immediacy of a live audience, that connection, the sense anything could happen. He wouldn't be tempted, unless something huge came along, a thing you did once, for the money. For kicks. Still, they wouldn't move to LA, they would keep it—

His phone buzzed on the coffee table. He opened a message from Dylan, laughed at the photo, an inexplicable number of Dutch Gold lined up on the kitchen island, and in the middle of them, a bottle of rosé.

Guess which one's for Rachel.

I'm not drinking that muck, Ben replied.

The rosé?

Obviously.

Dylan replied with a photo of himself, cans upturned at his mouth.

Nutters O'Neill?

Some lad for the Dutch.

Ben smiled. A burst of kinship came over him. He missed his friend. He hesitated over the next message, wanting to keep it light, while letting Dylan know he cared. These days there was always a third person in their conversations, the shadow of illness, surprisingly forceful for a shadow, able to commandeer just about any communication however jovial or banal.

How are you today? he wrote.

Dylan was typing, he wasn't, he was typing again, he disappeared.

Ben tried to bring it back. *Nothing Dutch won't cure!*

No reply.

He put his phone down and went into the kitchen, where Stevie had removed all the cutlery from the drawer and was now polishing each implement with a yellow cloth.

'You know they're IKEA?' he said.

'What?' She looked at him absently.

'They're not silver.'

'Clearly,' she said.

'You didn't give us the chance to get the good stuff.'

Her eyes darted up from the cutlery. He smiled to show he was joking, a lightness he still didn't feel, might never feel, over the fact that Stevie, after all their years together, refused to marry him. She didn't believe in marriage, it was a social construct designed to entrap women in the home, which made no sense to him because Stevie was a born homemaker: a fine cook, an organised, solvent, patient, decent human being, the type of person Ben had been beguiled by all his life.

'I'll buy you the good stuff for your birthday,' she said. 'Theatre tickets and heavy forks.'

'Deal.' He kissed the back of her neck.

'Do you want breakfast?' she said. 'A rasher sandwich?'

Rashers! On a day like today? He wanted champagne and lobster. Bordeaux and steak. Crêpes and café royale!

'Sure,' he said. 'Rashers would be great.'

Stevie took out a pan. She turned suddenly. 'Any word from Caroline?'

'No,' he said to the glistening cutlery. 'Nothing yet.'

*   *   *

Closing the door to the en suite, Rachel leant against the wall, giving herself over to its cool strength. She sank to the floor, which seemed as good a place as any for a rest, the mosaic tiles warm from the late afternoon sun that shone in patches through the dusty window. A source of beauty. Another thing to clean before the house was fit for company. Right now Rachel was supposed to be getting ready but she hadn't the will to move. The bathroom floor was perfect. Solid, safe, it asked nothing of her. The air smelled of earthy lavender; a buzzy silence. She felt alone for the first time in years.

At some point, soon, she would need to shower, though she might get away with a silk headband to cover the grease. Back in the day Rachel used to care about things like hair and make-up, she would get a blow-dry for a night out, a night in, for something *to do*, and she wondered what was wrong with that person, that girl who hadn't made more use of her free time when she had it—concerts, galleries, museums, etc.—who frittered it away, not realising there would come a time when she would never be alone again, that even precious minutes spent hiding in the bathroom would be undercut with a dreadful anticipatory sense of duty, not to mention failure for needing something as human as a break.

In a word, motherhood. And the thing was, she desperately wanted it again. Another child. Rachel was a planner and the plan had been to get pregnant on their wonderful American holiday of a lifetime that never happened, which meant she should have a child now approaching two, a boy ideally, but she would have been happy with either. Instead she was forty-one and they'd only recently started trying again. For the last few years her poor husband hadn't been able for sex, and though they'd eventually devised a method where she did most of the work, it could still leave him tired for days afterwards. But at least it was for some purpose, she thought, even the simple pleasure of union, not like his foolish solo trip to the off-licence this morning when he knew he needed to save his energy for tonight.

Rachel had nowhere to put her anger. It came out in strange ways. The other morning she'd snapped at the postman for not bringing her mail. She wasn't expecting something, had just seen him chatting to a neighbour and decided to question him when he passed the house without stopping. She ran down the driveway, the neighbour's terrier following her, both of them pursuing the man in the same yapping, overwrought manner, though perhaps she was being harsh on the dog. The postman responded kindly, if a little warily, promising he'd bring her mail the next time. Now she spent the mornings dreading the doorbell. She would like to tell him what was going on. But there were no easy explanations when it came to long covid, the term itself seemed to deaden interest, too imprecise and unsolvable, it contained too much of the past.

Was this her life now? Nurse, babysitter, shopper, cook, skivvy. His advocate on all things medical too. She knew she couldn't do it forever. She wasn't sure she'd last another month. The shape of him embedded in their living room couch, so that even when he wasn't there, lying down with his podcasts or asleep, there was the imprint of him on the cushions; the middle one that took the brunt of his weight had a dent in the centre, a scratch to the soft pink fabric that shimmered in certain lights. His pained face, his personality reduced to patient. Then the moods—she'd never realised Dylan had it in him, that darkness she remembered from her childhood, the force of its suction. Rachel had spent her adult life running away from miserable people, there was no other way to deal with them, and she wondered if their current situation was payback for her choosing someone as aggressively cheerful as Dylan. Before the bomb, as he liked to call it, her husband had been a supremely optimistic person, irrationally optimistic, it was something to do with professional sport, some ruse of management to get them to bounce back from one fixture to the next, to be hammered by Munster at home on a Saturday and go on to play Harlequins the following weekend. A child's logic of wiping out the past with hopes of the future. Well, there was no hope now, Rachel felt sure of it as she sat on the bathroom floor, the tears finally coming. She gave herself over to them. The print on the tiles smudged and replicated in dancing, broken patterns.

After her cry she felt more able. Pushing off the ground she went to the sink and washed her face. As the cold water gathered in her cupped hands she knew she would get her family through this. It wasn't Dylan's fault, she understood that. Just the uncertainty ahead that made daily life so overwhelming. But she had felt the same about motherhood at the beginning, that she was entirely unequipped for the role—the immutability of it, the mess—and things had worked out fine. She was a good mother. You couldn't admit that in public, it was all failures and self-reproach at the coffee mornings, but Rachel knew she looked after her daughter in the right way, which was by no coincidence the opposite to how her own mother had operated. Noreen was one of a small, sad cohort of women in twentieth-century Ireland who had sacrificed themselves to run a household then complained about it for the rest of their days, as if resentment could give them back their lives. By contrast, Rachel tried her best to be a source of love and comfort, not worry or fear. She had her own resentments, of course, she was human like anyone else, but she kept them to herself or saved them for the grown-up world. She knew the difference between an adult and a child, who was meant to look after whom.

Downstairs the doorbell rang.

She heard Leah's quick feet in the hallway.

'Rach!' Dylan called.

Patting her face with the towel, she smiled falsely at the mirror, her green eyes coming to life, reminding her of stage school, the hysterical woman who ran it, how she used to threaten to put matchsticks in their *peepers*. Rachel had enrolled for six months after her Leaving because everyone said she looked like an actress, but she'd quickly understood the futility of her efforts, it didn't matter what part they gave her, she was only able to play herself. *Beautiful, wooden Rachel,* she remembered a director saying in a whisper that carried down the rehearsal room. It wasn't one for the résumé.

'Rachel!'

'Mummy!'

She heard her daughter giggle, the slapping of hands against the stained glass panels. Leah was trying in vain to reach the lock, which meant it was either Dylan's mother or Suzanne from next door. Rachel ran downstairs, stopped Leah pawing the glass, swept her up in her arms, the weight just about tolerable. 'Who's there, Leah?' she said, though she could see it was Helen, loaded with dinners that nobody wanted, awful old Irish food of the 1980s.

'Nana,' Leah said. 'Nana Helen,' which was a funny distinction, because she saw the other nana once or twice a year.

Rachel opened the door. 'Hi, Helen. Sorry to keep you.'

'No bother at all. Hi, you!' Helen patted Leah's head. 'Are you being good?'

Leah burrowed her hot little face in Rachel's shoulder.

'She's the best girl,' Rachel said. 'Just don't mention eggs.'

'Yuck!' said Leah, wriggling to get down. But she was smiling now. Rachel knew her humours, they were past the eggs.

Helen laughed, already moving down the hall, a whirlwind of flowy fabrics that seemed to have no origin or end. She was a young sixty-seven, still worked three days a week in the credit union in Sallins. Helen had great drive. They were lucky to have her, even if the visits were mostly unannounced these days, the illness did away with things like manners.

In the living room Dylan was on the couch in a tracksuit and hoodie in varying shades of grey, a stain on his thigh. Rachel felt ashamed, like it was her responsibility to dress him too.

'Hi, love.' Helen went to sit beside him. He shuffled his legs into a peaked position he had deemed impossible earlier in the week when Rachel had tried to snuggle him, when she'd just wanted to be near him for a second in their old, easy way.

'What's in there?' Dylan pointed to the freezer bag.

'Your favourite,' Helen said.

'It's all the one to me,' he said despondently.

'Thank you,' Rachel said. 'That's what your son means, Helen.'

'Thanks, Mam, she's right.'

Rachel let the *she* go and went to put on the kettle, listening to Dylan divulge his most recent symptoms to his mother. Attempts to block out his voice were futile, she felt compelled to tune in, wanting to—what?—catch him out in a lie or exaggeration about this dismal, shape-shifting disease no one seemed to know anything about.

Most of the time, she believed him. It was only the last month or two that doubt had begun to burrow through her dwindling stores of compassion. She knew he was suffering, anyone could see he was physically cowed, but she wondered if his symptoms were as bad or as constant as he let on—illness was difficult to believe in all the time, to maintain interest in minute after minute. She couldn't just allow him his pain, this unbearable music, she felt the need to arrange it. So far Rachel had kept this to herself. Out of love for him, and for their marriage, the good years they'd had together, and could still have once more. She tried now to recall him as he once was. Kind, strong and agile, with a determination she had understood, even if she'd known little about the game of rugby. His confidence was so attractive, the way he'd seemed to know her body at once, none of the grasping clumsiness she had experienced with other men, most of whom had been older than Rachel, sometimes a good deal older, yet lacked Dylan's instinct, his wonderfully assured touch. He had made her feel wanted, needed, safe. What did it say about their marriage that only one of these things was still true?

They should be in couples therapy but they didn't have the money. The past few years had decimated their savings. Last month his parents had offered them a loan, which Dylan declined, afraid as always of being beholden to his father. Rachel was forced to acquiesce; hadn't wanted the issue of her spending to come up again. Her guilt rose now in tandem with the boiling kettle. A fact: Rachel loved to buy things, it gave her a great sense of well-being. She came from a family where money was withheld, or didn't exist, or was occasionally handed over with a meanness so entrenched it lodged in the dirty creases of the notes. The type of meanness that was easily inherited, if you didn't watch it. Her siblings were all misers like her parents, but Rachel had gone the other way, the metronome ticked too quickly, spend, spend, spend and give it all away was the impulse, because it only destroyed a person to hang onto it. And the truth was, when you hadn't earned the money yourself, this was frightfully easy to do. Rachel had always been able to spend

Dylan's money, first as his girlfriend in her thoughtless twenties, and later, when it became their money and she felt entitled to it as the furnisher of home and offspring. She thought again about her longed-for second baby, until the kettle clicked off. Presses started opening, the ceramic mugs Helen gave them last Christmas were on the counter.

'He's bad today,' Helen said.

'You think?'

'Pain in his legs, and did you hear his breathing? The wheeze is back.'

Rachel was familiar with the sound.

'When will it end?' Helen said. 'It's no way to live.' She put milk and a spoon of sugar in each cup. 'But I'm so pleased about tonight.'

'Yes, he's very excited.'

'Mind you don't stay up too late. I saw all the beer.'

Rachel rolled her eyes. 'Most of it will end up in storage.'

Helen smiled. 'Ben and Stevie are just the ticket. You know who your friends are in bad times. Tell Stevie the sweetheart I'm thrilled she's going to help him with physio.'

At that, she vanished with two mugs. Rachel picked up the coffee that was meant for her and tossed it in the sink. Just the thought of sweetheart Stevie was enough to reawaken her despair. She looked at the cuckoo clock on the far wall. It was almost four, the fridge stocked with wine. Though she'd planned to drink very little tonight, not wanting to mess with her fertility diet, a few glasses wouldn't kill her. The small wooden bird squawked on the hour, in full agreement and support.

*   *   *

After one can of beer Dylan felt the familiar throb in his head—always the left, the side of weakness in his game too, the illness knew where to target. The pain spidered across his eye before returning to the forehead. He told Rachel he was going to lie down, ignoring her reply about the need to get ready. As he went slowly down the hallway he tried not to panic. An hour and a half before Stevie and Ben were due. Upstairs in the bedroom he lay on the bed with the lights off and shut his eyes. Still the darting increased, and with it the sound of his own heartbeat until they were terribly aligned. At these times of intense pain he felt disconnected from himself, from the stoicism he'd had since boyhood that always seemed innate but now revealed itself to be merely a facet of his previously charmed life and the good health he had taken for granted. Any fool could be stoic about sprained wrists and pulled hamstrings because they were injuries that healed. Even his cruciate hadn't broken him. That was the rugby way: you did not complain. You just got on with it. Anything with an end was bearable, it meant there was somewhere to put the hope. He missed his sport so much, the routine of training, the buzz and camaraderie, highs and lows of competition. The simplicity of that life. A predictable weekly cycle, organised by management. Spoonfed so you could focus everything on the game. He missed his teammates, longed for the solidarity of the changing room, where even if you were out for multiple seasons there was the sense the others understood what you were going through. Now he was alone with his strange illness, his unfortunate exile, this useless, repellent pain. He could see clearly with Rachel that the more he complained the quicker she withdrew. She didn't like feeling helpless, it reminded her too much of her childhood, where there was nothing to do but wait it out. She was a plotter, a go-getter, always steps ahead of everyone in a room. She used her looks to her advantage, hid her intelligence in the sheen. He had always loved that about her. For a moment he was drawn out of his mood, he floated above the migraine to think about his wife, this clever, cautious person who had decided for whatever reasons to let him into her life. There was a privilege in that he too often forgot. He could hear her in Leah's bedroom, sounding out the words of the storybook, encouraging their daughter onto the next line. He smiled. Then the migraine returned with a terrific warning blast—pain vigorously renewed, strengthened by the brief respite. 'Rachel!' he cried. 'Rachel, please. Can you help me?'

*   *   *

From the bedroom window Dylan watched the taxi stop at the end of the street, the sign illuminating as the driver pulled away, neon digits suspended in the dusk. April was an odd month, it seemed to contain all the seasons or the promise of them, like right now, the give of summer evenings in the streaked sky. He focused on the colours until Ben and Stevie finished their kiss, which felt strange to witness, though he must have seen them do likewise a thousand times before. Ben put his arm around her and they walked down the footpath chatting, full of the ease of a couple in love.

'Quarter to eight,' Rachel said, causing him to jump.

'Don't do that.'

'What?'

'Creep up on me.'

'I wasn't. What's so interesting out there?'

'They're here,' he said. 'They got out by the road.'

'Finally.'

Rachel gestured to the zip of her navy shift dress halfway down her back. He moved it into place, feeling an unexpected tenderness at the terrain, the pale skin and fine hairs at the top of her spine, the triangle of freckles above the neckline. Dylan remembered the first time he saw her, weaving through the crowds on a dance floor in a glitterball dress with hundreds of metallic scales that flashed light in all directions, the sharp ends of her hair tipping her breasts. He tried to see that person now but could only see his wife.

She turned and kissed his cheek. 'Will I do?' she said.

'Gorgeous,' he said, which was true. His wife looked lovely, but equally, she was overdressed for a night in with friends compared to Stevie, the manly blazer he'd seen through the window. Classic Stevie, she'd had it for years.

The doorbell rang.

'Let's go,' said Rachel.

'Mummy,' Leah said as they passed her room. 'Who's there?'

'She knows rightly,' he said. 'Keep walking.'

Rachel hesitated.

Dylan said, 'Go to sleep, baby girl.'

The pair of them went quickly down the stairs, on the run from their own child. Rachel had given him a double dose of triptans for the migraine, and miraculously, this had worked.

At the front door there was a quick round of greetings before Rachel ushered them down the hall into the kitchen, leaving the door slightly ajar.

'Well,' said Ben, beaming. 'Thanks for having us.'

Stevie left their booze on the island beside the Dutch Gold display. She took a bottle of wine from a carrier bag and gave it to Rachel.

Dylan knew it was the wrong colour, too luridly pink.

'You're so good,' Rachel said.

'There isn't as many as before.' Ben pointed to the beer. 'Tell the truth, mate.'

Dylan laughed, patted his belly, wishing he hadn't as everyone looked at his midriff, or midriffs to be accurate, one on top of the other, he wasn't sure which was the original. To cover his embarrassment he gave his verdict on the Leinster match to Ben, who one hundred percent hadn't seen it, having a strict policy when it came to sport that it was only tolerable when Dylan was on the pitch.

'Oh, the match, the match,' said Ben. 'And how are *the lads*,' which was how he referred to Dylan's teammates.

'Haven't seen them much.'

'Really?'

'Jim called round last month.'

'What about Macca?'

'Ah they're busy,' Dylan said. 'Training, matches. I know how it goes.' When you left a team, you were cut loose. Didn't matter how many tries, medals or tours. Rugby was a business at the end of the day, he had learnt that early in his career through injury, though it was easier to rationalise back then, when there was hope for the future.

'Screw them.' Ben put an arm around Dylan's shoulder.

Stevie smiled, as she had at everything since arriving, a stillness to her that was at odds with the bright slash of lipstick, the hair in dark disorder. An angelic punk. As Ben went to help Rachel with the drinks, Dylan smiled shyly at her, wanting access, a hint of the private happiness inside her head.

He nudged her arm. 'What's so funny?'

She startled. 'Nothing, it's good to be out.'

'Is this out?'

'Beats The Palace,' she said.

'Those were the days.'

'You were barely there. Far too sensible.'

'Didn't have a choice.'

'Yeah, yeah. I know,' Stevie smiled. 'Dylan Turner is only boring by default.'

They laughed.

'Dylan,' Rachel said loudly. 'Where are the crisps?'

He made a helpless face. 'I forgot.'

'Seriously?'

'No hassle,' said Stevie. 'We've eaten.'

Rachel pressed the button on the fridge that released the noisy ice. Beside her Ben was doing something dangerous with a bottle of schnapps, holding it up so the liquid streamed quickly into a highball glass, the first in a row of four.

'Give us the vodka,' he said to Stevie.

'Already?'

'Something to get us on our way.'

Rachel declined at first but they badgered her into it. Dylan was pleased. She was too vigilant these days, with her mad diets and supplements, he wanted her to enjoy herself, to have a night off. When Ben was finished, they gathered around the island to toast how long it had been since they were all together. Dylan tried not to think about the reason as he drank the concoction. It tasted like perfume to him, but so did many things. The women seemed to enjoy the drink. Ben had worked as a bartender at various points over the years. So many jobs—doorman, copy-writer, fundraiser, call centre—while he waited for his break. Every now and then, Dylan tried to suggest, in a way that only best friends could, that maybe it was time for Ben to throw his admirable energies into a new career. For one thing, it would allow him to quit the Suicide Centre, which was what he called the phone sales job.

'Remember the call centre?' Dylan said.

'The one in Coolock?' Ben asked.

'Yeah.'

Ben frowned. 'What made you think of that?'

Dylan shrugged, it wasn't a dig, like.

'To Coolock!' Stevie cheered, saving him in a way that was intensely familiar.

'Where is Coolock?' said Rachel.

Stevie said, 'Are you a Dub, or what?'

'I'm not from *Coolock*,' Rachel said, which made it sound as if she was from Killiney like Stevie, not down the road in Drimnagh.

'Somewhere north of hell,' said Ben. 'At least that call centre was.'

'What were you pushing again?' Dylan said.

'Broadband that didn't exist.'

'Tough sell,' said Rachel.

'The longer you kept them talking the more chance you had. People sign up just to get away from you.'

'That's ridiculous,' said Rachel. 'I'd tell anyone who called here where to go.'

'Most people don't have your balls, honey,' Ben said.

Rachel gave her first real smile of the night.

Dylan was grateful for the banter, the glowy relief it brought to his wife's face. He was ashamed he was no longer able to do this himself. No longer tried. There seemed to be no right time for such things.

He went now to the utility to turn down the heat. When he came back he saw Stevie had moved to the grey picture wall at the end of the kitchen. With a tilt of her head she was studying the mounted photograph of him diving for the try line against Saracens some years back, a shot that made him look like a superhero without the cape, according to his mother. He'd laughed at the time, but he felt no connection to it now, as if Helen had framed a photo of a stranger and made them hang it as a centrepiece on their wall. He found it unbearable to have Stevie stare at the picture, a dazed, dreamy look on her face as she traced the blurred image of the rising crowd.

'Dylan,' said Ben. 'You'll have another.'

'I think I'll switch to beer.'

'Live a little.' Ben pointed to the poker set on the table. 'It will make losing easier.'

'We should probably start,' Rachel said. 'It's almost nine.'

Dylan said, 'Relax the head, Rach.'

'Really?' said Rachel. 'You're the one who won't be able to get out of bed tomorrow.'

Everyone went silent.

'Sorry,' said Ben. 'I wasn't thinking.'

Dylan gave his sunniest smile, the one he used in media interviews, the triumph-over-adversity nonsense the papers peddled back in the day: Dylan Turner, the Kildare wing who'd beaten the Dublin clubs to earn a place in the Leinster squad. Like Dylan's family were paupers because he hadn't gone to a private boarding school. It enraged his father, Sean, a civil servant and fluent Gaelgóir who, almost twenty years on, still hadn't forgiven his only son for choosing rugby over GAA. To banish the thought, Dylan clapped his hands. 'Let's get going,' he said, putting on a playlist.

They settled around the table, the pale wood covered by a green baize mat. Rachel chose the chair furthest from him, which meant she was practically on Ben's lap. She reached for the box and started to divvy the chips until they each had four stacks of assorted colours and heights.

Stevie remained at the far end of the room. Her attention shifted to the window, the long fall of dark outside. Dylan hadn't noticed the night come in.

'Earth to Stephanie,' Ben said in an American drawl.

She turned, groaning when she saw they were seated. 'Remind me of the rules again,' she said.

*   *   *

Leaning forward in the chair Ben checked his cards and tried to keep his face neutral. Pocket Jacks in the first round was an auspicious start to the night. He ran a hand through his hair, pretending not to watch the others, furtively alert, a skill he'd learnt as an actor, how to spot things with peripheral vision, how to pay attention, to tune out the soundtrack inside his head. Right now: Stevie was pleased with her cards, childlike incisors on display; Rachel had gone cold, shoulders curved inwards; across the way, Dylan was in an odd mood, a furrow in the space between his brows that didn't seem to fit with his jokey manner. *To smile and smile and be a villain.* Ben picked up his cards and gave a remorseful sniff. Dylan was no villain—he was classic hero material, from his cropped curls down to his nimble feet. Over the years at secondary school his bones and muscles developed in the correct way, they grew concurrently with each other to form a perfect figure, which was a weird thing to say about a man, maybe, but nonetheless true.

'It's on you,' Stevie said.

Ben zoned back in to a raise from Stevie, Dylan matched her, Rachel was out. She stood up. 'Anyone for a refill?'

'Don't be giving him time to think,' Dylan said.

Stevie handed over her glass, smiling gamely. She was in great form tonight and Ben wished he'd told her his news when they were alone. 'Reraise,' he said, throwing in two reds.

With a sigh Stevie folded and began to root in her handbag. 'Can I change the music?' she said. 'No offence, Dyl.'

'There isn't a thing wrong with Flaming Lips.'

'Sure,' she said. 'They're just a bit old school?'

Dylan looked wounded. 'I thought you loved them.'

'Years ago.'

'You know Stevie,' said Ben. 'Always after the next big thing.'

'That's me.'

Ben smiled at her but she was suddenly lost to him, gazing into the middle distance with dark, abstracted eyes. Something happened to the air in the room, some shift that had him back at a music festival nearly twenty years in the past. Felt the others were there too, yet he couldn't bring himself to name it.

Rachel returned from the fridge with the wine. Her chair was close to Ben's and he nudged it away with his runner so she could sit. She looked aggressively feminine in the dress and spike heels, her hair in a complicated knot. There was a small hole in her tights above the left knee.

'You alright, Ben?' she said.

'You look well,' he said. 'Nice dress.'

'Thank you,' she smiled.

Stevie linked her phone to the speaker and soon wordless electronic music began to play. 'Is it too loud?' she said.

Rachel said it was fine.

'By the way, Ben,' said Dylan, when the girls finished faffing, 'I'm all in.' He pushed his chips towards the centre.

'You sure about that?'

'Born sure.'

Sizing up his inscrutable opponent, Ben bottled it. He didn't want to be out of the game so early.

'Thief!' Rachel said to Dylan as he collected their chips. She gave him a comically seductive look, said if he had any spare to send them her way. They all laughed. Rachel had good timing, and the type of angular, aristocratic face that worked well on screen. Ben had said it before: if she'd stuck it out at drama school she might have made it. But so might hundreds of people he had met in the industry over the years.

The next few rounds passed quickly. Falling cards, hearts and spades, kings, queens, sequences appearing on the soft green mat. Dylan took over as dealer, a tyrannical move they all chose to ignore. There was a competitiveness to his game tonight, jerking forward when one of the girls did something out of turn, calling time on the chat between rounds, flipping the river cards with vicious dexterity. For the sixth round he sat in silence with his arms folded, a serious professional, all he lacked was the baseball cap. He won that round and the following two before Rachel got one back for the team, which was what it had started to feel like, the three of them against Dylan, the no-hopers banding together to see if they could take him down.

'Good woman, Rach,' said Ben.

'In your face, husband.'

'Take your pittance.' Dylan opened another can. 'This is the last of the Heineken. And you know what that means.' They looked at the island and laughed. The drink had worked its magic, the night was starting to unspool.

'If you could only drink one thing for the rest of your life,' Ben said, 'what would it be?'

'Dutch,' said Dylan.

'Yeah right.'

'OK, no, milk. Nothing like a cold glass of *bainne*.'

'Wasted in rugby,' said Stevie. 'You could have been the poster boy of the GAA.'

'Who would have me now?' Dylan said wistfully.

'Water, obviously,' said Rachel. 'Or sparkling water.'

'Tea,' Stevie said.

'Same,' said Ben. 'Overall a depressing indication that we're approaching forty.'

Rachel said, 'It's all downhill from there.'

'Ah, Stevie's still a child.' Dylan winked. 'Barely thirty-eight. Do you remember the bouncer in The Palace who would never let you in?'

'Until I scored him,' Stevie grimaced. 'At seventeen.'

'You did not!' Dylan said. 'The bald guy?'

'They were all bald. Do you remember the English lad with no teeth?'

'No feef.'

'Not a tooth in his head.'

And they were off, reminiscing about the early days of college.

As the stories showed no sign of abating, Rachel grew tetchy, her smile thinning. Ben decided to make another round of cocktails. They all protested, but only Rachel refused. He didn't argue with her. He knew they were trying for a second child, knew how hard it was to want something that seemed attainable but remained out of reach. Afterwards Stevie gathered the cards for a new round, messing up the shuffle. Dylan flicked them back across the table to her. Watching the antics, Ben felt it was time to tell them about the play.

'By the way,' he smiled at Stevie. 'There's some good news to share.'

'Oh my god!' said Rachel. 'Engaged?' Her hands clapped once, she began to stand.

'Oh, no, Rachel,' he said. 'Not that.'

Stevie's eyes slid sideways in her face.

'Sorry,' said Rachel. 'I just thought—'

'No dice.' Stevie shook her head. 'Still sticking it to the patriarchy here.' She gave a practised laugh.

Ben rattled a stack of chips, waited for the awkwardness to pass.

'What about kids?' Rachel asked.

'Rachel!' Dylan said.

'Screw it,' she said, 'in for a penny.'

Real laughter in some quarters now, bright and relieving.

'We've considered it,' Stevie said in a voice that was notably distant. 'But never at the same moment. That's not wrong, is it?' She raised an eyebrow at him.

Rachel swivelled in his direction.

'I would have gone for it,' Ben said. 'If you're talking about that time when—'

'You'd been cast as Hamlet?'

Cruel, Ben thought, she knew how gutted he'd been. They hadn't even given him Horatio. He glared at her. 'You weren't serious though, were you?'

'As a matter of fact, I think I was.'

'You were only twenty-nine.'

'Have your babies when you're young,' Rachel piped up. 'My gynaecologist said that to me last week. It's what your twenties are meant for. Not going out four nights on the trot.'

'Why were you seeing her?' Dylan said.

Rachel reddened. 'Um, Dylan, it's private?'

Ben was relieved the attention was no longer on himself and Stevie's reproductive choices, that it had passed mercilessly on to the next couple.

'So what's this news anyway, Ben?' Rachel said.

He gave Stevie a quick smile. 'Well, I've landed a big part.'

'Seriously?' said Stevie.

'What is it?' Rachel asked.

'The lead in a Pinter play, running at both The Abbey and the Royal Court.'

'Wow!' Dylan said. 'That's incredible stuff. Good on you.' He got up from his chair to hug Ben, but immediately bent over.

'What's wrong?' said Rachel.

'Are you OK?' Stevie steered Dylan back to the chair. He kept saying he was fine, though they could all see his body was rigid with pain.

'Sorry, Ben,' he said.

'What can we do?' Ben stood.

'It will pass,' Dylan said. 'I hope.'

The kitchen door was open, Rachel no longer in the room.

'Can of Dutch?' Ben joked.

'Don't be an idiot.' Stevie crouched on her knees beside Dylan. 'Just breathe in for four, out for seven.'

Presently the colour came back to Dylan's face. He said the pain had lessened. 'Give us that Dutch, mate.'

Stevie laughed at this, because the exact same sentiment was funny now, apparently. She asked Dylan if he was sure, then nodded at Ben to get the cans.

The three of them opened their beers in sync, the collective hiss resurrecting the evening. They were toasting Ben's news when Rachel returned to the kitchen with an excuse about Leah waking up. She took one look at the cans and said, 'Will we give up on the cards so?'

*   *   *

Outside in the garden Stevie exhaled a ribbon of smoke that drifted upwards in the darkness. A sizeable lawn for this part of Dublin, the manicured space given shape by the corner postings of two maple trees, their new fullness discreetly lit from small lamps sunk into the foliage below. Tiring of the view, she concentrated on the sky, which was starless and black with dimension, like looking into the hollow of a well. The night air cooled the back of her neck as she lifted her hair free of the blazer.

Though she had only taken a few drags, soon she began to feel dizzy. She wasn't a real smoker any more, usually succumbing at the end of a night in a self-sabotaging act of ensuring a hangover the following morning. But she needed one now, the effects of the pill were wearing off, tapering over the last hour in a way that made her miss the feeling before it was gone. She regretted not bringing more. It was like having a kind nurse take up temporary residence in her mind. She loved the little container they came in, the diaphanous amber plastic that allowed her to see the remaining number without having to upend them on the bed, which was something she had started to do lately, double checking her calculations, in case she was out by one or two. Ben knew she had a prescription, just not how often she was taking them; it felt too personal and silly a thing to burden him with, which is to say, she feared he would tell her to toss them immediately. And he would be right. The longer she took them—*dabbled* was the awful word that came to mind—the harder it would be to give them up. But it had only been a few

49

months, really, maybe six, if she cared to count. The GP had prescribed them after Stevie came to the surgery one day and unloaded a good three years' worth of minor problems on the poor man, because, like all health professionals, she didn't make an appointment with a doctor unless some part of her was about to fall off. In this instance it had been her mind; her restless, jumpy mind was hanging out of her skull and she just needed something or someone who could shove it back inside. She told him she was feeling stuck and overwhelmed. He had given her the prescription without enquiring much further, renewed it a few months later too.

Stevie lit another cigarette in the hope it might be laced with party spirit. Not long after, she heard the door to the utility open and wondered if it was Ben. He didn't approve of her smoking, never smoked himself since giving up the college weed, he was very precious about his larynx. She wasn't sure she had the wherewithal right now to hide her annoyance that he'd withheld his good news when she had asked him multiple times over the past few days. It felt deceptive. It belittled her enduring efforts to support him, to be the competent adult in the relationship while he rolled around in glitter. He had forgotten they were in it together. And she was mad with him too for calling her out on the baby thing, especially because he was right. Stevie had never really known her own mind on the subject. Even in that curiously fervent phase of her twenties the desire had been fuelled by Ben's disinterest, his blithe assurances they had plenty of time.

The back door latched. 'How do?' said Dylan.

Stevie moved off the step to let him out.

'It's lovely here,' he said. 'The house is too hot.'

'The house is perfect, as ever.'

He gave her a wry look, scuffing his loafer against the step. He had no coat on and the brilliant white of his shirt made her shiver.

'You're cold,' he said.

'The alcohol is doing its job.' She put up the collar of her blazer. 'How are you feeling?'

'Ah, grand.'

'What does that mean?'

'The back is OK again.'

'But?'

'I've had a migraine since the third round. It's always this side,' he pointed left. 'I don't know why.'

She stubbed out the cigarette on the decking. 'Is your neck tight?'

He clicked his shoulder in reply.

'Turn around,' she said, surprised at how quickly he obeyed. Putting her right arm around his chest to give her purchase, she palpated the smooth skin of his neckline for triggers. He smelled deeply of pine, a clean, cheering smell that made her conscious of her stale breath. She turned her head to the side and pressed into a huge knot near the curve of his shoulder.

'Jesus,' he said.

'Sorry.' After a minute she felt it disintegrate beneath her fingers, the satisfaction of that. She let him go.

Dylan gave his shoulder a rub. 'Thanks,' he said.

'Better?'

'A bit, yeah.'

'It will get better,' she said, looking into his eyes, the clear blue diminished in the dark.

'I know.'

'I mean the whole thing.'

'I know. It's just—'

'What?'

He stared at the lawn for guidance. A few seconds went by. 'It's not just the illness. I miss rugby. I don't know who I am without it.'

'You're you,' she smiled.

'But what am I going to do? I didn't finish college. Once I got the contract, I was out the door. At the time you said it was a bad idea.'

'I said lots of things in college. I was very talky back then.'

They laughed, broke eye contact, each preferring to watch the outline of the other.

She lit another cigarette. 'Just focus on getting better. You can figure the rest out later.'

'How are you anyway?' he said. 'It's not all about me.'

'Don't do that.'

He crossed his forearms over his chest.

'You've every right to talk about it,' she said.

'To moan.'

'Constant pain is hard going.'

'Others have had worse.'

'I mean in here.' She tapped her forehead. 'Pain affects the brain in the same way as loss or loneliness.'

'Thanks for the biology lesson.'

She smiled.

'You're in a great mood tonight,' he said. 'You must have known about the play.'

'I didn't, actually.'

'Oh,' he said. 'But you seemed so chummy.'

'This evening? When were we chummy?' She gave a loud chuckle.

'What?'

'It's a strange word.'

'Chummy? What's wrong with chummy?'

'Cut it out!'

'There's nothing wrong with *chummy*.'

'Like your man inside is a St Bernard.'

'I saw ye coming in tonight,' he said suddenly.

'Yeah?'

'Thick as thieves.'

Stevie humphed. 'I was probably comforting him. *It could be you*, and all that jazz. And he still didn't tell me.'

'Maybe he wanted it to be a surprise.'

'I guess.' She stopped smoking, not wanting the end, offered it to Dylan as a joke. With precision he flicked the butt from her fingers. She kept her eyes on it, following the trajectory, the pretty orange sparks.

'I better get that or there'll be trouble.' He ran across grass that had the slightest sheen of dew and came back smiling. 'What about that for a sprint?'

'Still got it.'

'I just need to shift this.' He touched his stomach.

'You look fine.'

'Come on,' he said. 'Three stone.'

'OK, you look normal. Not like a rugby player buffed to an inch of his life.'

'That's my normal.'

'Get over yourself,' she said. 'You're a ride.'

He laughed at that, and she felt pleased.

'Didn't you inspire a slogan T-shirt?'

Dylan groaned.

There was a girl in college who'd gotten the words TURNER: TOTAL RIDE printed on the back of the university jersey.

'She never missed a match,' he said. 'In fairness.'

'Until Rachel chased her off.'

They riffed about that night, in their mid-twenties, when Dylan met Rachel. She was working in the VIP area of a basement club on Leeson Street, the only promotions girl who was able to tempt him into a vanilla vodka shot. Stevie remembered her dress: backless, iridescent, flimsy. Leinster had narrowly lost the European Cup final and there was a sense of anarchy, as if they could drink back the win. Total Ride had been following Dylan from early evening, showing up outside the members' bar in the rugby grounds where the bouncers repeatedly turned her away, but the girl had staying power, she managed to track them to the nightclub in the wee hours, buzzing around their section like an inebriated wasp, stealing drinks with such brazen confidence you could hardly begrudge her the theft.

'She nicked the wine right out of the bucket,' said Stevie.

'Do you remember I asked you to pretend to be my girlfriend?'

She caught his eye.

'Just to scare her off, like,' he said.

Thank you for clarifying, Stevie did not say. 'She was disappointed in your choice, as I recall.'

'Didn't approve of your Converse.'

'Not WAG enough.'

'Then Rachel appeared,' said Stevie. 'What was it she said to her?'

Dylan shook his head. 'Something about the culchie bus and Coppers.'

'You don't mess with Rachel,' Stevie said.

'Certainly not.'

He hadn't been able to take his eyes off the dress, Stevie remembered that. Ben bet her a tenner that Rachel was a keeper, not just another of Dylan's conquests, the similar looking young women who would enter their lives for a week or two before vanishing again in a flurry of training schedules and away games.

'You didn't like Flaming Lips earlier?' Dylan said.

'Too cool for them.'

'You're too cool for everyone, Stevie Jones.'

The sound of her surname rang out in the darkness.

'Oh, yeah?'

'That's always been your problem. The coolest physio in town.'

Caught up in their laughter, they didn't hear Rachel open the door until her clipped voice interrupted the night. 'You guys,' she pointed to the bedrooms, 'keep it down.'

Stevie apologised, Dylan said nothing, and they all traipsed back inside.

*   *   *

On her way to the fridge Rachel didn't bother acknowledging Ben, who was muttering to himself at the table, his animated face flashing with handsome insanity. She'd enjoyed chatting with him earlier in the evening, dissecting the triumphs and casualties of the theatre world, the merits of reality TV, the very public breakdown of one of the rugby wives, and Rachel's relief that nothing like that had ever happened to her. They even talked about IVF for a while, whether she and Dylan might have to do this soon— whether they should be doing it already. Ben was surprisingly astute on the matter, the cost of it, financial and otherwise. He took the time to listen, to think things through. On a night out he was good company, his funny, malevolent charm hard to resist, a generosity of spirit, the way he engaged willingly, showed real interest in her life. Every enquiry he made seemed to highlight how devalued she'd become to her husband these past few years. And it had been nice—wonderful—to hear someone talk with perspective for a change, at a distance from pain. But sadly, after drink number whatever, he'd passed the threshold of attentively drunk to obnoxiously so and Rachel, who was relatively sober, had no interest in the fake rage arguments of world affairs into which he had chosen to distil his emotions.

Quickly she passed the table with its derelict air of half-filled glasses and debris, her gaze trained on the magnolia gleam of the island. Astonishing that he was still going, when she had literally left the room to get away from it. The endless environment. Negative tipping points and greenwashing and the earthquake in Myanmar that was far worse than anyone realised, which had made her want to say, *seriously?* What about the people who experienced it, the thousands who lost family and friends, who saw their homes crumble to the ground in a tremendous feat of reverse engineering? Ben was an expert on the environment, in his own mind, and like all secret experts, he was only ever brave enough to come out late in the evening when other people didn't have the energy or cunning to excuse themselves, to subtly change to a topic of conversation that might allow for two people to contribute instead of the unidirectional radio stream of invective she'd been subjected to for nearly half an hour while Dylan and Stevie hung out in the garden talking about god knows what. She had listened to their intermittent laughter, frustrated at her exclusion, as if the real party was happening out there and she was stuck in a perpetual queue.

'You OK, Rach?' Dylan came behind her at the fridge. 'Need some wine?' He reached to the top shelf to get Stevie's neon plonk. 'Here you go.'

'Lovely,' she said sarcastically.

Eyeballing her, he dug out a fresh four-pack of beer and closed the fridge. 'What's up?'

The other two were in frenzied debate at the table, Stevie somehow having managed to involve herself in the doomsday lecture.

'Rach?'

'Nothing's up. I'm fine. What's up with *you*?'

'Hey,' he said, offering a hand.

She shirked his touch. 'What were you doing out there for so long?'

'Having the chats.'

'It was rude,' she said. 'Grow up.'

The room was suddenly quiet.

Dylan clamped his mouth shut, snatched the bottle of schnapps off the island, brought it to the table. 'Will we have a shot, lads?' he said.

They debated whether it was too late, but Stevie never said no to fun—something Rachel resented, the way the woman's mere personality made Rachel look like a bore—and soon enough they were all preparing to do a shot, *one for the road*, she heard Ben say, in a voice that was fooling no one.

Although they cajoled her to join them she resisted, busying herself with glasses that could easily wait till morning. She looked at the clock. Just gone 1 a.m. The last few hours had played tricks with time, the excruciatingly slow seconds amounting to quick, sneaky minutes that meant they were now officially in tomorrow. It wasn't Rachel's call to ask people to leave. These were Dylan's friends—even after years of knowing each other that was true—and she would have to hang in there until they decided to go. To smile, to serve, to pretend to be chilled. The powerlessness of the situation was unpleasant, especially when she knew it would be her responsibility to get up when Leah woke at seven, trudge downstairs to make breakfast, clean up from the night before, which was in reality this current night, right now, time had done its trick on her again!

Rachel gave up on the dishes, returned to the table and did a quick shot, shuddering at the aftertaste.

'Well, hello,' Ben grinned. 'Look who's joined the party.'

Stevie cheered.

'Watch out Terenure,' Ben continued, 'Rach is on the tear.'

In his wild laughter there was an echo of youth, of insolent good health. Rachel had a flashback to the night of her hen party, her sister Emma doing the Macarena on the dance floor in The Academy, her own drunken awareness of how dated and mortifying this was, then from the haze of the surrounding crowd—Ben's grinning face. It was not a memory she enjoyed. She did another shot to shake it off.

'Wow,' Dylan said. 'OK.'

Rachel said, 'I'm officially resigning from breakfast duty.'

'Fine,' her husband said, 'I'll do it,' as if it was something he did frequently. He massaged the skin at his temples. His face was very pale, she noticed now. For a second all his suffering became clear to her and she forgave him everything.

But Ben was back talking about glaciers, how there was enough ice on earth for the sea level to rise by sixty-five metres, the height of the Makkah Royal Clock Tower in Saudi Arabia.

'The what?' said Dylan.

Time passed while they continued talking nonsense. Rachel watched them, not really following the agenda, just the flow, the brilliant bounce of their conversation.

'Water levels this high,' Ben was saying. He stacked the chips into an unstable column, then slapped the table to make his point, toppling the pile everywhere, so obvious and noisy an outcome that Rachel almost did the mocking, showy clap her father used to do when she was young.

The others were skitting, bending to collect the chips from the floor, before Stevie launched into a story about the time in college when they'd used foil-wrapped condoms for poker chips.

'The look of disgust on your flatmate's face,' Dylan said.

'Sandra.'

'Saintly Sandra,' Ben said.

'She was horrified,' said Stevie. 'Threatened to call campus security.'

'Thought it was an orgy,' Dylan barked. 'A threesome!'

They went into fits again.

'Guys!' Rachel said. 'Leah.'

The laughter tailed off, but Stevie still had it in her, her contorted face trying to contain it. Dylan looked at the ground, his shoulders giving small, involuntary shakes. He would glance at Stevie, Rachel predicted, and of course he did, the pair of them falling once more into peels of ungainly laughter, but at least Ben had stopped, he'd straightened up and was watching his wife—sorry, his 'partner'—with interest.

In a commanding voice, Rachel said, 'What's your big role, Ben?'

Stevie gathered herself. 'He was reading for Jerry.'

'In what?'

'Harold Pinter's *Betrayal*,' Ben said grandly.

'Brilliant,' said Dylan.

'Like you even know who that is,' said Rachel.

Woah! She tried to catch the meanness, to slow it down. This was another reason she didn't drink much nowadays. It wasn't a good look in your forties. She found herself staring at Stevie, resenting her the fortune of her birth a full three years later. So what if the little rich girl had started college when she was seventeen? It didn't make her special. Rachel was already working at that age, like everyone else she knew.

'Rachel.' Stevie waved. 'Are you OK?'

With effort, she composed her face.

'When the play is in London, how about we all go for a weekend?' Stevie said.

'Legend,' said Dylan.

'Sure,' Rachel managed. 'Who else is in the cast?'

Ben named an actress they'd never heard of and a moderately successful actor from a long-running cop show. 'He's playing Jerry, actually,' he said. 'I'm Richard.'

'Who's Richard?' said Stevie.

'He's the husband.'

'I thought Jerry was the lead?'

Ben gave a twisty smile. 'There are two male leads. They thought I was more suited to Richard.'

'Right.'

'Who cares?' said Dylan. 'London's calling!'

'Most of the rehearsals will be here though,' Ben said. 'We'll have the run at The Abbey first, then I guess I'll be a month or two over there.'

Stevie pulled a sad face.

'Don't worry,' said Dylan. 'We'll look after her.' He reached across the mess of chips and patted Stevie on the back.

It was an avuncular gesture, nothing that should have bothered Rachel, but added to the other stresses of the evening—the
endless small talk and exclusions, the many drinks of multiple
varieties, the fact it was nearly half two, and the exhaustion
of months, no, years spent caring for her husband was now, at
this most inopportune and public time, finally undoing her—
the intention alone induced a sour, primal loneliness that shot
through her body and brought her to her feet.

'I'm wrecked,' she said. 'Can we call it a night?'

The three of them gaped at her.

After a beat Stevie said, 'Of course. It's getting late.'

Getting? Rachel felt a pressure behind her eyeballs.

Stevie nodded at Ben to use his phone but he was too drunk
to understand so she scrambled in her handbag for her own
phone, pulling up the taxi app, in slow motion it seemed to
Rachel. To her left, without even glancing at him, she could feel
her husband's displeasure. She could neither leave the table nor
sit down, she was stuck in this posture of irate bouncer, which
she did not fully understand or wish to interrogate.

They walked them to the front door and said a sombre good
night. Rachel tried to recover by giving Stevie a hug but it was
all awkward angles and timings, their bodies had internalised
the strife. On the way back to the kitchen she could feel Dylan's
mood track her down the hallway like a half-starved wolf. He
closed the kitchen door behind them.

'Why did you do that?' he said.

'What?' She couldn't look him in the eye.

'Ruin a lovely evening.'

She apologised quickly, they were too drunk for anything else,
suppressing the feeling of injury, the urgent, childlike voice that
knew, like children always do, the shape of something wrong.

Dylan said her apology was useless, the damage was done. Sloppily, he filled a pint glass with water, left the tap running and stomped upstairs to bed.

As the hours ticked down to morning, Rachel lay awake in the guest room, wondering if there was any day in the fourteen years they'd been together where Dylan had loved only her. She couldn't call him out on it, she knew, had lost that right a long time ago. Instead she fell asleep thinking of their wedding, how the rain had lifted by evening and the ballroom glowed golden with a late and welcome sun.

DYLAN

AT THE CELEBRATION for their Leaving Cert results things have turned messy. Outside the nightclub in Sallins, Dylan discreetly checks his watch as Ben leans forward and retches. Nothing comes up this time. They've been here for nearly an hour, hiding down an alley beside the club, away from the bouncers. The wall of the building is splashed with a sickly orange arc. Ben tentatively straightens for a moment, before the retching starts again.

'Turkey farm,' Dylan says.

Another retch. 'Not funny.'

But it kind of is, Dylan thinks, that they're missing the big night out, the reward dangled for months to get them to study. He takes out his phone and checks the notifications. Five missed calls from Serena, and one very long text. He doesn't bother to read the full thing, the opening sentence is enough.

'I'm done,' Ben says. As he slides towards the ground, Dylan catches him, bears his weight over to the steps beside the fire escape. They sit down next to each other, the air around them a smoky blue, a corridor of dark sky above.

'Man,' says Dylan. 'Your breath.'

'I'll never get back in.' Ben buries his face in his hands,

presses the palms into his eye sockets with drunken purpose. His shirt has an obvious stain under the laurel wreath logo.

Dylan takes a packet of Extra from his jeans. He came prepared tonight: gum, tissues, condoms. This last item makes him feel like an imposter, as if having sex is something he does regularly. His teammates are always slagging him off for being a player. Only Ben knows the truth.

'You'll need to hide your shirt.' Dylan unties the jumper around his waist.

'Thanks,' says Ben, whose eyes begin to water.

Dylan looks at his scuffed Adidas, the little cracks like fissures in the earth. It annoys him that he can remember the term now, when geography is over and he got a low B.

'Sorry.' Ben rubs his eyes with the sleeve of Dylan's jumper. 'I'm a mess.'

'You just had too much vodka. We'll get back in.' He gives Ben a tissue. 'The bouncer knows who I am,' he says, meaning it to be of comfort but it sounds boastful.

'Serena will kill you for being gone so long.'

Dylan traces his runner in the dirt by the bottom step. 'I'm already in trouble for not noticing her hair.'

They laugh but underneath he feels mean, this is Serena's night too, he knows she's expecting big things. He wishes for a second they could just go home now, he and Ben, and play Grand Theft Auto until morning. Suddenly everything seems too dark, the pitch of the sky and potholed ground, even the strip of light from the street beyond, which shades rather than reveals the occasional passer-by.

'Will we go back in?' Dylan says.

'Serena's gorgeous,' Ben says. 'You're so lucky.'

Dylan smiles.

'Oh come on,' says Ben. 'She's the best-looking girl in school.'

This is not untrue, but sometimes Dylan feels that the reason they're together is because everyone thinks they fit. Serena's long red hair and obvious beauty, the fact she can sing, that she got the lead in the school show every year. His minor celebrity since the Leinster academy has shown interest. Another reason: Serena came up to him at the Halloween disco in fifth year, pushed him against the wall of the school gym and scored him in front of his cheering mates.

'Are you set for tonight?' says Ben.

'I think so.'

'Every lad in the school wishes he was you.'

Dylan gives a hostile laugh.

'What?' says Ben.

'Nothing.'

'No, seriously, what's wrong with that?'

'I just don't think it's accurate. The Cool Group, for example.' Which is what the lads in his year who have a band are called. 'They think she's an airhead.'

'Why do you care about those tossers?'

Dylan knows Ben hates The Cool Group, because he should be one of them, really, but wasn't allowed in way back in first year when these things were arbitrarily decided. 'You didn't say it was untrue,' Dylan says.

'What?'

'The airhead bit.'

As Ben starts to defend Dylan's girlfriend in passionate spurts, enthusing about the way she learnt her lines so quickly for last year's production of *Great Expectations*, Dylan knows he's baiting his friend in a way that isn't fair, soberish versus unsober, ice versus fire. But he can't resist, not since he figured out Ben is madly in love with his girlfriend, which Dylan realised one day during rehearsals when he arrived early to collect Serena. She was on stage doing a speech and Ben was watching her in raptures from the front row. Dylan was surprised at first, then as time went on and the shock lessened, he was confused at how little he cared. Other lads would be angry or possessive. He thinks there might be something wrong with him, that he lacks emotions that come naturally to his friends. When his sister Caitríona makes fun of him, she calls him *robot*. If he tunes out of one of her endless rants about the ever-shifting allegiances among the girls in her class, she says, *Robot is charging* in an auto-mated tone, and his family goes into hoots.

'OK, OK,' he says now, wanting to end Ben's paean. 'Serena is great.'

'Is she still angry about UCD?'

'You know the answer to that,' Dylan says.

'I'm sorry. Especially since it doesn't matter now.'

Ben convinced Dylan to put Trinity down as his first choice so they could both be in the same university. They've grown up together. Every seminal moment of their lives, every new phase, they've been there for each other, Ben said, which was a very per-suasive argument. But Ben didn't get through the interview stage for the drama course he wanted in Trinity, and now, even though he got five hundred and thirty points, he thinks his life is over.

'Single honours English,' Ben groans, as if he can read Dylan's mind.

'Better than information and communications technology.' Dylan picked the lowest scoring science course as his first choice. His scholarship—tuition costs and free accommodation in Goldsmith Hall for first year—is contingent on him getting the points for something. He seems to have scraped through, with the exact number needed, so he hopes it doesn't rise this year. His teachers have always said he has more in him academically, which put his mother on his case for years, but he reckoned they had to say stuff like that at the meetings, you couldn't just tell a parent their child was a dope.

Dylan's talents lie outside the classroom. Rugby, gaelic, soccer, running—he could have pursued any of them. He chose rugby because he can go as fast as he wants once he has hands on the ball. That's what he says publicly, and it's true, but another reason, that only Ben knows, is Dylan chose rugby to annoy his father, a former county footballer with a Leinster final medal to his name. He wasn't going chasing after that. Why would he want to live in someone's shadow?

'I might as well be doing ICT,' Ben says now.

'You can do drama on the side. Won't there be loads of it in Dublin?'

From the street beyond comes the sound of girls admiring each other. Dylan squints to see if he can make out Serena's bare legs.

Ben shakes his head. 'Not the same thing. It's like me telling you that you can switch to football if they don't pick you for rugby.'

Dylan thinks about this. 'Is it?' he says.

Ben clutches his stomach as if he might be sick again, though it's clear he's sobering up, they could actually stand a chance at getting back in. 'Drama is all I've ever wanted to do.'

'And you still can outside college.'

'What's the point?' Ben says. 'If I'm as rubbish as they think.'

'Let's go back inside.'

'You go.' Ben sniffs, like he knows far more about life than Dylan.

'Can't go without you. My best mate!'

Finally, Ben smiles. He always claims credit for their friendship, for sitting down beside Dylan on their first day of primary school. Dylan thinks it would have happened anyway. Their fathers knew each other, were friendly enough to call in a pint if they met by chance at the club, which was the closest Irish men of that generation came to intimacy. But then Ben's dad died suddenly when the boys were in third year. Dylan is lost for a moment, remembering the shock, the first person he knew who was there, then suddenly not.

'What's wrong?' Ben says.

Dylan hesitates.

'Go on.'

'I was thinking about your dad.'

'Why?'

'I dunno, the day like. It's a big day.'

'For *some* people,' Ben says.

'Ah, knock it off. We're getting to Dublin. That's what matters.'

After a moment Ben says, 'I did think about him today.'

'Yeah?'

'A lot, actually.'

'That's good.'

'No, it wasn't.'

Dylan looks intently at him.

'I know what would have happened,' Ben says. 'He'd have absolutely freaked that I didn't get my first choice. I can hear his voice. It would have been all my fault.'

'But he hated you doing plays. Remember? He was always on at you about football,' Dylan says.

Ben turns his head with animal alertness. 'I never thought of that.'

'That's what friends are for.'

'You're right,' Ben says. 'He might have been thrilled!'

'Come on to hell, I'll buy you a Jaegerbomb.'

He nudges Ben in the ribs and then they're laughing, standing, they even have a brief, ridiculous hug before setting off to face the bouncers with their best cocky strut. As they take the corner for the entrance, Dylan feels it again, the sensation of earlier that morning when he got the pink results slip, the start of a new life away from this town, where he won't have to carry the responsibility of being the rugby legend, where he can join other lads who are just as good as he is and see if he can make it.

*   *   *

Two months into college Dylan still hasn't been to a house party. This is either very smart (his coach, his father, his newly acquired agent) or incredibly stupid (Ben, Ben, Ben) so tonight, to please his friend, he has just arrived at a rundown redbrick in Portobello that looks to have lights on in every room and dozens of people inside.

Dylan lingers on the porch to catch his breath. The moon is hidden behind the peaked roofs of the terraces, the street unfolding in a glum orange light he has come to associate with the mazing city after dark. He ran from the bus stop on the main road, darting down in heavy rain, and now his jacket is the colour of cardboard. The wrong choice for a cold November night, but the only one he owns that doesn't look like training kit. Tonight's session was a washout, a gruelling endurance test on Trinity's waterlogged pitch. He was back in his room in Goldsmith in his pyjamas when Ben texted. *You have to come to this party. BIG news.* All Dylan wanted was to lie down in his compact bedroom and relax, but he hasn't seen his friend in weeks, so he made coffee, took two cans of Dutch from the fridge, then legged it as far as Nassau Street to catch the 15. It was embarrassing, the way the bus brought him halfway around the city before eventually landing him at a place he could have walked to in less time. Things like this happen to him often in Dublin, small reminders he's still green. He goes to ring the bell now but the door is on the latch.

Inside, the place is packed, older students at a glance. They have violently coloured hair, provocative piercings, clothes that are darkly shabby and artistic. Drama people. Ben was offered a place on the course a few weeks into college when someone dropped out. He's been busy ever since, catching up, he says, but this seems to involve socialising rather than lectures. In secondary school, even on training days, they always hung out at some point. After Ben's dad died, Dylan's parents stepped up. His mum Helen especially. She treated Ben like another son, and only very occasionally did Dylan find this annoying.

He does a slow loop of downstairs now, moving uneasily through the crowd. No familiar faces in the kitchen or adjoining sitting room, or in the group of smokers out the back. Upstairs there is music so he follows the sound, excusing himself to get by a girl in Doc Martens and fishnet tights who is sitting on the top step, rolling a cigarette with one hand. She says hello as if she knows him and he compliments her skills before moving on to a dimly lit room where clusters of people are talking loudly, some of them dancing to a song he doesn't recognise. In the far corner two girls are kissing, which he knows is fine, but it also makes him feel a hundred years old, like he's his father walking into a party of cool young people. He looks around in desperation for Ben but there's no sign. Taking out his phone, he calls him again, hangs up before the cringeworthy voicemail with the American accent that Ben says is for professional reasons.

Moving backwards towards the door, Dylan tries to blend into a group of four or five guys without having to contribute to their conversation. He opens a can, leans sideways against a free patch of wall, listens to them talk about a film he hasn't seen, that he didn't even know existed. Most of his evenings are spent training, if not with the team then a strength and conditioning session in the gym, or if it's a rest day, he tries to follow the advice of the coach and do nothing. He knows he has to let his body recover if he wants it to perform for him, that's what it frequently feels like, as if he's trapped inside a thoroughbred horse that requires constant maintenance and care.

The last few weeks, since the dark evenings came in, he's gone to bed at nine on rest days. He's lucky to be in a flat with four postgraduate students who are quiet and self-contained. A few of his teammates live in party flats and you can see it on the pitch. But sometimes he gets lonely; he's pretty sure his flatmates look down on him for his age and choice of college course. At the start of term, when he was only learning his timetable, the theoretical physics guy asked him what modules he was taking. The others were in the kitchen too, marginally interested, enough to hear that Dylan had nothing to say, his mind just blanked, he couldn't think of a single one. They've left him alone since. He doesn't care. None of them even like sport. The lads on the team are nicer, more inclusive, but most of them are from Dublin and have their own lives, their nights out and social circles already decided. More than once he's thought about calling Serena, or just showing up at UCD to see how she'd react. But he knows he would be using her, rekindling things for his own comfort. The last he heard she had a new fella anyway.

When he's drunk half the beer and there's still no Ben, he sends a text to say he's going to leave if his friend doesn't show his face soon. He doesn't mean it to sound aggressive, but that's how it looks, the little envelope fluttering away. He sets the can down between his feet, checks his credit balance, then opens the snake game and watches the line go slowly across the screen before it hits the wall and dies.

'Not a great effort,' says a voice behind him. He turns to see the girl from the stairs, whose pretty smile just about works to deflate the defensiveness he feels at having his phone spied on by a stranger.

'You have to use your fingers you know.'

'Yeah?'

'I think it would help.' Her low, brilliantly full voice makes her seem like an authority on the subject.

'Are you a snake expert or something?'

'Well, I'm only in first year,' she says. 'But pretty much. The Christmas exams are going to be a breeze.'

He laughs, glances shyly at her, likes that she's laughing too, the crinkled skin above her cheekbones. She's unusual looking, dark and impish, her short height is perfect for her face. It would look wrong on another girl, it would look wrong on Serena, he thinks, like she'd forgotten to wear heels. The girl smiles again; her teeth are small, overlapping in places. There is something familiar about her and he thinks that maybe she's on his course.

'What are you actually studying?'

'Physio,' she says. 'Sadly more difficult than snake.'

'I'll bet.'

'What about you?'

'ICT.'

She whistles. 'Fancy.'

'Not really.'

'How many of you?'

'Loads,' he says. 'It's not very high points.' He feels his face colouring, takes up the can again for something to do. The group of lads have inched away so that he's standing alone with this too familiar girl and he feels, perhaps because of the sudden sense of isolation, an undeniable charge.

She says something kind about points not being important once you're out of school.

'Did you smoke your rollie?' he says.

'Not yet.' She looks up at him. Lovely amber-brown eyes. No make-up, her lashes are long and soft. 'I'm waiting for my friend to come back,' she says, drumming fingers on the wall. 'I love this song.'

Dylan wishes he knew more about music, that he hadn't relied on Serena for cultural information. 'What is it?'

'"All We Have Is Now" by The Flaming Lips.'

'Cool.'

'The *Yoshimi* album.'

'I don't know a lot about music.'

'Right,' she says.

Horrendous pause.

He opens his second can of beer, which is to say, his last. 'Where's your friend gone?'

'The offie. He had to do an emergency run.'

Something rushes inside him on the *he*. As she tells him how much booze they've gone through already, she and this male friend, he thinks it sounds wild, enough alcohol for a week, and she'd never go for him anyway, he wouldn't be able to keep up with her partying, and also, maybe it was just the fact he'd seen her on the stairs that made her seem familiar, like she's been promoted straight to old friend in this party of strangers. Then all of a sudden her hand is on his hand and the room goes still, the voices rising above him. He gives her a sideways glance, sees her mouth moving.

'Gimme your phone.' She tugs the handset from his grip.

Dylan lets her take it and she busies herself with something. Her face is paler now, the line of her jaw more pronounced in the light of the screen. He wonders, in daft fashion, what she's doing, if she's going to ask for his wallet and keys next.

'So it's a hack.' She shows him the screen. 'You hold down the star and the hash key, then hit zero.' On his phone, the snake is heading for the wall but this time it glides magically through and reappears on the other side.

'Good hack,' he says.

'Not as good as Grand Theft Auto.'

'You play?'

'Nah, but everyone's heard of the hack.'

'I haven't.'

'Seriously?' she grins. 'Apparently there's one that lets your avatar have sex with another player.'

His whole body, head to toe, flushes now and while he's thinking of an appropriate answer, the door to the room swings open and he catches it just in time to stop it from hitting her. Ben is there in front of them, his hair slicked in a new style.

'Mental,' Ben says to the girl. 'How did you know it was him?'

'I didn't. This is your mate?'

'Brilliant.' Ben claps him on the back. 'This is Dylan, my best friend.'

'Hi, Dylan.' She puts out her hand, which feels different now. 'I'm Stevie.'

'Good to meet you,' he says. 'How do you guys—'

Ben tells him about an audition for the Players co-op where Stevie was given the part and had to come clean that she was only there for the free wine, she'd rather die than get on stage in front of people.

'But your friend here was sound about it,' she says, laughing. 'Not like the other drama queens.'

They talk in a zippy, booze-fuelled way about a range of things: the chicken fillet rolls at Centra, Wikileaks on Guantanamo Bay, the offie with the cheapest vodka, the state of the music at this party, which is a topic Ben elaborates on until Dylan eyeballs him.

'What?' Ben says.

'I chose that CD,' says Stevie.

'Awkward.'

'What's wrong with it?' she says.

'Nothing. It would be perfect at a funeral.'

Dylan listens to the banter, mildly surprised at this side to his friend, the clever wit and ease, the way he seems to have grown up years in a few weeks, the fact that Stevie's eyes keep flashing at the ribbing.

'OK, OK,' she says, 'I need a cigarette,' and takes the rollie from her blazer pocket.

'Bad for you,' says Ben.

'I know.' She gives a wicked smile.

Ben pulls a lighter from his pocket, teases her with the flame, letting it go out when she leans in. Dylan starts to feel uncomfortable. She puts an end to it by swiping the lighter from Ben's hand. 'Let's go,' she says. 'My mates are in the garden.'

They follow like they've been taking orders from her all their lives, but at the bottom of the stairs she meets a group of girls who sweep her into the kitchen in a commotion of drunken greetings and admonishments. As they wait for her near the front door, Ben nods towards the kitchen and says, 'Well?'

'Trouble,' Dylan says.

Ben laughs.

*   *   *

At training before the big Colours Match with UCD next week, Dylan has scored three times, set up another two, and just when they should be nearly done, the other side thoroughly defeated, he makes space out of nowhere, races the length of the field and dots it down between the posts to the sound of cheering. Even though he's on the weaker team they have won comfortably. He knows the coach did this on purpose—to test him, yeah, but mainly to show the firsts how far they have to go. Dylan doesn't like being used in this way. When the whistle blows and the coach comes over to praise him, he downplays it, not wanting the other lads to think he cares. His game has really come together this year, match after match of rave reviews, where he doesn't have to think about the right plays, they simply materialise, his body is ahead of his brain.

He says goodbye to his teammates, jogs down the path beside College Park, one eye on the students sitting in their droves by the pavilion bar. Since the start of April the weather has turned mild. Just gone seven, a generous lightness to the sky, grand old oaks in the distance towering green. Before going he suggested a beer to the lads to be sociable and was relieved when they declined. Everyone knows the match next week is the big one, the old rivalry with UCD, who usually beat them, but this year is different, people keep saying, because they have Dylan Turner on their side. Yesterday the coach let him know a Leinster scout would be in attendance. 'Play your game,' he said. 'That's all you have to do.'

Dylan looks again at the drinking hordes and thinks about messaging Ben. Not even for a pint, just to get away from rugby for a while, to hear about real student shenanigans, because no doubt Ben will have stories, he always does. Dylan has enough sports people in his life. On his bad, doubting weeks, he has far too many. Ben is a break from all that; treats him like a person, not an asset. At secondary school in Sallins, the rugby crew couldn't understand that, they had no time for anyone who faked illness to get out of PE. And they didn't get Ben's hilarity, which was the whole point of Ben. The way he could change his face into the child from *The Exorcist* or Nose the biology teacher without even trying. How he could capture the tone of a lame disco hall with a quick lift of his eyebrow. Their college friends get it though, Stevie most certainly gets it.

Turning left at the end of the path, Dylan quickens his pace back to Goldsmith, wondering if there's pesto in the fridge. He can see that people are watching him as he moves, an elegance to the way he runs, which is as effortless to him as walking or breathing. By the computer labs in the arches, a girl in a white shellsuit stares at him, waving as he approaches. He stops too late to hear her question, thinks it might be the time, holds up his bare arm in apology, about to continue on when she says, 'You were great this evening.'

'Sorry?'

'At training. You were the best.' A thick, northern accent. 'I had my eye on you.'

'Oh, right,' he says. 'Thanks?'

'I was on the sidelines, up at the far end.' She points in the direction of the college theatre, where Dylan recently sat through a three and a half hour production of some Irish myth called *Tawn* in which Ben played the main rock. 'You wouldn't have seen me,' she says.

Dylan thinks it would be hard to miss her.

'Gráinne Cunningham.' She sticks her hand out and he shakes it automatically. There is something worryingly forthright about her demeanour, like a teacher or guard.

'I better get going here,' he says, indicating his grass-stained gear. 'Have to clean up.'

'OK,' she says. 'Do you live in Goldsmith Hall?'

'Am, why?'

'Because it looks like you're going that way.'

'Right,' he says, embarrassed now, thinking she might live there too, which would make their exchange marginally less bizarre. 'I do, yeah.'

'OK,' she says. 'See you at the match next week.' She makes no move to leave so he goes first, speeding up after the first few steps, reaching the door to the lift terminal in no time. At the bins a trio of plump seagulls fight over a tinfoil tray. He stamps a runner at them, drawing the scorn of their pale eyes.

'Hey!' A girl seems to spring from the wall.

'Jesus Christ.' His hands go to his chest, but it's Stevie.

'What the hell is wrong with you?'

He glances behind him to where Gráinne Cunningham had been standing—waiting? 'I may have a stalker,' he says.

Stevie laughs. 'Male or female?'

'A girl, from Donegal, I think.' And when the shock has subsided, he looks at her properly, takes her in, the flared jeans and red hoodie, the small leather satchel with the long strap she always wears across her body. 'What are you doing here anyway?'

She groans. 'I'm hungover.'

He gets his keycard, buzzes them into the stale-smelling passageway to wait for the lift. 'At this hour?'

'It was a late one.'

'At Ben's?'

She looks miserably at him, shakes her head.

'Uh-oh,' he says.

Stevie and Ben have broken up multiple times since Christmas. It's hard to tell who is responsible for these breaks, only that each time they seem absolute, until they aren't.

She presses the button for the lift again.

'It's slow,' he says. 'What happened?'

'I'm not really sure. We were out—'

'Where?'

'The Viper Rooms. With his drama lot.' She rolls her eyes. 'And the parts for *Romeo and Juliet* got posted to their noticeboard and his classmate Sophie looked at it before coming in to meet them, and I can't really remember who got what, I was drunk at that stage, but Ben got Tybalt instead of Romeo, and basically, he lost it.'

'Tybalt?' Dylan says.

They start laughing at the ridiculous name. 'Doesn't sound great in fairness,' she says.

The lift arrives with a screech. Inside the lights are too bright. Dylan reaches a hand to the roof. Stevie leans against the back wall, another Stevie appearing in the mirror. He is suddenly ultra-aware of himself, as sometimes happens when they're in close proximity. He wishes the lift would hurry up.

'It's impressive,' she says, catching his eye.

'What?'

'Having a stalker.'

'Is it?'

'When you haven't even played for Ireland. Imagine what will happen then.'

'I can dream.'

The lift pings open and he pushes her playfully out the door towards the glass overpass to the student halls on Westland Row. Halfway across, they stop to watch the people below, office workers rushing to catch a Dart. People who don't look much older than him. Stevie raps on the glass, points at a group heading into Mahaffy's on the corner. 'I know them,' she says. 'There's a table quiz tonight.'

He could do without drinking this evening, but Stevie's plans have a way of working out.

'Come on,' he says. 'I'm hungry. Are you fed?'

She says she's ravenous and they head back to his flat to see what's left of his weekly shop. His flatmate Nigel is leaving as they arrive. He holds the door for them, leers at Stevie as they pass. Nigel is twenty-seven and has a fiancée back in Portumna who's waiting patiently for him to finish his PhD. She's a nice girl, a teacher who comes to stay most weekends. Dylan feels bad every time he meets her, as if he's cheating on her himself, rather than being silently complicit in her boyfriend's midweek adultery sessions with a staggering variety of women.

They head towards the communal kitchen. Once the door is closed, Dylan says, 'Do you think he's good-looking?'

'Yer man?'

'Yeah.'

She makes a face.

'I don't get it,' he says. 'How does he score so often?'

'Are you jealous?'

'Of that lad?' Dylan says. 'Don't be mad.' But as he watches Stevie fail spectacularly to find a comfortable lounging position on the hard student res couch, he thinks that maybe he is jealous of Nigel, of his unethical, ruthlessly pragmatic efforts to get himself laid. Dylan has slept with two women in the whole of first year, and one of them was Serena after an ill-advised trip to Belfield.

He takes the pesto from the fridge, bare scrapings on glass. 'Hmm,' he says.

'Go and change.' Stevie stands. 'I'll figure something out.'

In the shower he finishes with a cold rinse shock for the muscles and dries himself with his clean towel, which wasn't supposed to be used till Sunday. He dresses quickly, a pleasant urgency to his movements. Black jeans, runners, a light blue T-shirt that looks almost white against his freshly showered face.

When he returns, Stevie is chatting to Rajiv, one of his sound flatmates. He's doing a master's in sports medicine and she's quizzing him on the details, saying she might consider it when she's finished her degree. Dylan gets a kick out of seeing her talk to people, the way she can handle anyone, no matter the demographic, smart, posh, old, young, she finds some way to get a conversation going. He thinks it might be a Dublin thing, an ease that comes from remaining in your hometown.

'I'll let you eat,' Raj says. He rinses a mug, winks at Dylan behind Stevie's back as he departs. Dylan shakes his head. 'No,' he wants to say, 'You have it wrong. We're just mates. She belongs to my friend.' But these older guys he lives with think his life is a joke, as if everything that happens to a person before the age of twenty-five is an indulgence or a lark.

'Ta-da!' Stevie sits at the table where two mounding plates of pasta are waiting, full of ingredients he knows he doesn't own. 'Rajiv gave me the olives, and I nicked sundried tomatoes from the shelf.'

'Nigel will be after you,' he says.

She shudders, sticks a fork in the spaghetti and twists it expertly off the plate. Dylan pours them both a glass of milk. More details of the previous evening's carnage emerge: a very public row at O'Connell Bridge, a patently insincere threat by Ben to jump into the Liffey, an unexpected return to the nightclub for a shot of tequila, before Ben hitched a lift to Rathmines on the back of a motorbike driven by a barman who was maybe a drug dealer and most definitely drunk. At some point she tells Dylan that she's booked tickets for the nine o'clock showing of *The Hitchhiker's Guide to the Galaxy* at The Screen, asks if he'll go. He agrees, happy there'll be no injury to his liver.

'I didn't know they'd made a film,' he says. 'Good book.'

'Forty-two.'

'The meaning of life.'

'Exactly! And did you—'

As she continues, Dylan nods along, feeling like a fraud. It's one of only three novels he's read, pressed on him by Ben the summer they were in Irish college.

'Should we ask Ben to go?' he interrupts her.

'What?'

'Was the ticket meant for him, like?'

'So what if it was? He didn't want to go, he hates Martin Freeman, and also, I'm never speaking to him again for the rest of my life.'

'Bit harsh on Martin.'

She pushes the empty plate away from her. Leaning back in the chair, she yawns and stretches her arms above her head. Everything about her is smooth, it strikes him. He wonders what it would be like to touch the sparse hairs on her wrist.

'What?' she says.

'Nothing.'

He gets up quickly, clears the table, washes the plates and saucepan, hangs the damp tea towel on the oven door.

'OK,' Stevie says. 'Let's do it.'

'It's only twenty past eight.'

She smirks at him. 'Quick drink in Mahaffy's on the way?' and before he has time to protest, 'Just one!'

And the next thing he knows, he's standing at the bar, watching her eager face guess the table quiz answers while she downs a second beer, and he wishes, in this instant, he was a regular pint-swilling student too, not some lad on the cusp of a sporting career that might not even happen, standing there like a tool with his glass of tap water, wasting his current life because he's been promised there's a better one around the corner.

JULY

S TEVIE BEGAN WORKING with Dylan shortly after the poker night, and nearly three months into rehab, he was making good progress. On a slammed weekday of regulars and emergency appointments, she looked forward to this final session, had been anticipating it all day, but he was late, unusual for him, the clock on her computer read five forty-five. An uneasy quiet in the basement clinic, the weight of the Georgian building on her shoulders. The others were gone to collect their toddlers from crèche, or in the case of the boss, across the park to Holles Street for a scan. Stevie covered the evening shifts because she did not have the excuse of children. She didn't mind, not really, she enjoyed working with women her own age, the five of them clicked. But this evening the clinic felt lonely, just the odd creak from the accountancy business above as people left for home. Slits of summer sky teased her through the barred windows, the darkwood floors had a cold, unfriendly gleam.

Yawning, she roused herself and went to check the treatment room. The windowless space smelled faintly of vanilla from the candle she'd lit to mask the odour of the previous client. They came in to her in all states, the men, and the older they got the less they seemed to care. The peaceful atmosphere made her want to lie down on the fresh paper covering the bed. Wednesday was her longest day, a ten-hour shift in which she was rarely off her feet. She glanced once more at the innocent bed and decided there was no harm. Firing off a text to Dylan—*you alive?*—she lay back and checked her unread messages to see one from Ben, a rundown of the eccentric warm-up methods of his female castmate, described in this instance as *goat yoga*. She laughed out loud. Ben had always been funny, a master of pithy asides. She loved this about him, had found herself instantly drawn to it when they'd first met, as if, without ever agreeing to, they were speaking in code. It wasn't a very obvious humour, nothing soft or sentimental to it, rather quick, offhand, slyly charged, and you had to be ready, which she invariably was.

After replying she put down the phone and closed her eyes. So tired these days yet always struggling to sleep. The temptation was to take a pill in the evenings when she got home, a solution that worked so well it was heading towards a habit. For the past week and a half she hadn't gone near them, largely to prove to herself she could survive without. She didn't need pills. She wasn't in real pain, not of the sharp, headline variety. It was more of an ache, a wordless longing, almost friendly in its familiarity. While she could pin it to whatever she liked when the mood took her—the flat, Ben, their baby indecision, the weather, a sore throat or cantankerous client, Dylan too, occasionally, if she was feeling maudlin—really it wasn't about any of these things, it just felt good to have somewhere to put the blame. The problem, in simple terms: she was sleepwalking through life. At thirty-eight she had lost her sense of purpose. The purpose of her. Of her life. At that age her grandmother had five teenagers, her own business and went to mass every morning. Her mother had three young daughters and a job in a bank. Something had gone wrong with Stevie. The ache knew this about her. It knew everything. She was dissatisfied with her life for no good reason, dissatisfied with life itself, how arbitrary and sudden it all was, and she didn't know how to get over it. That there was no specific cause troubled her, that this was by any external measure a time of relative peace and few demands, no helpless infants or sick parents, none of that had touched her yet, and surely it wasn't possible to already feel the shadow of it to come? But even her work, which she used to love for the joy of helping people, had started to seem insubstantial, temporary—muscles tightened again, tendons weakened, bones depleted, yes, each and every one of her clients was in a continuous state of decline and decomposition that would, it was quite accurate to say, ultimately end in death. Panicked, she opened her eyes to the flickering orange of a smoky wick. Cloying vanilla. To be too much on her own made her restless. Physical itch. Horror: monastic cell, sickbed, prison, confessional. Alone with her mind, without the bright slap of other people. Naval gazing hell. Even as a child. Australia. Right now, this little room. Up, she thought, move.

As if in accord, the shock of the doorbell ripped through the clinic. Before it could ring again, Stevie hit the intercom on the wall. 'Hello?' she said.

'It's me.'

She pressed the button, blew out the candle, went to reception to greet him, laughing at the distressed, ruddy face, the shapeless hi-vis over his T-shirt and shorts.

'Where's your helmet?' she said.

'In there.' Dylan dropped his rucksack on the floor. 'Sorry I'm late. Rachel made—' He broke off. 'Can you still see me?'

'Of course,' she said. 'Let's go.'

In the treatment room he tossed the hi-vis on a chair and reclined on the bed. His T-shirt had patches of sweat in the shape of small islands. When she rolled up his shorts to start on his quad, her fingers slid across the muscle.

'You're warm, anyway,' she said.

'I raced down the canal.'

'Go easy, you don't want to push it.'

'I'm not,' he said shortly.

She pressed her fingers into the belly of the ropey muscle, tried an elbow, conscious of his face constricting in pain.

'Very tight,' she said.

'Yeah.'

'From our swim?'

'Dunno.'

'How have you been generally?'

'Grand.'

'Grand?'

'Yeah, grand. Fine. Alive. Whatever.'

'Helpful.' She meant it as a joke and when he didn't respond, she poked his knee. 'What's wrong?'

Dylan looked at the peeling cornice on the ceiling. 'Just lash on,' he said. 'Please.'

Stevie waited.

He swallowed a couple of times, the sound amplified in the stillness of the room. Eventually he said, 'I'm worried about going backwards, that I'll lose strength again overnight. Like Ireland back in the day—great one match, crap the next.'

Stevie laughed.

'Seriously,' he said.

'I doubt it.'

'So it's possible?'

'Anything is possible. Though the data suggests that if you've made the type of gains you have—over months now, remember—you'll continue to improve.'

'You think?'

'I do.'

'OK,' he said. 'Thanks.'

She worked in silence for the next while, her preferred approach, a deeper feeling for the body, the seemingly arbitrary connections that often left people with a sense of the miraculous, when really it was just plain old biology and a bit of discernment. Her elbow went deep into his quad, up the inner leg to the start of the hip flexor, which was inordinately tight. She heard him curse under his breath. 'Sorry,' she said. 'Are you stretching enough?'

'I'm doing everything you told me to do.'

She leant harder on the groin. This time he cursed out loud. As the muscles began to give, she massaged a figure eight along his thigh until it relaxed completely. He gave a sigh that caused some shift in the room, not unpleasant, just distinct and unexpected, in a way that reminded her they were alone.

'How's Rachel?' she said.

His eyes blinked open, the light, crystallised blue a breath of air.

'Not great, to be honest.'

'Really?'

'Yeah.'

'What's up?'

'Ah, nothing. Or everything.'

She didn't press him, just moved to the other leg, had almost drifted off again into the rhythm of the release work when his voice cut through the room.

'Rachel had a miscarriage.'

'What?'

'We did, I guess. We had a miscarriage.'

Stevie stepped back from the bed. 'That's awful, Dylan.'

'It was early on, like nine weeks. Happened shortly after that night in ours. She didn't know she was pregnant, then she figured it out, then it was gone.'

'I'm really sorry,' said Stevie, thinking of the amount of drink they'd put away at the card game.

Dylan stared at her and she wondered if he was thinking the same, until he said, 'And now we're trying again.'

'Straight away?'

'I thought it was too soon,' he shrugged, 'but you know Rachel. She was on it immediately. Like the miscarriage didn't happen,' he said. 'Like she can replace it.'

Stevie started on the knots above the knee, a shade falling on her thoughts, he had passed his angst to her. She was quietly in awe of what Rachel was willing to go through to have a child. What so many women were willing to do. The fear returned that she was making a mess of her life and would only fully understand this years from now when it was too late to change. Some of her friends didn't have children either, but they seemed more sure of the reasons; their childless states had the heft of family trauma, money woes, climate concerns, or simply the pragmatic detachment of people devoted to other causes. Her sister Laura, for example, had never wanted them, she just wanted to write, and while Stevie fully supported her in this, she also felt pressure as the next in line to fill the blank of grandchildren in her parents' lives. That it was mostly an internal pressure only made it worse. At least Elise said she wanted them, one day, in a breezy, conditional-tense kind of way. Stevie would love to feel so casually confident. Her strongest instinct came from the indecision itself: she would not bring a child into the world as a hedge against future regret. Yet the indecision was the painful part. If she could just decide, there would be no more wondering. Since the night of the card game it had been pressing on her mind, though not quite enough to broach the subject with Ben. She wasn't ready for the force of his personality to energise and persuade them both. No clear path from her imagination to reality. The truth was she couldn't see them as parents. In a way they were both still children themselves, still the age they were when they first met, which was one of the terrible beauties of knowing another person, intimately, for all of your adult life.

'You OK?' Dylan said. 'You're very quiet.'

'We'll need to get you back to full power if there's a baby,' she said.

'Think you can?' The way his eyes ran quickly over her face gave her a lift, a reminder of how she used to love her job. A strange thought occurred to her now that this was less about healing than it was about power. She gave an involuntary shake of her head.

'Stevie?'

'Sorry, yes,' she said. 'Definitely. You just have to believe it.'

'Ah, hear.'

'I don't mean like that. Neurons that fire together wire together. So if you keep thinking you're going backwards, you probably will.'

'Modern-day sage.'

'Enough of your guff,' she said. 'Roll over.' She started on the calves, working her way upwards to the lats, giving him the programme for the week ahead: a walk-run, two weights sessions which she'd send to him later, another sea swim with her, if he fancied it. When he agreed she felt relieved. These outdoor sessions were the highlight of her week, resurrecting a younger part of herself—the fun person she had been in the early years of college—that had disappeared into a masters then a permanent position in a hospital, which she'd thought herself lucky to get with a recession looming and many of her classmates heading for Canada. But these days she wondered what she had missed out on. Sometimes she went through old Facebook albums belonging to her friends—Cambodia, Queenstown, Iguazu Falls!—trawling through their experiences as if their youthful adventures could somehow transfer to her through mindless clicking.

'Am,' Dylan was saying, 'I think my head might be about to break off my neck.' His voice, through the donut cushion, was distorted.

'Wuss.' She released the pressure and ran her knuckles along the nape to ease the tension.

'Better. More of that.'

'I'm not a masseuse.'

'If you say so.' The bed shuddered with his laughter.

'Watch it or I'll take out the needles,' she continued to joke, but her hands were palpating the fragile skin at the back of his ears in a way that was oddly addictive, the smooth run down to the neck. An indeterminate amount of time passed in silence, nothing but fluid movement. When she was done, he sat up in a trance, all heavy limbs and lethargy. She busied herself updating his notes on the laptop, listened to his deep even breath behind her as he bent to put on his runners.

'I'm meeting Ben now,' he said.

'Is that right?' Her boyfriend was a busy guy these days, she never seemed to know his schedule.

'He's squeezing me in for a bite before evening rehearsals.'

'I know the feeling.'

'Ah, he's just committed,' Dylan said. 'It's a huge gig.'

'You don't need to tell me.' Since the start of rehearsals, Ben had been going around in a fug of his own incipient glory, but she didn't say this to Dylan, couldn't bear right now to hear him defend his friend again. Instead she led the way out to reception to do the awkward payment part. From the start she had offered the sessions for free, having intuited from Rachel that money was tight, but Dylan wouldn't hear of it.

As he was leaving, he turned suddenly and hugged her.

Her feet lifted briefly off the ground.

He let go. 'I'm sorry if I was moody earlier.'

'You weren't.'

'Seriously. I'd hate to—'

'I know.'

'I shouldn't be taking—'

'I understand.'

'What I mean is—' he looked out the open front door at the stone steps that led to the street—'you're important to me, like.'

Before Stevie could reply he disappeared up the stairs. She remained at the door, listening to the sound of him depart, the reverb as he removed his bike from the railing. She waited till he had cycled away to return inside.

As she tidied the treatment room in preparation for tomorrow's clients she thought about what he had said to her. It was not wholly out of the ordinary for close friends of many years. She was sure he had said as much before, to herself, to Ben, to the pair of them together.

Back at her computer, she decided to finish reading the research she'd started on her lunch break, a paper from a doctor in Toronto citing the positive effects of hyperbaric oxygen therapy on patients with post-viral fatigue. Dylan's case was challenging, no simple solutions, it gave her plenty to do. After reviewing the study—interesting, but as with all this new material, more anecdotal than scientific—she set the phone to answering machine, sent her lady who always forgot appointments a message reminder for tomorrow, then rebooked Dylan, thinking again of his words to her as he left. She would up his reps in the water this week, he was ready for it. In his company these days she felt the mild excitement of something about to happen, life moving on after so much stagnation. A wholesome feeling. To make someone better, to witness them at their absolute worst and best, which was true of all difficult recoveries. When she'd shut down the computer she sent him a text. Smiling at the message, she barely noticed that her earlier anxieties had lifted.

*   *   *

With Leah away to the neighbours for chicken nugget Wednesday, Rachel sat on the couch with a microwave lasagne and searched for her favourite show, the panel of middle-aged women whose outspoken, colourful chats she only felt comfortable watching alone. As she pressed play, the women's faces came to life, but the volume was down, the small remote missing. She found it beneath a pile of old magazines. The iPad was there too. Leah, no doubt. Her daughter had taken to hiding anything useful, which Rachel worried was a reaction to the pressures their family had been under these past few years. It could be worse, she reminded herself. Like her neighbour, courageously cooking chicken nuggets for the masses, when her youngest son had answered the door earlier on crutches, no further along the scoliosis waiting list.

On screen the women chatted about midlife career changes. In response to one of the panellists becoming a solicitor at fifty-two, the presenter with the long wavy hair smiled, her face took on a nostalgic bent as she recalled her mother's favourite saying: *life is full of surprises*. Rachel thought of her own childhood, which was also full of surprises, sudden violence or attacks on her character that seemed to relieve but never eradicate her mother's toiling misery. It had left Rachel with the sense of always being in trouble, a problem, just not right in some vague and intractable way. She'd carried this into adulthood, into her career as an almost-model, her fear over the constancy of Dylan's love, even into the rugby set, the feeling of never being on a par with the other wives and girlfriends. And now, worst of all, into the miscarriage she had basically brought on herself.

The programme was doing nothing to distract her, so when she was finished eating she muted it and took up the iPad to listen to the positivity meditation recommended by her doctor. It was supposed to help her focus on getting pregnant again, by which he meant, to forget about the baby she'd drunk out of existence. A vodka cocktail. Three glasses of wine. Two shots. The day after she bled out, Rachel read, with the masochistic impulses of an addict, every single link in dozens of pages of internet searches on the risks of alcohol in the first trimester. Some said one drink was enough to cause problems.

The pain of this was so great as to be almost unacknowledgeable. While her rational mind understood she hadn't done it on purpose, hadn't known she was pregnant, another voice, louder, shrewish, something of the puritan about it, undermined all reason with its bare questions: why hadn't she checked before the party? Why hadn't she thought to open one of the many boxes of pregnancy tests stacked in the press under the en suite sink like neat rectangular accusations? They were trying, after all, had been patiently at it for much of the year. But month after month of the red swipe shock in the bathroom had made her complacent, she who knew, from a very young age, the dangers of complacency, that letting your guard down, sharing some childish piece of excitement or hurt, only left you more vulnerable to attack later on. Since the miscarriage, Rachel could not stop thinking about her mother. Although she hadn't seen Noreen since Christmas and it made absolutely no physiological sense, somehow it was all her fault.

But who could she tell? Dylan didn't get it, not really. Her sister Emma lived with her wife and two kids in Melbourne, having opted for the safest and most literal form of freedom: geographic escape. As had her brothers—Leeds, Sligo, Aberdeen—who were older than Rachel anyway, in secondary school by the time she was born, the final mistake in the long sequence of mistakes her parents called a marriage. Until the miscarriage Rachel had been an expert in blocking out all of that noise. She even felt proud she was able to do this while remaining in the same city as her mother, only a few miles away, though in that very Dublin way where neighbouring suburbs could be entirely separate and ignorant of each other. As her mother coddled her old woes in Drimnagh, Rachel was safe inside her Terenure redbrick. But the miscarriage had done away with all that, somehow, it had left her porous, peeled, the shifting sands of the past salting in.

She wondered if her dead baby was a boy or a girl, which was the nearest she'd come to telling Dylan how alone she felt. He had held her and said not to think that way, she would only upset herself, a line that was meant to placate but landed like blame. Again now, for the torturous certainty of it, she returned to what she had drunk the night of the poker game. An obscene amount, especially for her. If only the others had left before midnight, as she was hoping they would. If only she had stuck to wine. If only her husband had stayed in the kitchen. If only Stevie had stayed outside. (If only she could always stay outside.) If only Rachel had hidden her jealousy. If only she hadn't snapped at Dylan at the fridge. And back to the start on the joyless merry-go-round: if only she had done a test before they arrived.

If only they had started earlier. Should have—straight after the wedding—except Dylan had been scouted by an Italian club that year and they'd seriously considered the move. Good money, first team guaranteed. A dream of life in Treviso. In the end the Leinster coach talked him out of it, the same man who would barely return a phone call these days.

Once they'd known they were staying she got pregnant so easily with Leah. They decided to go for it, she blinked at Dylan, a baby arrived. But five years had passed since then, and aside from the worrying biology of things, there was the more general issue of luck. Like all lucky people, they had thought it was inherently in them, of them, until it was gone. The gods were angry now, that much was clear, and Rachel had no training in the dark arts of how to appease them.

On the iPad a red notification popped up on the message app linked to Dylan's phone. Her finger hovered over it. Ordinarily she wouldn't go near his texts, she was not a person who went searching for trouble, but as her mind began to dwell once more on the loss, and the loneliness of trying again, which her husband seemed only grudgingly to support, the same husband who gave all his time to his own health and recovery, it suddenly seemed reasonable to check up on his whereabouts by accessing the surely insignificant messages.

One from Jim saying it was good to see him the other night.

Five from Helen that were all part of the same message about a new doctor she heard on the radio.

The last text was from Stevie. It read:

You are important to me too.

Rachel put the iPad face down on the couch.

After a few seconds she picked it up to review the message again. Unsteady hands. Words bounced in blue light. Not caring if he knew, she pressed into the conversation, scrolled down, to an innocuous exchange about swim times and meeting points. Stevie appeared to have sent the message from nowhere.

With peculiar logic, Rachel felt responsible. Her jealous thoughts just minutes ago had somehow caused the words to be written, a dire synchronicity, impossible to ignore, that, no— wait—her brain caught up with the mass of feeling, its gnarled revelations. She had things jumbled. The message, with that pitiful, condemning *too*, justified her jealousy, cemented it. There were clearly grounds for suspicion. Her fingers coiled tightly of their own accord. She stared at the Persian rug in front of the television, tried to make sense of the many threaded colours whose design had no beginning or end.

As tears broke down her face she went upstairs to the safety of the master bedroom, but the grey and lilac tones did nothing to soothe her. Into the walk-in wardrobe, she began to aimlessly catalogue her good dresses, most of which she hadn't worn in years. Her hands ran in nimble desolation across the rack: the navy shift from the night of the poker, the lacy mini with the awkward zip, obligatory stash of boring black, a structured two-piece in bright tangerine, a gold mesh affair, the gruesome taffeta from her sister's wedding, tartan pinafore with a jewelled pin, velvet creation with vampire sleeves, an office-grey A-line that Rachel had, genuinely, never seen before, and finally, finally, her favourite dress, the blue silk three-quarter length from the Mauritian boutique, which she could only wear two weeks out of the year because if it was too hot there were sweat patches to contend with and if it was too cold she could not show off the open back that was the whole point of the dress. Yes, Rachel thought, a real conundrum. She sank to the ground, sat very still and stared for a long time at the unquantifiable pile of shoes against the back wall.

After a while she was ready to go downstairs, retrieve the iPad and return without a qualm to their message thread, scrolling back weeks, all the guilty dates flitting by, only stopping when she got to December and the photo Dylan had sent of the three of them—their little family, Leah beaming in reindeer pyjamas—wishing Stevie and Ben a very happy Christmas. Before this, there was a gap of about nine or ten weeks, and before that, just a couple of generic messages from Stevie offering sympathy for his illness, and help, if needed, to which Dylan hadn't replied. The contrast with recent months was stark. It didn't take much to see that the communication began in earnest after the poker night. All these messages about rehab plans and scheduling she now feared had led to something more. Briefly she thought about calling Ben, the meagre comfort of having someone with whom she could share her suspicion, until she remembered that Ben was at this moment meeting her husband. And that was enough to land her, from the foggy heights of her hurt, back to reality.

Instead she stared at Stevie's profile photo and saw in the small circle the face of a witch. The first time they'd met, in the VIP lounge of Leggs, she had foolishly discounted her. A short, grungy kid with the prowling breath of a smoker. Dressed in an oversized T-shirt bearing the name of some nobody band, she'd looked so out of place Rachel had actually pitied her. Over the years that pity had turned to wariness, and now to outright distrust. Once more she went slowly through their communication over the last three months, which contained nothing obviously incriminating, just the ease, the pleasure of a back-and-forth between two people hopelessly in tune. Reading through the messages again and again she could see no discernible pattern; there was something dense and foreign about the simple language that couldn't be deciphered.

By the time the doorbell rang, with Leah's signature of three dongs in a row, Rachel had calmed down. A chance she was overreacting. It was only one text. While she didn't doubt Stevie was capable of treachery, she felt sure Dylan wouldn't betray her. He wasn't that kind of man. And if he suddenly turned into that kind of man, a mutation Rachel was familiar with from childhood, she was certain he wouldn't do it to Ben, his best friend. She hurried to the door, already a plan forming to get Leah to bed early so she could prepare for a cross-examination so polite and innocuous her husband wouldn't even realise it was happening. There were ways of getting people to talk and, as a former shots girl, Rachel knew them all.

*   *   *

Waiting in the noisy burrito bar for Ben to show, Dylan checked his phone. He had multiple messages he didn't remember reading, including one from Stevie that eased his mind. Apologising had been the right thing to do. It wasn't her fault the pain in his legs had returned. It wasn't even pain's fault, just the nature of

99

recovery, the ebb and flow of the dreary tide. As the minutes passed with no sign of his friend, he could feel himself slipping back into the murky, magnetic why of it all: why him, why this illness, why the earth, the sky? The wondering would drive you mad.

He decided to call his mother to thank her for the new health advice, but the seven exclamation marks in her final message put him off. He needed to be in good spirits himself to deal with her exuberance, needed to have time, which he was surprisingly short on these days, considering he didn't have a job. To appease his wife he had done a number of courses in recent months, earned a few badges, started to query his contacts. No returns as yet. Time was running out to be any of the things he had never even wanted to be.

In a bar across the street the green pitch of a television match was visible through the window. Reflexively he looked away. Probably soccer, but just in case. These days he found it hard to watch rugby. Such a taunt, to see your own youth in high definition on a screen. The formidable fitness and cheering crowds. He still watched the big games, of course, had to if he had any hope of coaching. He'd already spent too much time in the wilderness. Management were fickle. For all the talk of values and principles, rugby was ultimately a business: out of sight meant out of contention. Dylan didn't know if he would make a good coach, but he would at least like the chance to pass on his wisdom to the new generation. Because what were you supposed to do with all that knowledge otherwise—spend the rest of your life shouting abuse at a screen?

Rugby was a game of time and space. Now that he was no longer playing, Dylan understood this better than ever. Create space. Attack space. Focus on the basics, do the simple things well.

Eyes on the ball. Step early, square up. Look for soft shoulders. Hold depth and arrive late. Trust the body, sharpen the mind. Manipulate the defence. What are they thinking? What are they thinking you're thinking? Choose another way. The best coach he ever played under used to say it was like chess. The twang of the Kiwi tyrant: plan, act, react. Faster! At elite level, when everyone had strength and fitness, rugby IQ was what mattered. And working hard on yourself. Eating well, doing the extras. Train, train, train. None of this save yourself for the match nonsense, no keeping back twenty per cent. No minding yourself. Training hard was vital—especially as a back. Footwork. Speedwork. Evasion. Ability to win the contact. Even thinking about it filled him with adrenalin. He stiffened in the chair, eyes sunk into the room, softly scanning the field, tables, stools, counter, staff in black shirts, pink lettering; in mere seconds he had the whole place accounted for, he felt great, until a woman seated by the door glared at him and he became instantly pathetic.

Looking away from her, down at his dumb hands, he wished so much to be young again. Properly young, seventeen, eighteen, to have it all in front of him. What he would do differently. On the pitch, certainly, though more essentially, inside his head. If he could go back now he wouldn't doubt himself, he would just enjoy it. But the great tragedy of rugby—of life—was that you could not combine the hunger and stamina of youth with wisdom learnt over time.

As often happened at low moments he found himself back on the pitch playing for Ireland in that fateful match. Going up for the high ball just inside the twenty-two. Pivoting awkwardly on the way down to avoid the tackle. Getting sliced by the Welsh number eight. Shattered his right fibula and tibia, and worse again, shredded the cruciate ligaments in his knee; the pain was so intense he felt like he'd been knifed. Got the ball away, then the stretcher. When he woke up in hospital after an emergency knee op, he asked if they'd won the match. The team doctor said yes, they had, and that Dylan might never play rugby again.

Three surgeries and two seasons later, he proved the medics wrong. Dylan Turner was back. Papers, pundits, agents were all talking him up. It went on for months. Yet no matter how hard he trained, he couldn't return to where he had been before. Who he had been. On the bench for the Six Nations that year, the following one too, straining to keep the emotion from his face in case the cameras were on him. Physically he was improving all the time, but the part of his mind that worked on instinct, that processed information in nanoseconds, kept glitching during play in an unconscious effort to protect the body. His attempts to override it only made him worse. After two years of training, with no more caps for Ireland and increasingly fewer first-team starts for Leinster, Dylan was forced to accept his new stature. If he hadn't done this he would have had to leave rugby forever. So he'd told himself he was lucky to still be able to play provincial, to make a professional squad. It was enough, he had told himself over and over again until he'd begun to believe it.

'Hello!' Ben called from the entrance, his face a relief. Dylan waved back, but Ben's attention shifted to a group of elderly women whose matching yellow jumpers turned towards him like a bunch of daffodils turning towards the sun.

Ben stopped at their table to answer a question. They laughed heartily at his response.

'Hi,' Dylan said, when Ben sat down. 'Is that the fan club?'

'A charity group on a backstage tour earlier. Walter let them into rehearsal. We got to pretend we were famous.'

'I'd say that was hard for you.'

'Terribly,' Ben grinned.

'Who's Walter?'

'Our overlord. The director. Don't get me started. Hey, will we order?'

Dylan, who had been waiting twenty minutes to do exactly this, said fine. They both got pulled pork burritos, with a side of nachos to share. On their return Ben decided he'd prefer to sit on the stools by the window. 'To keep an eye out,' he said cryptically.

The evening Dylan had been expecting—a burger and a couple of beers somewhere nice, a proper catch-up—seemed to be getting further away even as they were here in each other's company. 'We could have done another night if you're busy,' he said.

'No way, it's good to see you.'

They ate in silence, devouring the food like when they were teenagers, as if someone might take it away. At the halfway point they stopped for a rest. Dylan wiped his orange fingers on a napkin.

'Famished,' Ben said, 'I was.'

'How's it all going?'

'Pretty good. We just moved from the rehearsal room onto the stage this week to get a feel for dimensions, and I can't believe it, I mean, I can, obviously, because I'm there every day, but it really is fantastic, to be standing on a stage like that, you know?'

'Totally.'

Was it just his face, or did Ben look askance at this, as if Dylan couldn't possibly understand. 'Like match days for me,' he said.

'Oh, the match, the match. And how are the lads?' Ben laughed at his old joke, but there was no humour in it for Dylan this evening. Recently he had been avoiding his teammates. The last time he saw *the lads* he'd only stayed for one pint. Through their rundown of games he kept imagining himself on the pitch.

'They're grand,' he said. 'I don't see them much any more.'

'That's harsh,' said Ben, which led him back to the director and his unsparing methods. 'The others don't seem to notice.'

'Your castmates?'

'Rosie and Sebastian. Seb is from London too, so maybe he's on the same wavelength, but Roseanne is from Limerick.'

'Right.'

'She gets a way easier time. I think Walter fancies her. He's a bit of a creep, actually.'

'How long till opening night?'

'Good few weeks yet,' Ben said.

At the mention of weeks, Dylan thought of the miscarriage. He hadn't meant to tell Stevie. Rachel didn't want anyone to know.

They returned to the food. Ben began to talk again, explaining the holes in Walter's approach, outlining his fear that the director didn't fully grasp the play, the intricacies of Pinter, so to speak, and there was nothing the cast could do except go along with him.

'Actually no, no,' Ben said, an errant kidney bean falling on his lap, 'that's too harsh. He understands the play, he just has the wrong read on Robert.'

Who the hell was Robert? There had been no mention of a Robert, Dylan was sure.

'My role!' Ben said, because he could be full of his own bluster and still manage to read his friend's mind. 'It's like he has no real vision for my character.'

'Poor Robert.'

When he finished eating, Dylan crumpled the burrito wrapper into a ball and wondered if he could make it over the heads of the charity ladies into the bin. He raised his pitching arm, lost his nerve as he felt Ben's attention on him.

'You would have made it.'

'You think?'

Surely his friend would show an interest in his life now, his boring life of recovery and sleep, but all he said was, 'Next time,' before returning to the trials of professional acting.

As Dylan listened, it reminded him of being a substitute on the bench—there but not there, a body, a husk, pretending he was enjoying himself but really thinking, when will I get on? Watching Ben finish his burrito in dripping, satisfied bites, he felt the abrupt pain of injustice, which he hadn't felt in months, not since Stevie started to help him.

'Stevie's great,' he said.

'I think that's my line, mate,' Ben laughed.

The blood ran to Dylan's face as he tried to explain. 'Her rehab has done wonders. It's changed my life,' he said, lowering his voice, embarrassed at the bald accuracy of the statement. For one thing, he no longer felt morally responsible for having acquired a mysterious, meaningless disease. Stevie had made it clear to him just how many people were still suffering. She'd done an amount of extra work on his behalf, contacted clinics abroad for the latest research, dieticians on gut health, respiratory consultants on lung physio, linked in with his GP to get him on statins and aspirin, she had even found him somewhere for red-light therapy. He told this all to Ben now. (And what he didn't say: the best thing about Stevie was that she understood his predicament without him having to explain. She just got it, she got him.)

'Great stuff,' Ben said. 'She knows her onions. Wait, listen— my god!—I can't believe I haven't told you this.'

With inexplicable heaviness, Dylan pictured a ring.

'I have a part on *Fair City*! Caroline got me in as a bigshot detective, I filmed the first scenes a few weeks ago.'

Dylan smiled. 'Unreal,' he said.

'I'm underplaying it massively, that's what you have to do with soaps, say everything in a depressed tone to counteract the drama. But it's working, the casting director told Caroline they were pleased.'

'That's some news, seriously. You deserve it.'

Warm words absorbed, Ben's face turned theatrically dark and he was off again about Walter's disapproval of the role, though it was clear Ben could manage both, hadn't missed a rehearsal yet, and on went the litany of wrongs from all these people who were trying to ruin it for him now that he was finally where he wanted to be.

Dylan didn't know what to say. His friend seemed to be living in a world of extremes where everything was either amazing or atrocious. He wanted to tell him to slow down, take a breath, to wake up and appreciate, for once, his fortunate life. Full health, incredible woman, dream job. As Ben gathered pace, Dylan's brain rewound and became stuck on the word *incredible*—a disturbance of static noise.

He came to his senses when his phone rang: Rachel, in a good mood, a rare occurrence these days, wanting to know what time he would be home and would she put beers in the fridge for him and would they watch a movie, he could pick after her awful choice the last time, and hugs and best wishes to Ben. Dylan was smiling again when he hung up.

Outside it was still bright, the heat of the day remained in the air. At the theatre he said goodbye to his friend, walked to the quays to retrieve his bike. Removing a Coke can from the rear rack and dropping it in a bin, he clicked his helmet into place and, remembering Stevie's earlier caution, began the slow ride back to Terenure.

Hurtful. Demeaning, disloyal and, above all, enraging. Ben was as far as the Customs House on his walk home before he realised he was outdoors. Powered by invidious sentiments, he had stalked down the street after rehearsals, thinking only of betrayal.

Now he stopped at the pedestrian lights before the Talbot Bridge and surveyed with contempt its flat arches, which were barely arches at all, wondering how any professional architect could have come up with something so banal. People were idiots! He felt like shouting the words over the stewed waters of the Liffey whose dungeony depths of glutinous river wrack revealed themselves in the draining light. As the green man stuttered to action, Ben continued down the boardwalk, in need of a pint before returning to the apartment, he couldn't go ranting in the door to Stevie.

Betrayal with a capital B, as in the play they were trying to bring to life. Increasingly obvious from rehearsals, really from the very first day, that things were not going to plan. They would get there, Walter had confidence, but in the meantime Ben was expected to endure hourly attacks on everything from his tonal consistency to the shape of his shoulder joints. Because Walter was confident, great, but he was also enigmatic, taciturn, terse, prickly, explosive and forbidding, which was a lot for Ben to handle.

This brought him to the lower case betrayal he'd experienced this evening. When he went back after the burrito, having said a goodbye full of gravitas to his elderly fan club, he walked into the auditorium to see Paul the understudy on stage speaking Robert's lines with disquieting, scriptless confidence in a scene with Roseanne. Right in the middle of a seminal speech that Ben had to be prompted on earlier that day. *Him at Cambridge, me at Oxford. Did you know that? We were bright young men. And close friends. Well, we still are close friends. All that was long before I met you. Long before he met you.* Gallingly unfair that he could remember the words perfectly now.

Walter cut them short, then pretended like it hadn't happened. Paul skulked off to the wings as Ben came forward to start the scene over. The mess of dropped lines, embellishments and throat clearing that followed was possibly some of the worst acting of his life, but he was thrown—anyone would be—by the treason. Why were they rehearsing when they were supposed to be on dinner break? Was Walter doubting Ben?

Drama was where he had found his voice all those years ago, where he'd discovered who he was, and thankfully, that this person wasn't nearly half as bad or deviant as he'd suspected. Now he wondered if it was pure delusion. Deep down he knew he didn't properly understand Robert, not yet. One of the issues was the part itself: in each of his auditions he had read for Jerry, had nailed, he thought, the cocky insouciance of a man who could callously sleep with his best friend's wife then have the temerity to feel betrayed when she confessed. He'd understood Jerry, turned him inside out, revealed the insecurity that manifested as arrogance, truly, he had found the juice. Robert, the betrayed husband, was proving much harder to crack. Where was the juice in being cuckolded? Where was *the gold*?

Walter didn't like to psychoanalyse a text and Ben was fine with this approach, had worked with worse, but weeks into rehearsals he still felt himself to be playing a role, exploring and interpreting rather than embodying whomever the poor man was meant to be. Time was the enemy in this regard. He knew from experience that the longer he spent trying, the more likely it was to elude him. Acting—real acting—was an opaque process that didn't like to be looked at too closely, it was secretive, protective, a dark transformation that stole in from the wings and floated out the door with satisfied audiences at the end of each night. It was art, it was magic, to be present and absent at the same time, to feel most like himself when he was someone else, at once filtered, protected and shamelessly exposed. Ben was still waiting for that uncanny shift. It hurt to admit it, summoned all the pain he had borne in his career to date, so much rejection in every little no. His looks, body, height, voice, his degree, diligence, his childhood, infancy, the first mewling sound that came out of his goddamn mouth. He thought he had put all that behind him.

As it always did at times of crisis, his brain flew rapidly through the previous decades of sporadic work, meagre accolades, understudy roles and various other delicious crumbs that formed just enough of a trail for him to continue through the wilderness. The highlights reel: his portrayal of Pip in a fifth-year production of *Great Expectations* that had left his mother Marian weeping in the audience. Afterwards in the school hall she had hugged him and kissed his face in front of his classmates and he had let her because he knew she was crying not just for the success of the play, but for his father, that every good thing Ben did also had some shadow attached to it, a reminder of their loss. Then the end-of-college showcase that snagged him his first agent who was supposed to be there for the star of their year but ended up being more impressed by Ben. His award-winning turn as the bartender in a fringe production of *The Weir*. A supporting role in a short film that won a Bafta. His debut at The Gate as a butler whose only line in a two-hour production was *Your umbrella, Mr Flynn*. The joy of being in the chorus for the Irish run of a hit West End musical, twelve glorious weeks of a huge professional cast, packed audiences and glamour. And then lastly, and perhaps most weirdly of all, given it was only an amateur production in his first year at Trinity, his role as the lead ogham stone in a dramatisation of *Táin Bo Cualaigne*, the first play Stevie had ever seen him in, the unmistakable pride in her voice as she congratulated him afterwards, as she said, and these were her exact words, *I never knew you were so good*. Ben would kill somebody (Paul, for example) to hear her say them again. Not in a contrived way, either, not because he was clearly thirsting for encouragement that she felt she had to give, but with genuine surprise and pleasure for this talent he had dangled so many years in front of her and was now, just maybe, about to fulfil. With *Betrayal*, Ben had landed the role of his life. He couldn't let it slip through his fingers now.

The most hurtful thing of all about today's rehearsal was when Walter said that Ben's face was *too extra*. What did that even mean? Marching down the quays, he found himself thinking of Dylan, who had the type of honest countenance that girls loved, a smooth forehead and straight, dignified nose, a high complexion that drew attention to his symmetry. There had been something off about their dinner tonight, some weirdness. In his mind's eye he saw the quiet shape of his friend in the busy burrito bar, realising as he sometimes did, and always after the fact, that he'd talked too much about himself this evening, had left barely any time for Dylan. This broke some ancient chivalric law that was best not to articulate, the transactional baseline of all good friendships: your turn first, now mine. Ben felt bad, wished he could do the dinner over, stop his yammering, just listen. But it was more than that, there was something else. Some oddness. Approaching the clean lines of the Beckett Bridge he almost had it, then The Ferryman pub came into view and it was gone again in the rush of relief.

BEN

FOR THE BIG COLLEGE rugby match at the end of term, Ben is undeniably late. He messages Stevie again when he finally arrives at Donnybrook stadium well into the second half. She won't be pleased but it's not his fault the auditions ran late, or that he had to walk here because his funds are so low. From the street he hears a whistle, then a loud collective roar, all these strange people who get so much pleasure watching a ball. He remembers what his classmate Sophie said about sport—an absurd activity that captured in microcosm the greater absurdity of being alive—and wonders if he could pass the line off as his own. Like most of the English students in his year, Sophie is a wonder of dry statements and mature quips, to the extent that Ben often feels as if he's living in a play, one of those bleakly funny mid-century dramas where somebody always dies.

Fixing the pocket chain on his jeans, he squeezes past the unmanned turnstile, crosses the car park, begins to traipse the perimeter of the pitch towards the far corner, to the bank side-line banner where Stevie has directed him. Some of the seats in the adjacent stand are free, long lines of tempting green, and he wonders why she chose to rough it. Getting through the stubborn mass of onlookers is difficult. It seems half the college has turned out: lads with cans, girls aplenty, a group of Trinity rugby shirts singing, if you could call it that, taunts at UCD. In the middle of them is an extremely drunk guy whose voice is a hoarse, demented shriek, as if he's been saving every emotion he's ever felt in his life just for today. Out of nowhere an egg flies high over Ben's head. He doesn't see where it lands, just jeering laughter deeper into the crowd. If this is what rugby is all about, maybe he's been missing out. He continues on, excusing himself past an old don shouting, *Come on College!* in a West Brit accent Ben has yet to perfect in auditions. He quietly repeats it to himself, tries to get the authoritative tone. Under his fake leather jacket his Nirvana T-shirt dampens with sweat. All the while, a few metres away, the real action is taking place.

In the afternoon sun the teams are distinct from each other, Trinity in white with trims of red, UCD in light blue. Ben moves closer to the sideline to try and spot Dylan, who as it happens has the ball in his hands, passing it backwards to another player. This is supposedly a good thing, Ben understands from previous games. Dylan's gear is more brown now than white. He shoots off in another direction, positioning himself to catch the ball again, taking it high in the air as three UCD players charge him, no bother to Dyl, a feint left and he's away down the pitch sprinting against himself until he stops behind the goal posts to touch the ball to the grass. Ben gives a high, tootling cheer, which Dylan somehow manages to hear above the other noise, looking directly at Ben before smiling and running back up the field. Another player sets up the ball to do the kick thing. A little jig, then he sends it soaring over the bar.

As the cheering subsides from the crowd, Ben reaches the corner, searches for Stevie. She is easy to spot, standing alone in her goth cardigan, smoking a fag. He doesn't like that she smokes, but his attempts to get her to stop are always met with a counterargument about his own smoking, a fallacy because he only smokes weed, in a pipe, or at worst, with the smallest sprinkling of rolling tobacco. Weed is natural, a plant grown in the earth, and he smokes at home, unlike Stevie, surgically attached to her Benson and Hedges.

Ben returns her wave, overcome with a sudden lightness at her smile, the feeling of hope that's been building since their chat on Wednesday, that if he doesn't do something foolish, he might be able to win her back. They met in the Buttery, a fittingly gloomy location for the negotiations; vaulted recesses and low lighting, the stench of overboiled vegetables wafting in from the canteen next door. Ben had begged. He isn't proud of this, or maybe he's a little proud, he isn't some Neanderthal who can't bear to admit he's wrong. So far this break-up has followed the pattern of others: fight, hatred, regret, pleas, vows, reunion. Today they are somewhere between pleas and vows, and he acknowledges this now by stopping short in front of her, when what he really wants to do is throw his arms around her and bring her in for a hug.

'Hi,' she says. 'You made it.'

'Sorry I'm late.'

'Trinity are leading, but only by three. Dylan's been amazing.' She pushes her hair off her face, which is a little pink. He considers mentioning sun cream—the girls in his course are mad for it—but decides not to.

'How was the audition?' she says.

'No joy.'

'Hard luck. Did you get the bus here?'

'Walked.' He taps his pockets.

'That's why you're late.'

'How did you get here? You hardly got a taxi?' Stevie's parents have money, a fact he's still getting used to. He's not sure how he feels about it, whether it's good or bad, just that it differs from his own life. When his father died his mother was left with a small pension, three children and sporadic depression that meant she was in and out of work.

'As if,' Stevie says. 'I got the bus with the team.'

At the sound of a whistle they both turn towards the pitch. The players do their crouched hugging thing, an arduous, interlocking manoeuvre. The ball disappears under the human canvas and there's a slow heave forward and back. Just watching it gives Ben a pain in his neck.

'How did you manage that?' he says.

'Dylan texted to say there was a seat going.'

'Oh, yeah?' Ben received no such text himself.

'I am a trainee physio.'

'But they have their own physio,' he says.

Stevie doesn't reply. For something to do he pretends to be engrossed in the match, concentrating on the players, specifically Dylan, who is set back from the huddle in a sort of spaced-out chorus line with a few other players. When the squatting dance is finished, the ball gets thrown wide to Dyl, who slips past two of the opposition to race towards the end of the pitch and over the line, landing less than a metre from Stevie's feet. The ref blows the whistle and the cheering begins again.

'Get in!' In the excitement Stevie hugs Ben, her breasts pressing against his chest. He holds on for as long as he can. Dylan is already running back up the pitch. The number ten does his dance again in front of the ball, takes a hard shot at goal, sends it wide.

'Shame,' says Stevie.

'Yeah.'

'But they're still ahead.'

The game resumes. Ben pretends to return to the action but really he's thinking about her breasts, how he misses them: large, buoyant, not boringly symmetrical, each has its own character and tilt. He can picture them perfectly through her top. Before they broke up he would sometimes notice other men discreetly scanning them when they passed her on the street, in the park, walking across the cobblestones of Front Square. He even saw Dylan do it, once or twice. A covert glance that was only obvious if you were his best friend, if you were right there beside him for every other girl he fancied from adolescence into manhood.

Trinity remain ahead for the rest of the match, which takes an age, so many stops and starts. The only interesting part is an argument over a high tackle just before full time, three or four players squaring up to each other until Dylan intervenes. At the final whistle onlookers spill onto the pitch for hugs and backslaps. Ben notices Dylan's parents for the first time, Helen marching towards her son.

'Come on,' says Stevie. 'Let's go.'

He hopes she means let's go and get the bus away from all this sporting prestige. But Stevie means no such thing. She's heading happily towards Dylan to offer her congratulations. Ben feels ashamed. He catches up, his long legs outpacing her so that he reaches Dylan before her, getting his own congrats in first.

'Thanks,' Dylan smiles.

'Benjamin!' says Helen. 'Aren't you good to come. We could have given you a lift. Sean, look who's here.'

He greets Dylan's parents, who are diametrical opposites of each other, Helen warm and garrulous, Sean quiet, shrewd. Dylan and his father have a strange relationship.

'He did great today,' Ben says to Sean.

Sean nods. 'How's the acting going? Are you in Hollywood yet?'

'Oh, practically,' Ben says, but his sarcasm is lost.

'Maith thú, a bhúchaill!'

As Ben tells Dylan's father about the Players' upcoming production of *Romeo and Juliet*, he can see Stevie being introduced to Helen. Dylan says something that makes both of them laugh, while Helen places a motherly hand on Stevie's shoulder, fingers squeezing the dark purple material. Ben is overcome by a possessiveness he doesn't understand, just feels it harden inside him, and it takes everything he has not to make it clear to Helen Turner that Stevie is *his* girlfriend, a statement that is true in essence, if not in the current reality.

He is saved by the burly coach who comes over to tell Dylan he's won man of the match. The women cheer, and even Sean manages a smile. An announcement comes over the tannoy. The players still on the pitch begin to clap. On the far sideline a girl gives a wolf whistle then waves madly in their direction.

'Christ,' says Dylan. 'Time to go.'

Stevie and he share a look, a joke or something, before she turns away, striking up a conversation with the coach about the demands of training.

As they walk towards the clubhouse, Dylan hangs back to chat to Ben.

'Thanks for coming today,' he says.

'Of course, I wouldn't miss it.'

They discuss plans for later, the upcoming exams, Serena's new boyfriend, a Sallins local known for selling bags of oregano to the kids in secondary school.

Dylan laughs. 'Weren't you one of "the kids" yourself this time last year?'

'I never bought it.'

'Yeah, right,' says Dylan.

Ben grudgingly smiles. The best thing about their friendship is they can both call bullshit on each other without falling out. Sometimes they don't even need words. If Dylan has twenty different types of looks, Ben knows them all.

'Anyway that feels like centuries ago,' he says.

'Yeah,' says Dylan. 'It really does.'

'Do you care?' Ben says.

'About Serena? Not really.'

'Fair enough.'

They spend the last stretch in contemplative silence, Ben out of breath as he struggles to keep pace.

'Listen,' says Dylan when they reach the changing rooms. 'I've to shower. But you head in for a few with Stevie. I've squared it with the coach.'

'Legend.'

'Better go chat to the parents,' he says. 'No doubt my father has a list of the things I did wrong. Might as well get it over with.'

Ben gives a sympathetic smile. 'Are you sure?'

'Yeah, they're not staying. Have to get back to Kildare.'

'Before sunset,' says Ben.

'Never know what they might be missing.'

'Big things could be happening right now in Sallins.'

'And the price of parking in Dublin.' Dylan throws his hands in the air.

Ben laughs. Over by the entrance, Stevie is beckoning him, or possibly doing an exaggerated drinking mime.

'There's a subsidised bar in the clubhouse,' Dylan says. 'But you won't be allowed to stay for the dinner. Too many alickadoos.'

'No hassle, we'll catch you back in town.'

'Cool.'

Ambling towards Stevie, Ben is seriously grateful to Dylan. He feels briefly embarrassed about the imbalance in their friendship, but mostly he's just grateful that by some trick of chance, whereby he chose a random seat in a classroom when he was five years old, he has ended up with a best friend as kind and considerate as Dylan.

Later, they all have a real night out, and, later still, Ben and Stevie get back together.

*   *   *

Second year at college is proving less enjoyable for Ben. The same faces at auditions. The killer hope spliced with dread. Rejection is no longer an external affair, something he can work on, but a mental state that gains more power from each painful *no*. As he leaves his latest failed attempt at The Abbey, the January sky is already dark, a grim sheen to the footpaths under the buzz of street lamps warming up from pink to orange, confirming it's evening now and he has wasted a day of his life sitting in line with dozens of other hopefuls, only to be told they're giving the part to an established actor, a lad from Belfast with an enviable résumé. A year and a half into college and Ben has barely had a decent speaking role; he even blew the Tybalt gig by turning it down because he considered it beneath him. Now he would love to be Tybalt. He would pay someone to let him play that part.

Walking listlessly up Marlborough Street towards the Sackville Lounge, he passes the grounds of a government department where a huge bronze sculpture of a hand reaches out in floodlit greeting, on the cadge, like everybody else. He figures he has enough funds for one reviving drink before Stevie arrives. There's the temptation, always, to spread his low mood to her after bad auditions, to share the burden, but it's not right—he's learnt this from her, actually, that being an adult means managing your own horrible emotions, not letting the cannibal out of the box to devour the ones you love. This is still quite new to Ben, and honestly not that easy to do. He came from a house where the weather gauge, even before his father died, was set to grey, and thereafter to perpetual rain. Any fun he had growing up happened outside his home, usually with Dylan.

The small pub is warm, virtually unoccupied, with inviting banquettes and low tables. A reassuringly ancient barman, fifty at least, a hardy man by the looks of it, short sleeves on a January evening. Ben orders a pint, notices the man study his face before citing the price. Digging a tenner from his pocket, he is pleased he hasn't been carded, never is, not since fifth year. His height gave him a pass, if he kept his mouth shut. The same height that seems to disqualify him now for so many parts. As he watches the slow pour of the pint, he tries to count them. To date, Ben has missed out on a Marina Carr; the Tom Murphy that cast two of his classmates; each of the seven brothers in an amateur musical production in Rathmines; Romeo; Bassanio; Ebeneezer Scrooge; Cú Chulainn; and finally, today, the lowest of the low, an audition for *Translations* at The Abbey, which he wanted to be in so much that he lied to the casting lady and said he'd gotten the part in the Tom Murphy, not realising the woman had cast the play herself. She made a big joke, in front of everyone, about his greatest role being that of the Invisible Man.

Ben thanks the barman, slides the change from the counter and takes the furthest table away from the only other customer, a man in an Aran sweater who is doing a crossword. Choosing the couch over the stumpy stool, he watches the head settle on his pint, wonders how long he can make the drink last. He's glad Stevie is coming to meet him. He doesn't want to go home yet, back to the flat in Rathmines where Dylan has replaced his drama buddy. This has mostly worked out well. Ben smokes less, reads more; the flat is tidier. Dylan brought two of his teammates round the first weekend of term and the four of them blitzed the place. But now there's always someone coming or going far too early in the morning. The noise of the blender for their protein shakes is like a car reversing over your head. This year Dylan has started to train with Leinster A. So many new friends that Ben struggles to remember the names. And the girls! You'd need a log sheet to keep up with that. In, out, in, out, like the flat has a secret trapdoor.

As he nurses the pint he takes in the room properly for the first time, the photos of famous actors and playwrights that hang in uneven lines on the walls. He's imagining how it would feel to have his own face up there when Stevie arrives in the door looking cold and lovely in the dark green coat she got for Christmas. He fights the instinct to show her his distress and uses every inch of his acting skill to smile. Turns out he's a little too talented.

'Oh, wow!' she says. 'You got cast?'

His face drops. 'No, no, sorry. I didn't.' He pushes himself up from the couch, kisses her. 'What would you like?'

'A glass of Guinness. Do you have—'

He waves away her question. They are still in the first half of the month, the stipend from the grant flush in his account. He can worry about the second half later, like he always does, for those perilous twenty-something dates. It is possible to live for a week on one euro a day, he has done it before.

They sink comfortably together into the couch, their drinks and, after the second one, briefly into each other for a while, until he gets the sense the weirdo in wool might be watching them. Stevie's commiserations on his audition are heartfelt and comforting. He asks about her day, the lesson on anatomy from the female lecturer she loves, the pair of Doc's she returned to Schuh on O'Connell Street before she came to meet him, the sales assistant she had to sweet-talk because she forgot to bring the box, and through it all, he wishes he had good news for her, to see again that transient delight on her face when she first came into the pub and thought he had got the part, only this time for it to be real.

Afterwards they're strolling to the Chinese that does an all-you-can-eat for a fiver on weekdays when Ben looks down Talbot Street in the direction of Connolly Station and is suddenly hit with an idea.

'Let's go away!' he says, pulling her into him outside Guiney's, whose gunmetal shutters are already a third of the way down.

'What—now?'

'Yes! Leg it to Connolly, get on the first train and mitch off for the rest of the week.'

'But where will we stay?'

'A hostel. Or B&B.'

'But we've no clothes.'

'Who cares?'

He swings her round the street, they're laughing.

'Who cares?' she says.

'Like why not?'

'You're crazy,' she says, but the brightness, the delight is back on her face.

'Come on,' he pulls her arm, 'let's go.'

'Wait,' she says. 'Should we tell Dylan?'

'Hardly his style.'

She laughs again, nods her agreement.

And then they do it, this madly impulsive thing, after a quick trip to Penneys for underwear and toothbrushes, off they go haring down the street towards Connolly Station where the solid stone clock tower, constant and forbearing, awaits the frantic rush of youth.

*　　　*　　　*

For a cracking start to third year, Ben has persuaded Stevie and Dylan to accompany him to Electric Picnic. Getting out of the car at the festival is like escaping from hell, five hours in the back of Dylan's banger, the Nissan his parents gave him for his twenty-first. They've been cooped up for so long it takes Ben a moment to acclimatise. A September sky that belongs in a foreign country, heat humming from the afternoon sun, and all around him, noise, laughter, music, thousands of tents pitched and being pitched in glorious stretches of colour.

'Here we go,' Stevie grins.

Dylan says, 'Have you ever seen anything like it?'

Their first time away together as a trio, the first year the music festival is being run over a weekend, the first time Ben plans to do real drugs, there are, in fact, so many firsts he can't take it in, the excitement is too much to bear, he needs to do something with his hands before it kills him. He opens the boot of the car and starts to unload their provisions.

'Come here,' says Stevie, brandishing one of five Kodak cameras she made them stop for in a chemist in Kildare. Ben was against the detour, keen to get down as early as possible, but Dylan overruled him. That's the thing about groups of three: bloody democracy at work.

Ben goes to where she's standing, takes the camera from her as she squeezes in between himself and Dylan. He stretches his arm as far as possible to make sure they're all in frame.

'Say fuckoed!' Ben says.

Brisk click of the camera.

'OK,' he says. 'Let's get down there.'

Between the three of them they manage to carry everything in one go: tent, booze, rug, clothes, the twelve-pack of Taytos also procured on the chemist trip. They pick the campsite nearest the action, which is full of people their age, most of the lads bare-chested, baking in the sun. After walking a field and a half, they find a clearing beside a large orange tent. Ben tests the consistency of the ground. An unbelievably hot girl walks past in denim shorts and a bikini top.

'Wow,' says Dylan quietly.

'I think I'm overdressed.' Stevie throws down her backpack, takes off her black hoodie to an equally black slip dress that stops a few inches above her army boots. Ben feels proud of her look, sexy, but not desperate. He leaves the crate of Dutch on the grass and blows her a kiss.

A couple of lads sitting in the shade under the canopy of the orange tent say hello. Paranoid Android plays in tinny bursts from a portable stereo at their feet.

'Is this space free?' Ben asks.

'Go for it. Our friends had to pull out.'

'Bummer,' says Dylan.

'Oh my god!' says Stevie. 'Noel?'

The guy on the left springs from his chair, half walks, half dances over to her. 'Stephanie!' he says.

One of her Killiney mates, older, cockier than her college crew. He has an Ace of Spades tattooed around his right nipple, and an eyebrow ring that would leave him nicely vulnerable in a fight. His buddy follows him over. Stevie makes the introductions, then disappears with the pair of them so they can show her where her girlfriends are camping, a row or two back.

'State of the tattoo,' says Dylan when they're out of earshot. 'Absolute state.'

Together they pitch the tent Dylan took from home, trying to work out the right poles and pegs, without guidelines, because Dylan's father doesn't believe in manuals.

They're at it a while when Ben says, 'Your da is a bollix.'

Eventually they stand back to survey the mustard yellow monstrosity. Although the tent appears to be standing, two poles and a fastening mechanism remain on the ground.

'At least it's big enough for the three of us,' Ben says.

'Maybe we should start again?'

'Not a chance.' Ben reaches for the crate of Dutch, rips the plastic, takes out two cans. They sit on the grass drinking, too wrecked to bother with the rug.

Dylan winces as he swallows. 'We should have brought a cooler.'

They get through them all the same, are onto their third by the time Stevie lands back, cigarette in hand.

'Get up,' she says. 'We're not here for the campsite.'

She's had a drink or two herself, Ben can tell, the glazed confidence in her voice, a woman with a plan. He's happy enough with this. The only band he cares about seeing is Röyksopp, who aren't on until the evening.

Dylan stretches on the grass. His top is off and the muscles of his lower stomach harden as his arms go back. Earlier this year he played for Ireland A in the Six Nations and his athleticism has increased at the same exponential rate as his attractiveness to women. He plays for Leinster A now too, as well as the big matches for the college team. It's actually hard to keep up with all his achievements; he's even getting paid, something which Ben has benefited from on more than a few occasions. He went out one night with Dylan after a home win in Donnybrook against Munster A and didn't buy a drink all night. The amount of attention his friend got after his four tries was close to oppressive. Ben glances at Stevie now to see if she's noticed the ripped physique lolling about on the ground, but she's busy rummaging in her rucksack, re-emerging with novelty gold sunglasses and a naggin. 'Get dressed you,' she says to Dylan, pushing the rest of her stuff into the tent.

'Should we not unpack?' he says.

'Spot the festival virgin. Look, we only have two days here, are you going to spend it folding your clothes or what? We've already missed Asian Dub Foundation. I told Jules we'd meet her outside the portaloos in ten.' She looks at the silver watch Ben bought for her birthday. 'Correction, nine and a half.'

Dylan laughs. 'Is she going to be like this all weekend?'

'Probably,' says Ben.

'Definitely,' says Stevie.

They close the tent, pick up the boys from next door and bounce on down to the portaloos, where predictably there's no sign of Jules. Stevie suggests giving her five minutes, but about two minutes later, she's had enough and they head off again, exiting the campsite, which is on higher ground than the festival. Without anyone saying a word, they stop in unison, take in the sight: stripy circus tents, formidable main stage, a big wheel in the distance, and everywhere you look, rollicking crowds. In the brief shadow of a passing cloud a river of people head purposefully in the same direction, before the blinding sun returns them to their anonymous fun.

Feeling Stevie's hand in his own, Ben squeezes her fingers, bends to kiss her, notices the Dublin dickhead giving them the eye. He kisses her again, a showy one this time that she pulls away from. She takes the naggin from her bag and between the five of them, they finish it quickly, two gulps a piece. Then off they go, down, down the sloping ground into the valley of the adult playground, chasing after Stevie who is racing ahead, arms in the air, roaring her head off, and he thinks, not for the first time, that he's lucky to have found this girl.

*   *   *

At quarter to something, Ben is in the queue for the burger van, the burnt sweetness of onions too enticing to ignore, he needs to eat, Stevie told him with a wild look in her eyes that meant trouble or business, he can't remember the context, just the tone of voice, a warning: he was not to ruin the party. Yes, there had been a jaunty altercation between himself and Noel in the Bacardi tent, when Noel managed to convince Stevie and Dylan to go to The Flaming Lips, who happened to clash with the legendary Röyksopp. Come on! They were amazing, by the way, he says out loud, causing a girl in a pink wig to turn around and say, 'Are you talking to me?' Ben shakes his head, busies himself with his phone, which has no signal most of the time, except when you're near the Vodafone tent and a volley of bleeps arrive like homework. The girl considers him then goes back to her crew. He feels he should make an effort to be friendly but finds it hard to focus. Too many drinks, no drugs to counter the effects of the alcohol. Dark now, velvet sky, winding routes with fairy lights, and not a drug to be had, of any variety, even weed, though he watched Noel and his mate smoke a fat spliff earlier outside the mellow lounge tent. With a deeply ful-filling obstinacy, Ben refused a drag each time it came his way. He won't take anything from that tosser, not if he has to spend the entire weekend sober.

But he is not sober, a fact that is becoming clear to him the longer he stands in the queue, people wiggling in and out of his line of vision. He remembers Dylan asking him if he was sure he wanted a double vodka, how Ben had answered with some quip that belittled his friend in front of the Dublin lads, regretful, but there was no other move at the time—Dylan had checkmated him with kindness. The sky was still light then, his friend's flushed face obvious to everyone.

Ben feels guilty, then remembers Dylan sided with Noel about the schedule. This was a betrayal. He didn't mind so much about Stevie, who can never resist a new band, but Dylan doesn't even care about music, he only said yes because Stevie wanted to go, which is something he likes to do, step in and act the good guy when Ben lets her down. For a while he wasn't bothered by this; he saw it as a peacekeeping effort, it was sort of helpful, frequently preventing an argument, getting him out of trouble he didn't think he deserved. But the longer they're all friends, the more it irks him, some falseness, an unnatural undertone, because it's easy to be the good guy when you're not the boyfriend. You can just walk away back to your own life whenever you like.

'Alright there, mate?' a guy with yet another Dublin accent asks him.

Ben is leaning forward, the guy is telling him in a very loud voice that this is happening. 'You're leaning into us,' he says. 'Woah, man. Can you, like, stop?'

'Sorry,' Ben says, attempting to straighten, which makes him light-headed. He drops to his hunkers, apologises again.

'You're grand,' says the girl in the wig. She nudges his knee with her flip-flop. Her toenails are sparkly black. 'Are you OK?'

He stands up and is about to answer when she throws her arms around him. 'This is the best festival ever!' she says. When she lets go, he looks into her eyes, two dark, dimensionless circles. The guy's pupils are similarly enlarged.

'The best,' says Ben, introducing himself.

'Jess.' She gives a little curtsy.

Ben really wants to ask for some of whatever she's on, but he's asked approximately five hundred people already in the last four—seven, ten?—hours. So he waits, listens to the pair of them go through what bands they've seen, who was brilliant, which is everyone, they are bursting with goodwill about it all. The portaloos are the cleanest they've ever seen, there was actual toilet paper in one.

'The organisers thought of everything,' says Jess. 'I'm going to come back every year till I die.'

'It's like a foreign festival,' her friend says, 'almost as good as Burning Man. I'm Rob, by the way.'

'Nice to meet you.' Ben sticks out a hand, but no, here it comes, another interminable hug, the guy's bare chest sticky and warm. Who wears a waistcoat to a music festival with nothing underneath but a blaze of ginger hair?

By the time he stops boasting about Burning Man, they are almost at the top of the queue. A girl in front is arguing about the price of a bottle of Lilt and Jess wades in, telling her to hurry up.

'Are you coming to the rave?' Rob says.

'Which one?' says Ben.

'Seriously, man?' Rob takes money from his shorts, passes it to Jess. 'Two bottles of water.' He turns back to Ben. 'There's a rumour of a rave in the forest behind the main campsite.'

'Cool,' says Ben. 'But I'm going to Kraftwerk.'

Rob starts to laugh.

'What?'

'Man, Kraftwerk were hours ago.'

'They were not!'

'You're a riot,' Rob says. 'Here.' From the same pocket as the money, he produces a baggie of white powder. 'This might help you remember.' He wiggles the packet coquettishly. Ben snatches it away. Now that he has it in his hands, there is an overwhelming desire to leg it, which wouldn't be entirely ethical, and besides, he doesn't even know what to do with the powder. 'What is it?' he says. 'Cocaine?'

'Molly,' says Rob.

'What?'

'MDMA, man,' he says. 'Lick your finger and dip it in the bag.'

Ben follows his instructions, taking half a forefinger of powder.

'Go easy!' Rob retrieves the bag, quickly seals it. 'That's enough to fell a horse.'

Excellent, Ben thinks, that's exactly the amount he wanted.

*   *   *

When he comes back into his body they're in the middle of a wood, uneven ground beneath his runners, twigs, leaves, wonderful nature, crackle, crackle, snag, it is all just wonderful. Bouncing off the ground, no effort, he could climb a mountain right now and not break a sweat. His hands tingle; the sound of Jess's voice is like a song drifting in the night, pink head bobbing. 'Oh my god,' says Ben. 'Oh. My. God.'

'Are you buzzin?' Rob says.

Ben says some words in the wrong order.

'He's buzzin!' says Jess, fairy girl.

The three of them run towards the thumping bass, he doesn't understand why they don't fall, the woods seem to part, the trees swing back to let them through, the sky lightens as they pass under it or into it, like a computer game, a simulation, when suddenly they're in a clearing with hundreds of people who look insanely lawless, half-naked, jumping up and down.

Then: the music courses through his body.

'Is that?' says Jess. She's shouting, pulling him into the crowd.

'Fat Boy Slim!' Rob roars.

Up and in they go. Ben feels himself lifted by the noise and heat and for one split second of a second he wonders if he'll ever come down again.

*   *   *

After the set they sit with a group of strangers who are now great friends. Jess is talking at fantastic speed to a girl stretched out on the ground beside them. Rob has skinned up and Ben is about to take a drag when he hears his name—Stevie! He feels her voice spread warmly through him, jumps to his feet in anticipation of an almighty hug, but then Stevie's face comes into focus. Pale, cross. Stern brilliance of her eyes. She wastes no time getting to the point.

'What have you taken?' she says.

Ben smiles, there is nothing else to do or say. Behind her, Dylan and the Dublin lads, the girls too, collectively stare at him as if he's a freak show, which in fairness is probably what he looks like to anyone who isn't high.

'Hi, beautiful,' he says to Stevie. 'How was the band?'

He means it sincerely but she snaps, 'Are you for real? Because I wouldn't go to Röyksopp you don't answer your phone all night and now you're off your head?'

A bolt of clarity: Stevie does not approve of drugs. Her prudish physio classmates have turned her against them. She tolerates his weed smoking, that's about it. He hadn't meant for her to know!

Now his new friends are watching too. Ben tries to take her hand, pull her away from everyone, they need to talk, to sort this out, he can explain. Instead she presses her fists against his chest, pushes him back and thanks him for ruining her festival. She walks off, posse in tow. Dylan stalls behind. He puts a hand on Ben's shoulder, asks if he's OK.

'Man,' Ben says. 'I'm amazing!'

'Will I stay?' says Dylan.

'You want a dab?' Ben is thrilled at this turn of events, even if he senses Rob is not.

'I'm good,' says Dylan, who appears to be sober. 'I just don't want to leave you like this.'

Ah Dylan—kind, tired, selfless Dylan who would stay at a rave in a forest to help his friend. Ben is overcome with love.

He pulls him in for a hug, tells him he's the best. Dylan draws away too soon. 'Look,' he says, 'will you come back with me? It's nearly four. There's always tomorrow.'

'I'm grand,' Ben assures him. 'I'll see you later. I love you, man.'

Dylan smiles and tells the group on the ground where they're camped. 'Take it handy,' he says to Ben, then he's gone.

'Who were they?' says Jess. 'The fun police?'

*　　　*　　　*

The sky is light when he gets back to the campsite. He said goodbye to the others at the portaloos, Jess intimated she was going to be in there for ages, which ordinarily would have grossed him out, but why should she have to hide an entirely natural biological process, a biological *necessity*. People are so judgemental, preoccupied with insignificant worries and cares, if only everyone could feel the way he feels right now, it wouldn't even have to be a regular thing, he has a new perspective on the world he knows will continue long after the drugs wear off. Ben can't believe this is what they're like. All the scaremongering from parents, politicians, guards. For what? He was wasted in the burger queue, not enjoying the festival, barely even present for Röyksopp, he only remembers the sweaty crowd and some headwrecker in a Roscommon jersey who kept shouting the lyrics to a Chumbawamba song. Taking drugs was like an awakening, a rebirth to all that is good and miraculous about the world.

He wanders along the haphazard rows of the campsite, clueless as to the location of their tent. It doesn't matter, there is much to appreciate, an early morning silver lit serenity to the sea of zipped tents, thousands of bodies inside, cocooned, preparing to hatch for another day. Every so often he comes upon a human or two, similarly *monged*, a word Rob kept using, by which he meant people with feral hair, whitened lips and oddly elastic jaws. Ben cordially greets these kindred spirits, but he doesn't stop, his voice is hoarse now, tongue parched, the muscles in his face ache. None of it matters. His bladder? All night he has forgotten his bladder. The thought brings it ferociously to life, a boulder in his lower abdomen. Happily, he's right back at the portaloos where he left the others ages ago. He goes to enter the first cubicle—quite the cowshed—lets the door bang, pleasing, on down the line, bang, bang, bang, each and every door, he can't remember what he's looking for, there is no one inside, just wads of wet paper and foul odours of cleaning fluid or worse, on and on he goes, a compulsion, bang, bang. Bang. In the last cabin there's a guy asleep on the toilet seat, his head balanced awkwardly on the soap dispenser. Ben regards him with fascination. A prompt: his bladder, which has gotten much worse since he last thought about it, painful and swollen. He allows himself one final bang then goes round the back of the portaloos to pee. Slow, painful, glorious release.

By the time Ben spots the canopy belonging to the Dublin lads, people are waking, there is a ghastly daylight to the place, a sober sun on the rise. Although he's gone to the toilet twice, his bladder is still sore, he is, in fact, aching all over. Now that he's back at base, the need to lie down is urgent, yet when he reaches their tent, he freezes. Everything is quiet, no sign of Noel and the lads, but then suddenly, as if tuning in to the frequency of an alien station, he hears the sound of giggling, of low laughter and togetherness inside the mustard-yellow cave.

Through the gauzy front window, he can see a shadow of a person lying down, just one, not two, which makes no sense as there are definitely two voices, the tones and inflections of which he knows as well as his own. He steps towards the tent, crouching silently, carefully reaching for the zip, knocking an open can of Dutch with his foot, which falls over with a thud—wet, ashy liquid spreading over his runner. Ben curses, kicks the can away, looks in disgust at the soggy cigarette butts that have landed on the rug.

'Hello?' He hears Stevie say. 'Ben?'

It's a while before he's able to speak, the festival seems to vanish, a pop-up planet collapsed. She has the zip open, he doesn't know what he wants to say, what he is allowed or able to say, her sleepy bedhead is peering out the entrance at him, they look into each other's eyes for a gaping moment, and in the background, Dylan turns away.

OCTOBER

AFTER WEEKS of gruelling rehearsals, opening night for *Betrayal* at The Abbey was finally here. Ben could not believe it. Having borne reluctant witness to two, three, even four of the ghastly small hours, he was still in bed now, wild-eyed and pale, paralysed by tiredness or fear. He called out for Stevie, to silence. Futilely he tried again, his abject state echoing back to him in the deserted apartment. Perhaps she had slept well in the boxroom, where he'd banished her around midnight for excessive breathing, and was out to the bakery now to bring him back a soothing cappuccino and one of those sunshiny Portuguese tarts. Ben needed as much sugar and caffeine as possible to get him through. He needed a whiskey. A saline drip. He needed a break.

Last night's preview had been full of errors. Following the pathetically lacklustre curtain call, Walter marched into the dressing room and said in his cutting accent, *With respect, folks, it simply wasn't good enough—time to iron out the kinks.* He looked directly at Ben when he said the k-word, which cut far deeper than Walter could possibly have known, unearthing a memory that should have been lost to the horrors of time, a question Ben's father had once asked him, prompted by nothing more than his son's love of acting: *Do you have a kink in you, or what?* And because it was

Ireland in the nineties, and because Ben was only thirteen years old, he'd said, *No, Dad, I promise I don't*, instead of telling the old homophobe where to go. Well, his father was dead now, wasn't he, which at least meant one less person for Ben to worry about in the shadowy depths of discombobulated heads otherwise known as the audience. The Abbey was sold out tonight—sold out for the run—even after a mediocre early review in *The Irish Times* where *tall* was the only adjective used to describe Ben's presence on stage. He was learning a brutal fact about life, that even when you thought you had it made, there was always more pain ahead. Maybe he should have listened to Caroline years ago, when she'd tried to persuade him to drop *one teeny syllable* from his surname to make it Brosnan. He had refused. The 'ah' was very special to him, he'd said. Ben Brosnahan would not lose the 'ah'.

Fuck the review. Fuck the fucking reviewer too. He had to stop fucking cursing. It happened at times of great stress, his vocabulary deserted him, replaced by weak language and clichés, a mockery of his education, his memory, the fact he could do twelve accents and knew thirty-one Shakespearean monologues by heart. Again he thought of the packed house this evening, his friends and family looking proudly on. Stevie waiting nervously. He couldn't disappoint them, he had to deliver. The pressure was motivating, but it was also obscene.

Pulling himself out of bed, he moved around the apartment in his gloom. On the fridge he found a note from Stevie saying she'd gone to Half Moon for an early morning sea swim with Dylan. Ben was almost jealous, until he remembered he hated swimming, could never get the breathing right, his limbs refused to synchronise. And he was thrilled to see the improvement in Dylan, everyone was. His friend's life was slowly returning to normal, the malaise had finally started to lift.

Last weekend they'd sat in the pub through a rugby match, a hurling final and an hour of darts where a humourless Dutchman outmanoeuvred his opponent so conclusively he was largely playing against himself. Even this egregious amount of sport hadn't spoilt the fun for Ben. He'd forgotten how much he liked Dylan's company, how easy he was to be around, how they knew each other's moods, lives, histories. Ben had missed their friendship more than he'd realised, in a way that was only now becoming apparent with its return. In the pub they'd matched each other pint for pint, had chips and gourmet burgers, much later, questionable kebabs from a place on Camden Street. Dylan's senses had revived and his childlike wonder in this awakening—the cherry scent of a vape! the sour crunch of an onion!—was lovely to witness, all these ordinary things that had become for him extraordinary through their absence over time. It was like watching a puppy let loose on a beach. For the entire day there had been no mention of pain. No back problems or migraines or breathing issues, no ringing Rachel for a lift. Like the old days. Dylan and Ben. Ben and Dylan. No need for anyone else.

Bringing his coffee over to the window now, he watched a Luas approach the stop at Spencer Dock, the burst of life as the doors parted. He sat on the couch, pulled his pyjama sleeves over his hands and cradled the hot mug. As he rattled off his biggest speech in the play, the living room felt chilly. His own fault: he'd badgered Stevie into keeping the heating off until November, though he really shouldn't have bothered, because for the first time in his life Ben was making money. The Abbey production paid well and Caroline, true to her word, had turned the *Fair City* gig into a recurring role. They had written an arson scene into the script just for him. Ben was managing to do both gigs concurrently, had never once been late for play rehearsals, a small source of pride that helped to mitigate against Walter's directing—*wrong, wrong, more, less, wrong!*—and the absolute bollocking he'd given Ben one afternoon for napping in the jacks. Still, it was worth it, he reminded himself. Finally he was getting to do what he loved. No greater feeling in the world than being wholly, electrically someone else. The promise of new beginnings and second chances that he rarely got in life. The audience no longer seeing him but whomever he wanted them to see. A kind of power, to make the man in the fifth row, the woman in the second, look up at the ceiling or down at their feet. He loved sinking into character, the deep immersion so freeing it had traces of the spiritual—when he got it right. The annoying thing about the preview was that the last few weeks of rehearsal had gone really well. He had finally inhabited the role, the shift occurring almost without him noticing it, his lines sparked and soared. The tech rehearsal had been particularly good. Each line, cue, light, came exactly on time, all building precisely and with discipline to the final scene, so stunning, as they walked offstage in the glimmering pool of night. Even Ben had been fooled for a second into thinking he saw the moon.

In the bedroom, Stevie's spare goggles were on the dresser. Beneath the nerves and excitement, the other feeling returned. Not jealousy, no. Exclusion? On a whim he decided to throw on his running gear, get out in the fresh air. Quickly he downed his coffee, clipped his old iPod nano on his T-shirt and bundled himself out the door, realising as he heard the click that he'd forgotten to take a key. He cursed loudly, then cursed again for cursing. The lady in the apartment across the way appeared and asked if he was OK. Apologising, Ben went to leave.

'Fella,' she said.

He turned back.

'I seen you on the telly.'

'No way.'

'I told my daughter we have a celebrity in the building.'

'Hardly,' he laughed.

'Do you think it was the mechanic's wife?'

He stared at her.

'The fire.'

'Oh,' he said. 'I'm afraid I don't know. They don't tell us anything until we get the scripts. It really is a mystery.'

'Handsome *and* funny.' She proceeded to tell him he was better than two of the regular actors and definitely better than the mechanic. Ben hadn't a clue who she was talking about. He'd never seen a full episode of the show. When the script landed in his inbox he read the scenes he was in and not a page more. Only a modicum of cunning was required to conceal this fact. It wasn't exactly Brecht. Something bad happened every three or four pages and as long as you got the gist of the drama—robbery, murder, affair—it was easy to play along.

'As for that one Dolores,' the neighbour had barely taken a breath. The floral pattern of her housecoat started to bleed before his eyes.

Ben backed a few steps away, the soles of his runners padding the carpet. 'I better go here.'

'Wait,' the woman said. 'Just a tick.' She disappeared into her apartment.

He did a calf stretch to pass the time, ignoring the slight sting of his right Achilles. She returned, pressed a takeaway menu and pen into his hands.

'It's the only thing I could find.'

'Right,' said Ben. 'You want me?'

She tapped the menu. 'Your autograph might be worth a fortune someday.'

'Here's hoping.'

The woman laughed.

Ben put the menu against the wall, signed beside the price list for the sides.

'No,' she said. 'On the front.'

He flipped over the page and did a totally different signature in the yellowy space beside the Peking Duck. There was a brown splotch of what he hoped was soy sauce directly underneath. She took the menu, held it to the light, satisfied. He walked away feeling delighted with the bizarre encounter. Perhaps it was the start of things to come, an omen for the night ahead. He couldn't wait to tell Stevie, must remind her to get a programme as a keepsake.

Outside, the city was fully awake, streets industrious with suits, seagulls already in combat, kamikaze swooping over the river. The rough pink tarmac of the cycle lanes stretched in long tongues across the bridge. Ben did one last flamboyant stretch against the railing then jogged towards the south quays, over-taking car after car of solo drivers in gridlock, heads turning to follow him, he was sure of it, all the eyes drawn to the free cut of a man who was gloriously alive, weightless, not even a house key to his name. Physically lifted by the imagined admiration, he picked up the pace till he could barely feel his feet touch off the ground.

*   *   *

They locked up their bikes and walked through the industrial wasteland where large, autumnal coloured shipping containers loomed in the distance by the port. In recent months they'd discovered this last stretch to Half Moon was easier on foot. Initially Dylan was unsure of leaving their bikes chained up in a remote location, but Stevie decided to risk it so he followed her lead, and sure enough, not a scratch on either one all summer.

'Look at that,' she said now, as they reached the beginning of the chalky walkway that separated port from beach. 'We should have brought a surfboard.' They stopped and watched the swilling water, white strips flashing through the grey. At the far end, kilometres away, the big red lighthouse was braced against the wind. On the wild horizon even a large tanker seemed lost and insubstantial. Putting up his hood, Dylan looked at Stevie in her thin check shirt, the outline of her togs visible.

'Are we mad?' he said.

'Let's find out.' She gestured to the changing area halfway down. A high curve of water splashed onto the path a few metres from where they stood.

He shook his head.

'Move.' She pushed him forward like some sadist pirate.

Through occasional bursts of rain they soldiered on towards Half Moon, less fun adventure, more emergency services and helicopter rescues. But Stevie was transfixed by the water, the way it kept sloshing over the path, wetting their runners. Every time it happened she shrieked in delight. There wasn't another human in sight, which was thrilling in a way he had long associated with her, the irresistible draw of good times before the bad. Dying without witnesses was pretty bad.

When they reached the sheltered area for changing, Dylan hunkered down on the white-washed bench. His shorts rode up to the pale skin of his thighs. There had been no holiday this summer, despite Rachel's pleas. Needed to watch their spending, and he didn't want to mess with his rehab, which was going so well. Stevie had him doing all sorts, not just sea swimming. There were oxygen tanks, vagus nerve lessons, breathing like a goddamn bee. These days he gave himself a lymphatic facial massage in the mornings and wore a microcurrent device around his ankle at night, like a criminal in his own home. Anything was worth it if it worked, and it did seem to be working, this mad programme of hers, in tantalising increments. He felt guilty about Rachel and her holiday, especially after what she'd been through earlier this year. But he was angry with her too. She had claimed all the sorrow for herself, making it clear as the months wore on that he was not entitled to mourn.

'It will be grand once we're in,' Stevie was saying, to herself or to him. 'We'll stay close to the shallows.'

'Hmm.'

'OK?' she smiled.

'I dunno.'

'Trust me,' she said, and he knew what was coming. 'I'm a health professional.' With that she whipped off her clothes and ran down the ramp.

He watched her wade into the rough sea until her knees were covered, at which point she usually did one of her lithe dives, resurfacing somewhere further out. Instead he saw her stall, she took a step back and looked around, a show of doubt that reminded him of Leah. 'You don't have to do it!' He headed towards her.

She pushed into the water, vanishing in its high folds. Reappeared. 'It's like a bath!' Her voice was taken by the wind. White bubbling froth and dirty backwash splashed up the ramp before retreating.

Dylan unzipped his hoodie, fired it towards the shelter, cheering when it landed on his bag. Still had the eye. One of his favourite tries, when he came on at sixty-seven minutes in a quarter-final against Toulouse, was a neat chip over their back line, which he'd caught on the run. Pure pleasure of following a ball meant only for him. The thing he'd loved most about rugby, that feeling of running blind.

'Dylan!'

Happy as a seal, she was beckoning him into the water. He refused to look at her, it would only make the task more daunting. Darted down the ramp, flopped into the cold, gasping, some elemental barrier broken, nature disturbed; searched for her as he came up. At the level of the whipping wind he couldn't hear a thing. Swam towards her, stopped at the kick of her foot.

'Isn't it lovely?' she shouted.

'Are you not seasick?'

'Don't be a baby.'

'Was I the one looking around for her daddy before she got in?'

She laughed at that, her face wet and wild, eyes shining. Stevie was lucky, she had easy parents, the only one of the four of them who could say that. As he attempted to tread water against the current, he thought of his most recent phone call with his father. They were always at odds with each other over trivial matters—a match result, car manufacturer, the evils of craft beer—which seemed to stand in for some greater argument about life and family that neither of them was able to broach.

'My folks are coming this evening,' he said now.

'Ben will be thrilled.'

'My mother wouldn't miss it.'

'Your dad will be asleep before the interval.'

'Helen has sharp elbows,' Dylan said.

'Sharp everything.' Stevie splashed him.

Before Dylan could get her back she went under. He tried floating. Asphalt sky dipped downwards. She came to the surface soon enough, circling him, he could only see the top of her head.

'You're making me dizzy,' he said.

She lay back beside him. 'I'm worried about Ben,' she said.

'Yeah?'

'I ran a scene with him yesterday and he forgot his lines.'

'Nerves,' said Dylan. 'Pre-match jitters.'

'I don't know, he never forgets lines.'

Then she was off again, quick strokes in parallel with the faraway strand.

Dylan continued bobbing, wondering when she'd have enough, he was ready to get out, but there had always existed some class of competition between them that made it impossible to admit defeat, to admit anything, really. For all that he knew her over decades, their relationship was one of shadows and glints.

When she finally turned around she had a distant look on her face, which made him remember a sea swim from college, a trip they'd taken one hot autumn a few weeks into term. Sandycove. The best day. Their best day, that had ended so embarrassingly—all these years later he still felt the seizing heat of shame. Sandycove was the only beach they hadn't been to in their rehab sessions. Stevie, who was in charge of the itinerary, must have decided against it.

Swimming up to him, she said, 'Have you had enough?'

He stared at her.

'What?'

'Do you remember that day in Sandycove?'

She blinked a couple of times, rubbed water out of her eye. 'It's getting cold,' she said. 'We should go.'

Turning towards the ramp, she misjudged the tug of the current and bumped against him. Dylan left his leg against hers for a moment, that was all it took. He felt a pull the length of his body that seemed linked to the surrounding swell. No gap now between thought and act. Managed to look at her—a deadpan expression that confused him.

Doggy-paddling away, he remembered his wife and daughter, as he often did in these instances, seconds after the physical urge subsided. He had never, in all his years of professional rugby, cheated on Rachel with the many women who had offered themselves to him as easily as if they were offering to buy him a drink. Again he thought of his father, how disappointed he would be if Dylan confirmed his suspicions that rugby was a godless sport played by philandering peacocks.

He quickened his stroke so he could get out of the water first, not wanting to be behind her as she went up the ramp in the threadbare swimsuit she'd had for years. That felt weird now, when moments ago it would have been fine. He hated his mind, what it made him think at times, or he hated the feelings that produced these clearly destructive thoughts, hard to say which came first, to figure out the match from the fuel. It was linked to his illness, he knew, to the fact she'd helped him recover when everyone else, including his wife—including Dylan himself— had given up. For the difficult initial months of rehab he'd been able to pretend the feelings were benign, nothing more than gratitude, but alone with her in the water today he understood that all the while it had been there, a writhing creature below on the seabed, his wilful attraction to the one woman he knew he could never have. Lumbering up the ramp he felt deeply ashamed; since his health had returned, he was a married man who kept forgetting he was married.

Back at the bench he hid in his towel for as long as he could, listening to the rustle of her bag, the slap of her swimsuit hitting the ground. In silence they got dressed. She sat beside him to dry her feet.

Suddenly she laughed.

'What?'

'You're like a cockatoo.'

He patted down his hair and feigned a smile.

She was fully clothed now, in as much as she ever was after their swims. Shirt, leggings, runners, she rarely bothered with a bra. Look away. That day in Sandycove he had held them in his hands—incredible to think of that now. Putting on his runners he tried to shake the sensation of loss, all those shimmery, wasted days.

They set off for the port, walking briskly along the path to warm up, squeezing through the gap in the bulrushes that led back to their bikes, the wiry stems yielding to the pressure, parting left and right. For the final stretch Stevie did the talking. He was still somewhere inside his head, trying to reckon with what had happened in the water. By the time they reached the bikes he was beginning to doubt every life choice he'd ever made. All around the eerie grounds, nothing but weeds and broken glass. In a daze he watched her struggle to get her lock open before bending to help.

'I can do it,' she said, her fingers pink from pressure.

Without a word he uncoiled them and removed her hand. Still she stayed crouched beside him, a coolness coming off her skin. He jammed the horizontal bar tight against the shackle, jigged the key till it opened.

'My hero,' she said, but neither of them laughed.

He felt the sting again, whatever it was, the feeling, not love, no, nothing like what he felt for his daughter, for his wife— oh god, his wife—it was demanding, aggressive even, wanting explanation, to know, after all these years, this person once again. He pulled her silver racer off his own bike, a cheaper, clunkier affair bought for his rehab. She took the handlebars of the racer, busied herself with the gears, clicking them up and down, without reason it seemed to him. An atmosphere had crept into their morning, for which he was entirely responsible. Sandycove: a place they didn't mention. A place that didn't exist. There were one or two others, basement nightclubs and early morning tents. Their friendship had endured all these years because they didn't talk about those places. He understood now, too late, that it could not survive them.

'Will we bounce?' Stevie rolled onto the road, started down the slope. Unaware or indifferent once more. He felt his sorrow harden, shifting now to something meaner—unfair but easier. Why couldn't she let him be? She had chosen Ben long ago, he was her life partner. Dylan put on his helmet, pressed hard on the pedals and soon passed her, not looking back as she called his name.

*   *   *

In the bathroom Rachel combed her daughter's hair, eased out a wet tangle, not wanting to hurt her. Traces of steam clouded the mirror. The clean scent of baby shampoo filled the air. Leah hummed the song she was learning in school.

'Is that the one about the animals?' Rachel gave a quick tug as the knot neared the ratty ends.

'Mummy!'

'Almost done.' She freed the hair. 'Hard part over.'

Leah drifted back into song. Reaching her hand into the sink, she played with a smear of toothpaste, swirling it across the porcelain.

'Oi, messer,' said Rachel, tickling her ear, to giggles. She watched her daughter's face in the mirror, so entrancing, the elfin profile and quick green eyes. People said she was the image of Rachel, which was true in one sense, the same colouring and lines, but Leah had a playfulness, an energy, all of her own. Rachel would never have been allowed to mess toothpaste across a sink, for one. As a child she'd learnt quickly how to behave, to freeze, to disappear into walls if necessary. Leah was free to live in her imagination, to ignore the adult world unless she wanted something.

After a quick change into princess pyjamas, they went into the master bedroom to dry Leah's hair at the low marble dressing table Rachel hated but affected to like because she couldn't admit to Dylan that she'd spent nearly a grand without bothering to properly check the dimensions. Back when the money was coming in, one reliable monthly chunk after the next, these things didn't seem to matter.

With the warm air of the blow-dryer Leah grew sleepy, her head drooped every so often before lifting again. Dylan came in and out asking about shirts. Where was the pink one? Not that one, the nicer one. Was it ironed? Did he need to wear a tie? Rachel didn't understand why he cared so much. They would all be sitting in the dark, except for Ben of course, up on stage living it large.

The next time Dylan appeared he had a beer in hand, a cartoon bear on the can, because men were just like children when it came down to it.

'So I guess I'm driving?' Rachel said, though there was no choice in the matter. She had to drive, she was—whisper it—six weeks pregnant, but waiting until the proper hospital test before she told him.

'Well, you're not really drinking these days, are you?' he said, continuing into the walk-in wardrobe, re-emerging with a white shirt that was meant to go under a tux.

Rachel turned off the dryer, kissed her daughter's head. 'Time for bed.'

'Night-night, furball,' said Dylan.

'*You're* a furball, Daddy.' Leah hugged his leg then vanished.

'Will I do storytime?' said Dylan.

'I really wish you wouldn't drink up here. Especially in front of her.'

'It's one can, Rach.'

'Isn't it always?'

'That's not fair.' He left the beer on a bedside locker.

'That will stain.'

'It won't,' he said. 'Are you going to be like this all evening?'

Her eyes went to where he stood in the tuxedo shirt that came halfway down his denim thighs. 'Like *what?*' she said.

Wisely he withdrew, wandering off to Leah's room where soon the jocular, easy laughs of fatherhood began. When you were in charge of a child, when they came out of your body like a vital organ you had to carry around externally for the rest of your life, a laugh was a more layered affair.

Rachel put the dryer away, threw on a silk blouse and sat at the dressing table to do her make-up. Her face was like the surface of an old boreen, more spots on it these days than skin. It was worth it, she reminded herself, just annoying that Dylan couldn't share the burden. She would happily carry the baby if he could take on a few things, like the acne, pelvic pain, insomnia and labour. With one last squint at her face she decided to ignore her complexion, focusing on her eyes, which were still that deep mossy green he'd fallen in love with years ago. No amount of hormonal upset could leach the colour from her eyes—that was something, wasn't it? Wiping an excess of gloopy foundation onto a tissue, what she wanted was for Dylan to comfort her, to mother her, but for that she would have to tell him, and something, aside from the hospital test, was holding her back.

Only when she tried to do her eyeliner did she notice her hand was shaking: an uneven black line across her lid, which was still puffy from the afternoon bout of tears. Rachel had taken to calling them 'naps', these disturbingly frequent stints where she had to run and smother her face in a pillow to stop herself from screaming.

Stevie, Stevie, of course it revolved around Stevie. Yet Rachel had unearthed nothing during her interrogations, it was all innocent recovery. And she could not—how could she?—complain about that.

'Mummy,' Leah called from her bedroom now.

'Coming.' Rachel relinquished the eyeliner and zipped up the make-up bag.

In Leah's bedroom, with the curtains drawn and the low, hypnotic music of the turning carousel, it took everything she had not to nestle in beside her daughter. The sweetness of the air, soft comfort, Mr Cuddles in slumped happiness against the rainbowed wall. 'Where's Daddy?' she asked Leah.

'On the phone to Aunt Stevie.'

'Since when?'

Leah's eyes widened.

Rachel forced herself to smile.

'He didn't finish the story, Mummy.'

'Bad Daddy.' Rachel sat on the bed, read from the beginning, when the poor old bear loses his hat. If they missed the drinks reception and preamble of opening night, she didn't care.

At the end she read the last page twice in keeping with tradition, then bent to kiss her daughter's forehead. Downstairs she could hear the babysitter, the Ugandan pharmacy student whom Leah loved.

'Night, darling,' she said. 'Chioma's in the living room if you need anything.'

'Mummy?'

She turned, anticipating a negotiation. 'You know it's bedtime.'

'But Mummy.'

'Yes?'

'Why don't I have a sister?'

Rachel froze.

'Or a brother. Like the girls in my class.'

Rachel gave a huge smile and said, 'One day soon.' She blew a kiss, closed the door halfway, unable to bear the hopeful face. It had absolutely been the wrong thing to say, to promise, and she went down the stairs in a rage. No one knew whether this pregnancy would take or end up like the last one. Dylan had once again put her in a position she was unable for, the man couldn't even finish a ten-page book.

In the kitchen he had a face on him. 'We need to leave,' he said.

'You look fab,' the babysitter smiled at her.

'Thanks, Chi.'

The girl went off to the living room.

'Let's go.' Dylan herded Rachel out the door.

'Hold on a second,' she snapped. 'You didn't bother—'

'Rachel!' he said. 'You don't understand. Ben has done his Achilles.'

'What?'

'He's freaking out, Stevie's freaking out. We need to get there.'

'Like ruptured it?'

'I don't know,' said Dylan, from the hallway. 'But it doesn't sound good.'

Rachel picked up her bag, called to the babysitter to raid the fridge, then followed her husband outside. As she closed the front door he leant over from the passenger seat, blasted the horn and she contemplated going straight back up to her daughter's room without even acknowledging him. Another toot, shorter this time, apologetic. She braced herself, walked steadily towards the car.

They didn't speak until she'd reversed out the driveway, travelled the length of their street and made a quick turn onto the main road, the headlights from an approaching double-decker flashing in the back window.

'Jesus, Rachel!'

'Thought you were in a rush. Stevie's freaking out, remember?'

'It would be nice to get there alive.'

'Would you care to walk?'

Dylan sighed.

'No?' she said.

Another sigh.

She turned on the radio to the station he hated ever since their sports guy had given him a four out of ten rating for a match against Edinburgh.

A minute later he switched it off.

'Hey!' she said. 'I was listening.'

'Rachel.'

'What?'

'It's not my fault.'

'What?'

'You're acting as if it's my fault.'

'What do you mean?' She knew well but she wanted to hear him say it.

'The miscarriage.'

She sped up the canal road towards Portobello Bridge through lights that flashed orange-red in her line of vision, down to The Barge where a backlog of cars at the next set of lights put an end to her joyride. The first car was slow to get going and only a few behind managed to get through. Shifting into neutral, she found her voice.

'I never said it was.'

'Yeah, but you're so angry at me all the time. Stevie says it's not good for the rehab.'

'You talk to her about me?' Rachel said. 'About our marriage?'

'No,' he said quickly. 'I don't. It's just that from a health point of view, Stevie says—'

'I don't care. Don't want to hear another word about her.'

'Excuse me?'

Some time went by before he asked her again to explain herself. What was her problem with Stevie? What was that all about? They were, as it happened, just passing the smooth cream walls of the National Gallery, turning onto Lincoln Place, the disjointed back of Trinity College, the old fortress Rachel could never enter. Sure, as an adult she could walk into the grounds, her legs worked just fine, but you could not walk into the past.

'Stevie's been great,' he said. 'I've improved so much. Do you not understand that, or what? You know how bad it's been for me.'

Relenting, she said, 'Yes. Of course I do.'

They drove the rest of the way in silence, with Rachel visualising the cool glass of white wine from the theatre bar she was no longer allowed to have.

*   *   *

Loud, excitable chatter filled the upstairs area of The Abbey, which was busy with people enjoying their drinks, all the tables taken, leather couches too, bodies perched on the curved ends. Rachel spotted a famous playwright in a long brown coat that made her hot just by looking at it. She felt a glide of foundation on her forehead, the creepiness of a second skin. From behind, Dylan put a cool hand on her shoulder and steered her towards a corner. He took her jacket, hung it on a nearby rack.

'Will I get you a sparkling water?' he said.

She nodded gratefully. 'Lots of ice.'

He joined a queue where two impeccably dressed men turned to talk to him, pumping his hand, the Leinster stalwart greatly missed by the team, she could imagine the conversation with no effort at all. Looking around, it seemed like everyone was in costume: silky outfits and pressed suits, indoor scarves, the air rich with perfume.

When Dylan returned, his phone was ringing in his pocket. He gestured for her to take the water. She looked longingly at his pint, the swift dip of the golden liquid disappearing into his mouth. As she downed her tepid water she had an unseemly craving for a bump of cocaine, which she hadn't done in years, not since the night of her hen.

Dylan was talking into the mobile in the calm, decisive manner that everyone, which was to say his mother, assumed would bag him a lucrative management contract with the IRFU. Ireland maybe, Leinster surely. That's what Helen believed. Yet there was no sign of an offer. No indication one might appear. The organisation wasn't known for its transparency on these matters. Rachel couldn't say that out loud, but it was true.

Two men came over to the wall beside her. The younger one had a phone flat in his palm, voice recorder zigzagging across the screen. Even without this Rachel would have sussed him as a journalist. They had a look that she'd learnt to watch out for over the years, a scruffy professionalism that typically included a wrinkled shirt or inappropriate shoes, stained fingertips, a milky, sun-starved complexion. The other man was someone important, maybe the director.

Dylan hung up the phone. 'That was Stevie. She's outside with Ben now trying to calm him down.'

'So why was she on the phone to you?'

'She put me on to him,' he said. 'Obviously.'

'Obviously.'

'Ben is in—'

Quickly she shook her head and Dylan stopped speaking. She nodded at the director, the hack, casting her eyes upwards. Dylan understood. Finishing his beer he said, 'Will we go?' She left her water, reached for her coat and took his hand. He charged into the crowd, keeping a tight hold of her. A group parted to let them pass; a moment of normality. Dylan was her husband, she was his wife. How good it would feel to be here alone with him, like when they were first together, before the complications of other people.

Outside the theatre a man in a sleeping bag was crouched by a pillar, heckling the smokers. He shook the coins in his cup. 'Are you enjoying that wine?' he asked a woman in her sixties who gave him such a disdainful look that Rachel reached into her handbag for a fiver. 'Thank you, gorgeous,' he said, but she was gone, following after Dylan towards the quays.

'Wait up!' she said. The heel of her right stiletto wobbled. She had only worn them to outshine Stevie and now she wished she was in runners. Her husband's broad back disappeared around the corner.

On the quays, waiting for a break in the traffic, she caught the show on the far side of the road, the three of them huddled on the boardwalk, backlit in orange from the street lamps. Ben was gripping the balustrade, shaking his head in violent denial at whatever Stevie was saying. Dylan had a hand on Ben's shoulder.

'I'm so sorry, Ben,' Rachel said when she reached them. 'How are you?'

To which Ben broke into a howl.

'He's not going on,' said Stevie.

'I am!'

'Maybe it's not ideal?' Dylan said.

'I'm fucking doing it.'

Ben looked mournfully at Rachel as if she should support him. 'What happened?' she said, her tone shifting, all business, which is what mothers had to be able to do, switch identities to nurse, guard, teacher, depending on the trouble. The entire civil service in one human. 'Tell me from the start.'

'It's just tendonitis,' Ben said.

'I think it's close to rupture,' Stevie said. 'You need a scan.'

Ordinarily Rachel would have deferred to her opinion but there was a vague look in her eyes this evening, a lack of authority in the slump of her shoulders. Rachel had never liked that blazer.

'Listen, guys,' she said. 'You need to decide. This dithering is helping no one. Is there an understudy?'

'It's my call,' Ben said. 'I'm going on.' And off he went limping up the boardwalk.

Stevie gave a final, futile shout after him. Dylan mumbled a platitude.

Rachel felt her patience dwindle. 'We should find your parents,' she said to Dylan.

'Alright,' he said robotically. 'Let's go.'

'Marian is here too,' Stevie said. 'I think they travelled up together.'

This was news to Rachel. Generally Ben's mother was either in the Canaries, at work, or on retreat somewhere deep in the border counties. Beyond that Ben didn't like to talk about her. There was an alcohol dependency, which was maybe in the past, Rachel couldn't remember the details, just that she and Ben were bonded in that way, adults who had carried from childhood certain psychic wounds they had no interest in reopening.

As they made their way back to the theatre, she began to feel worried for Ben, her friend, whose dire predicament was only now beginning to dawn on her. She'd been so caught up in her own woes she hadn't really thought about it: barely able to walk he had to go on stage in front of hundreds of people. After working towards tonight for years. It hurt her heart to think of it, that a person's best efforts so often fell short. These two goons in front of her—because of course Stevie and Dylan had gone ahead, stopping every so often to wait for her heels to catch up—didn't have a clue. They knew nothing about the stage.

At the entrance to the theatre, her in-laws were suddenly upon them, kisses from Helen, Sean stately in tweed, letting his wife do the greetings for the pair of them. Ben's mother stood morosely beside them in an elegant velvet coat, a gaunt, attractive woman who was nearly as tall as Ben. Stevie's parents were conspicuously absent, Rachel thought; even if the Lake Garda trip had been booked before Ben got the part, he was practically family. They could have postponed. That was the Jones' for you, they looked out for themselves. Over Helen's animated head, Rachel gave her father-in-law a smile. He sidestepped Stevie without saying hello and came to hug Rachel. She didn't know whether he did this deliberately, whether he also viewed Stevie as a troublesome presence in Dylan's life, but she deeply appreciated it either way and clung on to him for longer than normal.

'There, there,' he said, misunderstanding. 'I hope you're doing OK. You've had a tough year. Our Rachel.'

The *our* did her in. Rachel, who never cried in public, felt her eyes warm with unwanted tears that went quickly down her face, leaving a wet trace on Sean's shoulder. She rummaged in her bag for a tissue. 'Hay fever,' she said, realising everyone was watching.

'In October?' said Helen.

'Mrs Brosnahan!' Rachel seized on Ben's mother for distraction. 'It's lovely to see you.'

'Yes, dear, so lovely,' Marian said in her deadpan way. 'Is my son all set?'

'Not quite,' said Stevie.

'What's wrong?' Helen said.

'He went for a run this morning and messed up his ankle.'

'That's terrible,' said Marian. 'Truly awful.'

While the women fussed over the news, Sean clapped Dylan on the back and said, 'Does this here place do pints, lad?' Rachel could see Dylan stiffen at the 'lad'. He hated when his father countrified his accent, which he did every time he came to Dublin.

'Yes,' Dylan said. 'I imagine they do.'

'Let's all go in,' said Helen. 'I've every confidence Benjamin will pull this off. I'm feeling very optimistic.'

Rachel caught Stevie's eye and they shared a smile. As Dylan guided the others in through the thronged foyer, they hung back.

'So everything's going to be fine,' said Stevie. 'What a relief. In the Land of Helen, at least.'

'Better than Marian, angel of doom.'

'True.'

'We could bail,' Rachel joked. 'Do a runner. Could you imagine?'

'You wouldn't get far in those.' Stevie pointed to the heels.

Laughter over, fellowship gone.

Rachel felt her lips press together. Back again, the mask, locking into place. 'Will we go in?'

'Sure,' said Stevie. 'Race you to the bar.'

'I'm not drinking.' Rachel flashed a hand over her midriff. 'Because we're trying?'

'Oh, I'm sorry. I forgot.'

'Of course you did.'

Stevie stared at her, open-mouthed.

Many things happened to Rachel in that moment: relief, regret, fear of reprisal, but mostly the realisation that there was no going back now, not if she wanted to keep her dignity. She could see Stevie puzzling over what to do, her fingers began to clutch at her frayed sleeve. Eventually she said, 'I'm not sure what you mean by that.'

'Aren't you?' Rachel said.

'No.'

'Maybe you should think about it.'

'The mis—'

Rachel held up a hand. 'About the fact I've tried for years to be friends with you, I've really made an effort, and still you see me as an outsider. Someone to ruin the fun.' She felt her voice go hoarse. 'Someone to make fun of.'

'That's not true,' Stevie said.

'Yeah?' Rachel did an unintentional eyeroll, a dormant gesture last needed when she was in school and direct conflict with other girls was a weekly, sometimes daily, occurrence.

'I don't know what else you want me to say here.' Stevie looked back in the direction of the river, confirming for Rachel that the woman really didn't like her.

Emboldened by the rejection, and by the presence of her in-laws inside the theatre—real, physical proof that she was married to Dylan and he was married to her—Rachel said, 'Dylan is my husband. He's been my husband for years now and the sooner you accept that, the better for everyone involved.'

Stevie flushed a deep pink from her neckline to her forehead. She opened her mouth, closed it again. Her eyes squinted at Rachel.

In the foyer there was an automated announcement that the play would start in ten minutes. People around them began to move.

Rachel unfolded her arms and said in a chirpy, utterly fake voice, 'Right then, I guess it's showtime.'

In the large auditorium the trundle of theatregoers finding their seats began in earnest. Stevie let the crowd take her, a polite swell that stopped and started as people checked their tickets against the lettered rows. She wished they would all keep walking down onto the stage, over to the fake bar counter, the suspended glasses of the fictional English pub, right through the painted windows scenery, the building itself, until she could get away from everyone she knew and run off into the night to absorb the shock of what had happened.

Firstly, had it actually happened?

When they'd gone back inside to the others, Stevie had downed a wine, and along with the pill she'd taken to deal with the tendon fiasco, plus the supplementary half right before leaving, it had left her mind addled and uncooperative, her sense of honour battling fiercely with the sedating effects of the tablets, thoughts dragged downwards to the dark primordial space where nothing mattered. She took in her surroundings, the sleek wooden slats that lined the walls, the scarlet rows losing their uniform colour as here a person, there another, sat down.

Beside her Helen was fussing over seat numbers that Sean had managed to mess up online. In his excitement at seeing Ben's face on The Abbey homepage, he hadn't booked enough tickets, and when he went back to get more the good ones were gone. 'Here,' she said to Stevie, pressing two into her hand. 'Row P, I'm afraid. Will you go with Dylan, and we'll take Rachel? I think she needs some looking after.'

Stevie went to tell her that Ben had saved front row seats for herself, Dylan and Rachel, but her current mental state was no match for Helen's stream of consciousness on old men and the internet.

Mercifully they parted ways at G, Stevie trudging up the remaining steps alone, relieved that her seat was over to the right of the auditorium, at the edge of a row behind the shelter of a partition. She sat down quickly, tried to make herself small. No sign of Dylan; she left her bag on the free seat. Below at row G, she could see Rachel sitting between his parents and Marian. Rachel said something that caused the older people to laugh, then she looked around, left, right, over each shoulder, her high ponytail a bright comet as she tried and failed to spot Stevie.

Secondly, how had it happened?

Just before, Stevie was sure, they'd been outside the theatre colluding together over the contrived happiness Helen tried to generate wherever she went. Rachel had winked at Stevie on the sly, or at the very least grinned at her, some fleeting connection notable for the fact it was so rare. How could a person go from that to an unprovoked attack? Stevie had said it before: she didn't understand Rachel Turner. She did not understand how Dylan, of all people, had ended up with the woman.

Magnetically her eyes found him in the crowded space, in the front row, sitting in the middle of two free seats. Slouched, you could say, for a man of his stature, which reminded her she hadn't been alone in knocking back the booze. When he'd gone to the bar to get her the wine, he'd come back with another pint for himself though he had a half yet to finish. This was unusual for Dylan, but possibly linked to his father. He was always on edge around him, a side to his personality that Stevie didn't often see and therefore found intriguing.

As the audience settled she felt her phone buzz in her handbag. She took it out, grateful for the reminder to switch it off before the show. Dylan's name flashed on the screen. She saw him stand, handset to ear, clearly visible to all the other rows in his starched shirt. She was now watching Rachel watching him call her, even if Rachel couldn't possibly know who he was calling. She would presume of course. And she would be right. Which answered the third question: why had this happened? Why had Rachel Turner, who was viciously sober, accused Stevie of having feelings for Dylan?

Stevie knew why.

Worse than that, she felt like everyone else knew too.

Her finger declined the call, which she regretted even as she was doing it. Did she remember that day in Sandycove? His question this morning she hadn't dignified with an answer, because how could someone forget a day like that, it was like forgetting you had a pulse. She looked at the chair beside her and wanted him there and in the same breath didn't want this at all.

In the end she got no say in the matter. Dylan somehow spotted her, he sought her out in a way that made her forget her reservations, he was bounding up the steps towards her row, bounding past his own wife and parents, with a wide, artless smile. Before she put her phone on airplane mode she sent, as if to a sickly uncle, a text to Ben to wish him well. In her lap, the programme she had bought at the last minute, on the cover a monochrome image of a pretty woman with fraught, despairing eyes, flanked by two men facing the other way; Stevie couldn't bear to turn the glossy pages, shoved it now into her handbag, out of sight.

'Hi,' Dylan said when he reached her. 'Budge over.'

She moved her knees to the side and he went gingerly past. The look he gave her seemed loaded, but maybe it was her own twisted mind. The not knowing was a kind of pleasure.

'Did you forget about the front?' he said.

'Your parents got us tickets too.'

'I told them,' Dylan said. 'They never listen.'

'I'm just following orders.'

'Sensible.'

Both of them remained looking forward. She got a trace of pine, and underneath, his quintessential scent, his skin-scent that was impossible to describe but nevertheless known to her in a way that made the fine hairs on her body stand to attention.

The audience quietened as the lights dimmed.

'Where's Rachel?' he said.

It took effort to point to the midsection of the auditorium.

'Right,' he said.

They moved their arms onto the shared armrest at the same time. She felt an odd burning up her forearm, which settled into a pleasant heaviness as it became clear neither of them had withdrawn. Dylan shifted in his seat, a small, nothing movement with a seismic impact. How was she expected to put up with one hundred minutes of this? There was no interval, she knew from Ben, and she wondered if she should make a break for the front row. Or the exit. Or the bar.

'I think we're better off here,' he said psychically. 'Less distracting for Ben.'

She let that one stand.

The announcer reminded everyone to check their phones, prompting some commotion, then the lights went down. Right before the actors appeared on stage, Dylan leant in and whispered, 'Are you OK?' They looked sideways at each other, were still looking as the lights came up and a man, Ben's castmate Sebastian, passed a glass of wine to a woman and said, 'Well…'

Much of the first scene hurtled by without Stevie hearing a word because once the actors started to speak, Dylan moved his thigh against her own. The warm press of it in the dark was exquisite. She wanted very much to close her eyes. They stayed like this for who knows how long, until the woman on stage said, 'I think we're going to separate.'

With a mild vibration his leg was gone. Soon Stevie's leg drifted of its own volition in his direction, seeking reconnection, and from there things sped up, there was no doubt about it now. He pressed back stronger than before, she could actually feel his quad muscle straining as it tightened, then he reached his hand across and gently took her fingers, moving them off her lap till they were entwined with his, their hands joined in guilty union under the shade of the armrest in the narrow, sticky space between their seats. Two conflicting impulses: she feared the people in the row behind might be watching; she wanted to get out of her chair and climb on top of him. Instead she squeezed his fingers and he squeezed back. Things inside her began to quicken, blood rushing in various directions. He let go of her hand—bereft!—only to change position. Turning it face up, he began to rub the sensitive middle of her palm with his thumb. Stevie became disconnected from her thoughts, she was nothing but feeling, her body, so often forgotten amid the grinding worries of life, reasserted itself. She went lower in the chair. Her legs stretched in front of her under the partition and she felt sorry for Dylan that he didn't have the space to do the same. She could see his left knee trembling. His thumb pressed deeper into her palm, a jerky referral up the length of her arm, almost a physio technique, which reminded her that her hands had been touching his body for months now, knew every muscle in his legs and back, the ferocious knot always in the lat dorsi, the grunt he gave when it released. It felt right that things should finally be reversed, that he should be the one to touch her, his fingers now trailing the skin of her inner wrist, in a way that was clearly visible to anyone who cared to look. What was it to her, who had already been accused of worse? In this brave new world, Rachel's outburst seemed weirdly like permission.

On stage the lights suddenly flared. Sebastian said, 'I mean, I picked his own daughter up in my own arms and threw her up and caught her, in my kitchen.'

Dylan's fingers stopped moving. They cuffed her wrist, then they were gone. She understood he was thinking about Leah, which in turn meant she was thinking about the little girl too. For the first time in a while she felt her own childless state as a lack that seemed to reek right now of her intrinsic delinquency.

During the deft set change, a sense of shame settled between them with the solidness of a wall. Dylan leant to the far side of his chair. Stevie mirrored him. Two men appeared on stage, one of them her life partner, the person she'd been with bar the odd break-up for twenty years. The backdrop to this new scene was a grand old study with dark mahogany furniture, the type of room she knew Ben wanted whenever they could afford to buy a house. A place to put all his plays and novels and acting manuals, most of which were stored unlovingly in Marian's attic in Sallins. She watched him track across the stage now in a loose approximation of a man with two working ankles. He was being handed a fake whiskey by Sebastian, whose poised appearance gave no sense of trouble or alarm. Stevie was further reassured when Ben began to speak. He leant against a table but his lines were distinct and fluid. His bright eyes had conviction, his tone a commanding allure; he was fully in character. The skills which she had mostly seen in audition monologues or minor roles seemed to fit naturally in this grand forum, he appeared to be at home.

But a few minutes later he had to walk downstage and his body went into visible spasm. His face smiled, then flattened. A drastic rigour to his movements as he tried to regain control. Sebastian repeated a line, buffered with an ad lib that didn't work. There was a long pause before Ben replied, his voice noticeably altered, lowered in growling pain. Heads in the audience began to turn. The fiction was broken—they were out of the dream.

'What the hell?' Dylan said quietly.

She shook her head, unable to look at him, unable to partake in the horror of what was happening to Ben in front of all these people, which seemed perversely but definitively linked to what she and Dylan were up to moments ago. Just what, she wondered, were they up to?

'Oh for god's sake!' Ben said. 'Look, what exactly do you want to *fucking* say?'

A nervy titter started up in the auditorium, surely only from people who were unfamiliar with the play, who didn't realise, as Stevie did, having been through the script multiple times, that this was supposed to be a serious meditation on the consequences of betrayal.

The scene continued, one despairing response after the next, a mutation of the physical injury. By the look on Ben's face he was aware of it too, could hear the words gargling from his mouth, the increasingly stiff responses of his stage partner, and that he would continue on despite this fact, he would double down on his efforts, it was just the way he was built.

'I think I will sit down!' Ben said. Stevie wasn't sure if it was part of the script, maybe he was improvising, but at least it seemed to work: once he was seated, his voice steadied, the rhythm of the conversation returned. You couldn't call it acting though, not with the strained face, grisly focus, the faltering gestures of a body governed by pain. There was the sense he was barely staying upright in the large armchair where he had taken refuge. The audience were invested solely in his fortunes. They had stopped following the play. Some people were visibly leaning forward in their seats, waiting for the climax, and the fall.

When the scene ended the lights went darker than the previous set change. An ominous quiet. Stevie could picture the ructions backstage. Straining her ears, she thought she caught the staccato cry of refusal. What were they to do? If the understudy was still in the building, he could replace Ben and carry on, but in a play with only three characters this change would be confusing, an admission things had gone badly wrong.

As the wait grew longer, people began to mutter and rustle their belongings. There was an incipient giddiness, a crowd about to turn. A man in a row behind said that if he'd wanted to see a farce, he would have gone to the Oscar Wilde at The Gate. Those around him laughed with abandon, thankful for the release. 'Shall we leave?' the man said to his seatmate. The pair of them rose with grandiose indignation, excusing themselves in authoritative voices that carried across the auditorium. Once they made it to the end of the row they walked proudly down the stairs towards the exit. An usher told them they wouldn't be readmitted if they left now, to which the farce man responded, 'Thank God for that!'

All the while Dylan sat silent beside her, a silence that was getting difficult to bear. She turned her head. He rested both hands flat against his thighs before looking at her. Their eyes locked.

'Stevie,' he said.

She tried to hide her face with her sleeve. The drugs had worn off, she was no longer immune to the world and its demands, felt the effort of the long day and evening overtake her, the madness of the morning swim when she knew she had to follow it with work and a big night out. The rough water, the stupidity of that. What was wrong with her? What was she looking for in all the worst places?

'Hey,' Dylan said. 'Hey, it's OK.'

To her surprise she found she couldn't speak. Quickly he put his arm around her, gripped her shoulder, kissed her temple. She leant into him, stayed there a second too long, as the lights came up and heads began to turn.

Down below a velvet curtain descended from the rafters, sealing off the stage and its failures. Not long afterwards a man in black walked onto the proscenium and announced, with regret, that the show was over for the night.

*   *   *

Stevie couldn't remember the specifics of leaving her seat, the boring mechanics of it, just the rush of transportive feeling that had landed them here together in a cubicle of the theatre's gender neutral bathrooms whose delicate lighting and blonde wood furnishings felt dangerously European. His mouth was hard against hers, her back pressed against the cool divider. She opened her eyes. A strip of raw light at the join of the cubicle door.

'This is,' he said quietly, 'so nice.' Then he traced a finger over her lips, unbearably tense.

On went the kissing, for seconds or years, until they both stopped at the sound of someone entering the bathroom. They stayed close together, in shocking collusion, his hand on the curve of her jeans.

As they listened to the tap turning on, every painstaking splash before the powerful dryer, she tried to access some plane of reason that might allow her to walk away, it wasn't too late, not really, but her mind was no match for her body, which didn't even have to argue back, all it had to do was exist. The desire was biological, grounded in impulse; the very fact of it won the argument.

Two ladies came into the bathroom, one offering to hold the other's coat, and even this sense of decorum couldn't penetrate their new world, the delicious pressing. When they kissed again his hand went roughly through her hair, a sensation so intense she was almost relieved to hear the dread notes of a familiar voice, that of Sean Turner, thanking someone *as gaeilge* for— what? Stevie didn't catch it, only the feeling of Dylan drawing away, his head inclined towards the door.

Taking a chance his father was safely inside a cubicle, he kissed her one last time, released the slatted lock and left with his shoulders hunched forward. Some confusion arose when a man tried to access the cubicle. Stevie had the wherewithal to pull a tampon from her bag and brandish the flimsy wrapper. Apologising, the man backed away. She locked the door, stayed safely inside until her heart slowed to a pace that was probably human.

*   *   *

In the upstairs foyer she waited by the stairwell, watching the slow morass of people still exiting the auditorium, their hushed tones adding an edge of menace to the more general aura of mayhem. Standing on her toes, she looked beyond the crowds to the corridor that led to the bathrooms, the doorway an oblong of white nothing. Just moments ago Dylan had separated from her, told her to go first to meet the others. She knew he didn't want to face his family. Stevie didn't want to face them either. She tried to behave normally, as if nothing had happened since they'd last seen each other. Nothing had happened and she was on her way to an affair. The more she obsessed about this, the more it would come true. Dylan Turner, a married man, her friend, her closest friend, no—wrong—*Ben's* closest friend. Suddenly floored by urgent thoughts of her forgotten boyfriend, she took out her phone, tried to call him but it went to voicemail. He hadn't responded to her well wishes before the curtain rose.

Stevie looked towards the bar, scanned the shelf of amber spirits, though she knew she didn't want another drink. She didn't even want a pill. For the first time in months she had no interest in them. The safari to the bathroom had shocked her sober. Lingering, the fresh effect of him all over her body. A pure sensation, not veiled with synthetic feeling. As she sank back into the surreal pleasure, a man with a crisp English accent ordered a double shot of whiskey at the bar.

'That's the director.' Rachel's voice came from behind.

'Hello!' said Stevie. 'Hi.'

Rachel had her jacket on, a light pink bolero zipped to the neck. Dylan's father stood beside her.

'That's Walter?' Stevie said.

Rachel ignored her.

'God knows he needs that drink,' Sean said. 'What a shambles. Poor Ben.'

Another man approached the bar. Walter joined him, their conversation unfolding in earnest spurts.

'And that's a journalist,' Rachel said to Sean. 'A critic, I think.'

'How do you know all this?' Stevie said.

'I'm an observant person.'

Stevie gave the briefest of nods.

'Not a lot for him to criticise,' Sean said. 'Except,' he trailed off.

'Where are the others?' Stevie asked.

'You know women,' he said.

'Where's Dylan?' Rachel deigned to look at Stevie. 'We need to get home. The babysitter.'

'But you're early,' Sean said. 'We're not supposed to be done for another hour—more.'

'Where is Dylan?' Rachel said.

'Toilet.' Stevie couldn't bring herself to hold her gaze, the tension was too much. Even Sean caught the atmosphere and the three of them spent a good ten minutes in near silence punctured by the occasional expression of pity or regret. 'All his life leading up to this,' Sean said at one point, almost to himself.

More unbearable emotion assaulted her. Sean was right. Poor Ben. This was the worst night of his life, and only she and Dylan knew the full extent of it.

From the inside pocket of his blazer Sean produced a programme, wound it with big hands into a tight roll. Stevie knew already, before she even opened her bag: her own programme had fallen out somehow, it was gone. She was about to take off for her seat when Marian and Helen came through the doors, the latter apologising for the delay. 'We've been trying to get backstage,' she said. 'But they won't let anyone in.'

Stevie felt wrongfooted for not having thought to do this. 'I'll go,' she said, nonsensically.

'No, dear,' Marian grimaced. 'There's no point.'

The crowd began to thin, only friends and family of the cast remaining, Stevie guessed.

'Where's Dylan?' said Helen.

Everyone looked at Stevie.

'Bathroom,' she said, just as Dylan appeared at the doors of the auditorium with a dishevelled Ben propped up against him.

'Sorry,' said Dylan. 'It took us a while to get going.'

'How are you?' Stevie said to Ben.

His devastated face was streaked with orange foundation, as if he'd partially taken off his make-up before giving up. He shook his head, bit down on his lip, which had an unhealthy purple tinge. Dylan manoeuvred him onto a nearby chair. Ben put his head in his hands. Stevie went over, crouched beside him and patted his stage-gelled hair. 'It will be OK,' she said softly.

Marian said, 'Well, at least you were in it. We saw you up there.'

Helen was quiet, an indication, should Stevie need it, of the grim situation. A few of the stage crew came over to sympathise. One of them asked if Ben wanted an ambulance.

'Thanks,' said Stevie. 'We'll look after him.'

When they left, Ben opened his mouth to speak, closed it again in wordless horror. Then: 'Was it bad?' Looking only at Stevie. 'I mean, just how bad was it? Come on, tell me how bad.'

At the third *bad*, Helen came to life with a succession of words that were English in theory if not in a syntactical sense, assuring Ben that no one noticed a thing, praising his presence on stage, his inimitable talent. They should blame the cancellation on a scenery malfunction. Technology. Faulty lights! In the distance Stevie could see the journalist gather his notes and make quickly for the stairs. As he passed their group he kept his head down.

'Do you realise who that is?' Ben whimpered. 'He was here. Jesus Christ. They were all here—even the *Guardian*.'

'I think,' said Stevie, 'we should get you to a hospital.'

'Rachel can drive,' Dylan said.

Rachel's lips disappeared. She gave him a look that said, 'Really?'

'Will I stay?' said Marian.

'I'm fine, Mam,' Ben said stoically. 'You go back with the Turners.'

Sean said, 'The hospital in Naas would see you far quicker than this Dublin brigade.'

'Yes, Dad,' said Dylan. 'There isn't a good doctor to be found in the whole city.'

Ben stopped nipping his lip and actually smiled. Dylan leant across to pat his arm. Stevie drew back, too late, the pine scent had infiltrated her senses and was sparking through her with wounding desire. She felt the guilt come in again. The shame, rather. Guilt was when you felt bad about something. Shame was when you felt bad about yourself.

'The Mater is closest,' she said.

'Could you,' said Rachel, 'think about getting a taxi?'

'Rachel!' Dylan admonished.

'The babysitter, Dylan.' An edge to her voice.

At this juncture Walter chose to introduce himself. 'Listen,' he said to Ben once the formalities were done. 'You get that leg looked at. It's your health that matters. I'm not angry. Don't give it another thought. You might not believe me right now, but I've been involved in worse.'

Stevie thought it was a lovely thing to say, until he followed it with, 'We're lucky to have a super understudy in Paul. He'll be able to step in straight away.'

'But—' said Ben.

'Clearly you're not going to be able to do the run,' Walter said. 'I'm sure everyone here is telling you it will be OK, because they love you, but I'm afraid it's my job to be a realist.'

'What about London?' Ben croaked.

'Don't even think about it!' Walter said. 'Focus on your health. That's a good fellow. Now if you'll excuse me everyone.'

Once he was gone the men helped to lift Ben downstairs. Those going to Kildare said their goodbyes, with promises of hourly check-ins. Then it was just the three of them, Ben, Stevie and Dylan, alone in the deserted lobby, waiting in bewilderment for Rachel to retrieve the car.

STEVIE

Six weeks into stevie's third year at college, Dublin gets a heatwave. For days the sun is high and constant over the city, a strange, clutching heat so unusual for autumn that talk is of nothing else. All week she's sat in lectures and looked out the windows of the sciences building at the cricket pitch, the yawn of students accumulating from mid-morning, enjoying the windfall of a brief second summer. She has texts from flatmates, classmates, siblings, all essentially asking the same question in various degrees of civility: Is she mad? A loser? Doesn't she know she's missing out? Many of her lecturers have joined the party, cutting classes early, or in one instance, not showing up at all. The campus seems to be in agreement that a freak weather event lets everyone off the hook.

Even without the admonishments of friends, Stevie knows she's punishing herself, that her perfect attendance since the beginning of term has a manic bent to it, a foolscap-filling urgency, penance for what might be going on in the rest of her life.

But today is Friday and she has had enough. Enough lectures with empty chairs, enough stuffy indoors, enough repenting for sins that don't exist. With her swimsuit already on under her soft denim beach dress, bats and towel in a bag, she's leaving her digs in Irishtown before any of the others can ask her where she's going, she's hopping on a Dart out home. Stevie is going for a sea swim, then she's going to see her mother. Barbara will know what to do.

Waiting on the warm bench at Lansdowne station, she takes out her phone and calls home. When no one answers she tries her mother's mobile, her sister, lastly her dad, who has no interest in technology, the inactivated voicemail reminds her. On the train she gets a window seat facing south, leans her head against the rubber rim until the doors close and they depart, the long shadow of the carriages moving backwards on the tarmac platform.

Approaching Booterstown a low line of sea wavers in the distance, the ridged strand is slick and hard. Her phone buzzes: her mother.

'Hi,' says Stevie.

'You're up early.'

A jokey accusation but it makes Stevie bristle. 'Eleven? My lectures start at nine.'

'So why aren't you at them?' her mother says, enjoying herself now.

'If you must know, I've been the only one going to classes all week.'

'Is that right?'

'Yes,' Stevie says. 'And I've had enough. I'm coming home for the day. I might stay actually,' she adds, though she has no intention of this. 'Why didn't you pick up before?'

'We're in Wexford, love.'

'What?'

'Having lives, you know,' Barbara laughs.

'Am I on speakerphone?'

'No, but your father is here beside me in the café. Say hi.'

'Hi, Dad.'

There is a muffled enquiry about money.

'I'm grand, Dad.'

'She's coming home, Joe,' her mother says. 'But she never gives us notice.'

Stevie feels suddenly too hot. The train has stopped at the platform at Booterstown, the sun is in her eyes. She shields her face with a hand, realising she's forgotten her sunglasses.

'Laura will be there this evening,' her mother says.

'OK.'

'If you stick around till Sunday we'll see you then.'

'Right,' says Stevie. 'Maybe.'

They talk for a while, mainly about the success of the new bed in the holiday home in Ballymoney, until the train passes the colourful crescent of tall terraces in Monkstown and Stevie says she has to go.

'Is everything OK?' her mother says.

'Everything's fine.'

'Is it about Australia? Are you having doubts?'

'What?' says Stevie. 'Why would you say that? Of course not.' Stevie has opted to go abroad for her placement after Christmas, six months on the other side of the world, when she could have picked London, Edinburgh, Stuttgart, or indeed any of the Dublin hospitals where most of her classmates have ended up. She made the decision in a moment of pique her first week back at college and she realises now, listening to her mother's incessant repetition of the word Sydney, that she's been deliberately not thinking about it ever since.

Her mother changes tack. 'Is it Ben?'

'No,' says Stevie. 'It's nothing to do with him.' Which is a lie, obviously, her mother has forced her to lie.

'Right then. Say goodbye to your father.'

After she hangs up, Stevie thinks that even if her mother had been home it would have been impossible to explain the problem. Her mother, a respectable and sensible person, would not have understood. Yes, it's about Ben, but it's largely about Dylan, which is about Ben, which is about Dylan, which is to say, there is nothing relatable about her feelings at all.

Ever since the music festival, barely six weeks and yet a lifetime ago, Stevie has been going slowly insane. On the face of it, she probably looks to be managing—she is her mother's daughter, after all—but her mind is troubled, unsure of itself, constantly overthinking and rethinking, in a way that takes her half an hour to make a cup of tea. There is no space for normal things.

As the train slows for Dún Laoghaire station, she thinks, for the thousandth time, about what happened in the tent during that long night into morning—the slow creep of light over Dylan's face; his tired, lovely eyes; the soft mouth telling her everything would be OK, he was consoling her, they were laughing about how angry she'd been at the rave, the state of your one in the pink wig, then they weren't laughing any more, they were right up close and she was leaning into him, he had his arm around her, and parts of his body were touching hers in a way that was incredibly gentle and hot. They did not kiss. Or rather, they did not kiss on the lips. They did not take off their clothes. They did not have sex. They didn't do anything together, really, except hear with alarm Ben's sudden, staggering footfall outside the tent, the kicked can and cursing, the river of dirty beer that ran onto the canvas floor when she opened the entrance flap to be met with his wild druggie head. Before she let him in, she had one clear thought: enemy soldier, the belligerent invading the base.

Ben pushed past her to get inside and root through his things, an overwhelming dark edge to the silence in the tent. Dylan rolled in his sleeping bag towards the left pocket near the supplies. His eyes were closed. He went overtly still and appeared to be holding his breath. Ben didn't bother with pyjamas, just grabbed the old rug they'd brought for outside, threw it down on the centre of the floor and soon he was a long, snoring, bifurcating line between his girlfriend and his friend. Stevie curled up in her corner, stayed painfully awake until she heard Noel and the lads get up across the way.

She spent day two of the festival with them, furiously avoiding her tentmates. Entirely without sleep she managed a jacuzzi for breakfast, a ride on the Ferris wheel before lunch, a DJ set, four bands, an impromptu sing-song on the picnic tables in the food area, and to be back in the yellow tent blessedly unconscious long before the headline act appeared on stage that night. The fact that Ben and Dylan had a brilliant day together, catching all the bands Ben wanted to see, seemed to carry them into the third morning, allowing for a breeziness, an air of reconciliation, Stevie thought, as they began to recount the highlights of the preceding day while packing up for home. She was wary, guilty, ready for peace.

During the arduous trek back to the car she asked if she could carry anything else, the tent, the leaking cooler or rug, the leftover beer? The guys wouldn't hear of it, they had become superhuman in their attempts to compete with each other's manliness, and she was left with their sleeping bags, her own rucksack. Right as they got to the car she decided, on seeing the exit queue, that she needed a toilet, begged permission to race back to the nearest portaloo, which Ben reluctantly granted, a note of anguish in the way he jangled the car keys, having only recently remembered he was driving home, that he'd lost the rock-paper-scissors to Dylan on the way down.

On her return the mood was subdued, the tough journey ahead had landed like a hangover squared. Ben revved the engine. Dylan sat motionless in the passenger seat. The fermented sweat of the unwashed permeated the car. When Stevie lowered the back seat window, Ben told her to wind it up—he had the fan on full power!—and neither she nor Dylan had the courage to point out that all he was doing was recirculating the stagnant air. As they inched out of the car park towards the stationary queue, Ben began to see this for himself, then realising that they'd known before him, he rolled down the driver window in a sulk, cursing Dylan's banger, asking why he didn't own a better car. After that outburst silence reigned and time grew even slower, every minute on the dashboard clock seemed to take ten to turn over. To rekindle the ease of earlier, Stevie tried to talk to Ben about the Mercury Rev gig she had missed the previous evening. Dylan made a half-hearted effort to describe the music, which ended the way his descriptions of music always ended: with him apologising for his ignorance. Usually this perked Ben up, but he was lost to them now, Stevie could see the embittered slit of his face in the rear-view mirror, he had gone deep into the cave of his mind, all the furry bats were scarily awake. The atmosphere in the car became so oppressive she began to wonder if the Dublin crew could give her a lift back, when suddenly Ben pulled out of the line of traffic over to a grassy bank beside the railings and cut the engine. Dylan made the maddeningly rational point that they would lose their place in the queue, nearly an hour of waiting. Ben opened his mouth to respond but no words came out, just drops of saliva landing on the handbrake. Simultaneously they looked down at the residue and up again. Stevie closed her eyes, it was too intense, she wanted to not be in the car with them, she would prefer to travel home in the boot, to live there for the rest of the year.

'What's the matter?' Dylan asked with clear nervous dread.

That was enough to do it. Stevie heard Ben tell her to get out of the car. She opened her eyes at the instruction and stared at him with an integrity she found difficult to muster, a woman trying to compose herself as she turned to face the firing squad. Reluctantly she followed Ben from the car, leaving Dylan inside. What happened next she would prefer to forget: a terrifically nasty fight in front of dozens of onlookers whereby all manner of accusations and past misdemeanours were dredged up, until eventually Ben said he was breaking up with her—*FOREVER*—and stormed back towards the festival tents. When Dylan got out of the car she was crying, from the shock or the hangover or the feelings of self-loathing that were so concrete and absolute it was like something inside her was turning to stone. He reached out to touch her shoulder. She squirmed from his hand, bolted for the back seat, lay down and placed Ben's discarded hoodie over her face, her body shuddering in unison with the engine as Dylan turned the key in the ignition and uttered a sound so completely devoid of happiness that it seemed to represent all the things that had gone wrong at the festival over two lousy days, in their friendships over years, and in the world at large, which was still out there beyond the increasingly narrow prism of their preoccupations, still spinning on its axis day after miserable day.

The same world that is passing her now in distinct frames through the train window. How can something so vast and imperative be irrelevant to the majority of thoughts in her head? Or to reverse the equation, why do the contemptible decisions of her puny life feel vital and urgent when she could die tomorrow and the universe wouldn't blink? In a bid to forget her worries, she makes eye contact with a young boy sitting opposite her, sticks out her tongue, gets a smile. He does it back to her and she's about to go again, when her phone vibrates. A text from Dylan:

What you at?

She replies instantly. *Swim at Sandycove. Fancy it?*

Now?

Yes now.

A heartbeat of nothing, then: *Jumping on a Dart.*

Foolishly she looks behind her down the carriage, as if he might have the ability to break the laws of physics. She reads the exchange one more time, slips the phone in her bag, bounces towards the door to wait for the train to pull into Glasthule station.

As they slow for a tunnel, the light in the carriage dims and she shivers in the murk. Any meetings in the last six weeks—and there were more than a few—have taken place on campus, surrounded by people they know or could know or who might know them. Whether it's coffee in the JCR, lunch in the thronged canteen, a snatched hello between lectures or training, there is always the feeling of being watched, at least that's how it seems to Stevie, as if she swallowed a camera at that godforsaken festival and will never be free or alone again. But this is different. So far from college as to be almost in another county, literally closer to Wicklow than the city centre. Her imagination goes into overdrive. All at once there is the sense of possibility, of mischief and adventure.

At the promenade in Glasthule the sun nearing noon throws shapes across the bay. She walks slowly to the short swipe of beach at Sandycove, resists going straight in the water when she arrives, it seems important she wait for Dylan, that they do this together.

The cove is busy with people, dogs, pockets of children playing at the shoreline, wet sand streaked on their bodies. She watches a father chase after a fugitive toddler. In her pale swim-suit onesie the little girl wriggles like a prawn, shrieks of protest as he lifts her in the air. The dramatics remind Stevie, somewhat unfairly, of Ben. They haven't spoken since the festival and it feels weird that this person she saw nearly every day for the last two years is suddenly gone from her life, a living ghost. This is perhaps not as simple a situation as her anger has allowed her to pretend.

With a dip in energy, she settles for a free stretch of beach a few metres from the shoreline, spreads her towel, uses her red slip-ons to anchor the corners. The surrounding noise seems to lessen as she sits, voices refracted by the water, tossed up in the warm air. She hugs her knees to her chest, the denim sundress bunching against her thighs. Surely she is old enough to make decisions for herself, to take responsibility for her own life. Even the little girl beyond, who shoots off again towards the shoreline the moment her father lets her go, even she knows what she wants. Our bodies tell us what to do, if we're willing to listen. Isn't that what they're teaching her in college? Listen to the patient but look at the body. The body is the evidence. The body never lies.

She is miles away when she feels hands on her shoulders.

Dylan comes around the front of her towel.

'Hiya,' he says.

'Hi.'

He's in an old grey T-shirt and swim shorts, his feet already bare, aviators hide his eyes. She still hasn't quite caught up with the pro athlete look of him. Sometimes she wishes they could go back to that night she met him playing snake in Portobello. Before the buffed body, the female fans.

'How are you always tanned?' she says petulantly.

'Dunno.'

'*Dunno.*' She tips her foot to his knee to topple him onto the sand.

Laughing, he rises quickly and rolls a towel out beside her.

'Have you been in?'

'Do I look like I've been in?' She fingers the hem of her dress, barely covering her crotch.

Dylan pushes the sunglasses onto his forehead. Slowly he scans the length of her legs as if he's going to reach out and touch the shaved skin, but instead he says, 'You were chicken without me.'

'As if.'

Stevie lies down, scoots her bag under her head. Something hard hits the base of her skull. The beach bats. If she was only going for a swim and to her parents, why had she thought to bring them?

'This is the life,' Dylan says.

'Yeah,' she says, but she can't get comfortable against the bag. Before he has time to look at her again, she lowers the straps of her dress, quickly removes it to use as a pillow, pulls a loose black thread at the leghole of her swimsuit. Reclining, she feels happy she undressed first.

'I've never been here before,' he says.

'Really?'

'Nearly got off at Seapoint by mistake.'

'You've never been to the Forty Foot?'

'I have not.' He sits up to look at the beach. 'But it's lovely.'

'Fool,' Stevie says. 'The Forty Foot is over there.' Opening her eyes, the sun blinds her. 'Gimme those.' She points to his aviators.

'Not a chance.' He shifts onto his side, propping himself up with a hand under his head. 'Turn towards me,' he says.

It takes a moment before she can do what he's suggesting, some resistance, but when she does she finds his torso is blocking the sun. A narrow patch of shade lies between them and she looks at that instead of his face. The end of his T-shirt has ridden up, a neat line of hair visible from his belly button and further down. To break the tension, which he doesn't seem to mind, she tries to snatch his sunglasses. His reflexes are quicker than hers and her fingers are squashed in his hand before she can object.

'Thief,' he says, not letting go.

Now she finds herself drawn towards the hand till there is barely any space between them. He comes down to her level, their heads flat on the ground, and she has to close her eyes from the sun, which proves a mercy as his body moves against hers. She has a brief thought about the children playing on the shoreline, their attentive, disapproving parents.

'Hi,' Dylan says.

'Hi.'

She feels his lips on her forehead, her nose. A trace of toothpaste. She leans in, puts her lips against his, surprisingly dry, then opening and dry no more. They spend a while at that.

'Okaaay,' says Dylan when they stop.

A loaded quiet has descended on their patch of beach. Sitting up she looks behind to a group of four middle-aged women, who proceed to roar laughing at her probably horrified face.

'Having fun?' one of them says, and they're off again.

'Shoot me,' says Stevie.

'What?' Dylan smirks.

'Stop it.' She hits his chest.

'What can I do if I'm happy?'

'Get up.' She takes the beach bats from her bag, reaches for her dress.

As they go down to the hard sand she glances back at the women but they've lost interest, engaged now in a new drama of a crying child. She positions herself away from the sun, neon-pink ball in hand. Dylan is still smirking and she takes great pleasure in smashing the first shot at his chest, which he manages to return, still smiling, he cannot stop smiling at her. They thrash out a good old game before setting off for the Forty Foot, nudging each other up the dry sand, stumbling, messing, utterly in their own world once more.

When they reach the footpath he takes her hand and they walk like a couple towards the swimming spot, talking about college, her flatmates, his teammates, even her parents, basically everyone they know except Ben. She almost wants to mention him just to get it out of the way, but whatever is happening between them feels too new to go there. Instead they stop for ice cream.

Afterwards, as they round the corner for the Forty Foot, she asks him how training's going. He looks left at the blocky shape of Dún Laoghaire pier in the distance. 'Still no call-up,' he says.

'For Leinster?'

'For anywhere. But yeah, they'd be the hope.'

'It will happen.'

'I dunno, the talk last year after I played for the As never came to anything.'

'You were brilliant,' she says quietly.

'Thanks.' He puts his arm around her shoulder and they walk the rest of the way in thought.

'Ta-da!' she says when they arrive, breaking free of him to take the stone steps two at a time down to the flat expanse of the bathing area. The water looks cool and vigorous.

'So this is it,' Dylan says.

'Impressed?'

'Busy enough.' He nods at the queue of swimmers by the handrail.

'Come with me,' she says.

They go over to the right of the main area, behind a tall jutting rock with a dry ledge, a steeper drop into the sea but still accessible.

She takes off her shoes. 'Straight in?'

Dylan considers the craggy sides of the rock and shakes his head. 'Like jump?' he says.

Dress discarded, she goes to the edge, peers into the deep clear water and allows her body to fall forward. She swims towards the horizon, only stopping once she's warmed up. Wiping her eyes, she looks back, expecting to see him dawdling but he's already in the water, swimming quickly towards her. Things continue at this surprising speed. He swims under her, lifts her up, pretends he's going to drop her. She lurches against him, pounding his shoulder with her fists, water in her mouth. Then the playacting is over, his movements are slower, full of purpose. Her legs grip his waist, arms circle his neck and they kiss while he keeps them afloat. Here in the water there is a different feel to his mouth, his hands, a cold vehemence. One goes under her swimsuit onto her left breast and within the shot of pleasure that goes through her, there is something else, a memory of Ben, who is the only person she's slept with, how he preferred the right breast. She feels her legs detach and drop. They are no longer kissing.

'Sorry,' Dylan says. 'Full on.'

'It's not that.'

'What?'

'Nothing.' In the wide open space with only the cormorants on the faraway rocks for company, there is suddenly too much of him and she dips under the water.

They get out after a while, sit dripping in the sunshine on their towels, snug in the warm air, skin tingling dry. Without thinking she says, 'I'll have this every day from January.'

'How?'

Oh, she thinks, uh-oh.

'What do you mean?' Dylan says.

She starts to pat her toes with the towel.

'Is your family going away for Christmas?'

'No,' she says.

'I don't understand.'

'My work placement. I have it after the break.'

'Oh yeah,' he says. 'On the doss.'

She does him the dignity of turning towards him. 'I'm going to Australia. In the draw, I got a hospital in Sydney.'

When he doesn't respond, she tells another lie. 'A few girls in my class are going too.'

'Right,' he says.

'It's only for six months.'

A fat bank of cloud drifts in and she covers her shins with the towel.

'You can have my sunglasses now if you want them,' he says in a jokey tone, which she appreciates, this valiant attempt to ignore her news, to not let it ruin their day. It is so unlike Ben's reaction in similar situations, his response to anything unsettling or new, that she finds herself, once again, thinking about her ex. She feels strongly then that Australia isn't a bad plan.

Dylan walks over beyond the rock face.

'Stevie!' he says sharply. 'Stevie, look.'

'What?'

In lieu of an answer they both listen to a siren blaring repetitively from the beach beyond, a squad car approaching, joining the ambulance already parked beside the slope. Everyone on the beach is standing. Even the children have a terrifying stationary quality. Down by the shoreline paramedics kneel on the sand, a stretcher laid out behind them. She pictures the little girl in the onesie.

'Come on,' she says. 'Let's go over.'

'I don't think it's a good idea.'

'Why?'

'The ambulance men are there,' he says.

The 'men' part riles her and she finds herself snapping at him, seeing for the first time the downcast of his eyes in relation to her, a wounding. Scrambling off the rocks she hears him follow behind; resents his obedience. Why is she always in charge?

At the cove they can't access the sand, a guard has cordoned off the area while his colleagues further down the beach herd the last of the onlookers towards the road.

'What's going on?' Stevie asks the guard.

'An accident, miss,' he says. 'In the water.' The radio on his walkie-talkie crackles with distant voices. 'Move back,' he says. 'Please. If you weren't on the beach keep going.'

Feeling Dylan tug her arm she resists, recognising two of the women from earlier, holding their children to their bodies.

He continues to pull her away from the crowd, back towards Glasthule.

At the crossroads there is a break in traffic, a clear line of sight down to the shore. On the stretcher a child lies motionless, not the little girl, an older boy, impossible to say how old, but his thin legs are nearly the length of the canvas.

'Christ,' says Dylan, taking her hand again. 'It's not right,' he says. 'We shouldn't be watching.'

They continue their doleful walk back to the station, each of them trying to get the conversation going, without much luck, continually returning to what they've just witnessed.

'Do you think he'll be OK?' she says.

'I don't know,' Dylan says. 'How can I know?'

At the station she changes out of her togs in the toilet by the kiosk, appreciating the alone time. They wait on low benches for the northbound Dart back to the city. On the opposite platform a train slows to a halt, people disembark, make for the village, no idea they're walking into tragedy.

'Life is so random,' she says.

He gives her a look.

'What?'

'What about Australia? Was that random?'

'I guess.'

The air goes out of the day. She takes her phone from her bag, can't believe it's only half past three.

Dylan stands as their train approaches and it's easier to tell the truth to his back. 'I picked Australia,' she says. 'I put Sydney as my first choice.'

He stays watching the train. 'Right,' he says.

In an almost vacant carriage, he takes a window seat facing south and when she goes to sit opposite him he takes her hand, draws her down to sit beside him. She's relieved but doesn't understand why he's not mad. Leaning her head against his shoulder she watches the coastline go by in reverse, feeling as if years have passed since she left her house this morning.

They don't talk for the rest of the journey, until they're almost at her stop and the inevitable awkwardness is upon them. Part of her wishes this was an ordinary day, any other day of their lives so far, where they wouldn't have to think about whether he'd come with her, it would just be a given, the sort of endless, aimless, sexless, fun-filled college day that is no longer available to them. Stevie needs to be on her own for a bit. Too hard to think with him beside her. She is all reaction, no thought. Like right now: she can feel him about to offer to come back to her digs and she tries to pre-empt it, to take some of the burden.

'Are you hungry?' she says.

He turns towards her. 'I could come with you.'

'Sure.' She reaches for the knitted handles of her bag and stands. 'I can cook. The girls might not even be home.'

'I mean to Australia,' he says earnestly. 'I'm way behind at college, I hate my course. There could be a club over there that would want me for the season.'

The misunderstanding throws her. Gaping at him, she moves in from the aisle as other passengers begin to rise and the train shudders to a stop at Lansdowne. She feels his eyes on her, knows she needs to help him, but she can't find anything to say except, 'I better go,' which is true, as the doors are open and soon to close.

Then she's standing on the platform, watching the shape of him recede, the train departing. He doesn't look out the window, doesn't lift his head, just travels steadily away from her. She waits at the station for the pedestrian gates to separate. On the walk back to her digs she pulls dried leaves from the boxwood hedges of the neighbouring houses and crumples them to dust in her fist.

*   *   *

Though Stevie intended on calling Dylan later that evening, though she intended on making everything right after she showered and was clean again in body and soul and they could start over—or preferably continue where they'd left off in the privacy of her bedroom—what happened instead is that her flatmates were in the back garden in various states of undress, drinking unwise amounts of supermarket-mix margarita. Delirious with sun and drink, they descended upon her, dragged her into their slick, coconut-scented disorder. They wouldn't listen to her protests, she had been far too studious already that week and must therefore be cajoled, or in sober-person language visibly forced, to catch up with four successive cocktails on a stomach that only had a ninety-nine for lining. Of course it was hell. But it was, in another way, a relief.

Time elided that weekend, the beginning of a more general quickening, a merging of weeks and months and years that would drive her unwittingly into adulthood. She didn't realise it then, that life would never be slow again.

Margarita Friday rolled into Monday, into a week bringing good news and bad. Good: her phone wasn't lost, she still had her wallet, and the boy on the beach hadn't died, which she discovered in the queue for the ladies of a nightclub on Camden Street. Bad: Dylan, having tried to contact her multiple times over the weekend, now wouldn't speak to her, not even when she

193

sent him a message about the boy. This she considered cold and peevish, traits that seemed common to all men.

Eventually they made up—just in time for him to get the nod from Leinster. It was a few weeks before Christmas, not long before she left for Australia. There was nothing to discuss. They were not a couple. Living in the same city for months they had failed to get together. An old story then: she went and he stayed.

More time elapsed, enough time to disappear to Sydney, into a flatshare with a chef who was never home, on rotation at a hospital where everyone seemed older and busier than her, where no one had time for questions let alone lunch or a drink, leading to a period of sustained loneliness, the first she'd experienced in her life. One wretched work week into the next, relieved only by the boxes of wine she discovered in the local supermarket, a novel Antipodean invention that made the long hours before bed each night tolerable, even if it increased the anxiety the following morning, so clear a cycle it didn't bear thinking about.

Any news from home came only from her mother, her sisters, flatmates, until one particularly low weekend in April, there was a surprise email from Ben. She devoured it for news of Dylan—success at Leinster, a new houseshare with another player, talk of dropping out—then reread it slowly, appreciating Ben's wit, the detail in the long paragraphs, the insights and character assassinations, the fact he had bothered to write to her at all.

Their correspondence continued apace, switching to instant messenger, where their knack for making each other laugh, for anticipating replies, became once more apparent to Stevie, reminding her of the good times they'd had together, making her doubt her previous doubts, to lose connection with the version of herself who had been so sure of the break-up. At the start of June, when she had only four gruelling weeks left at the hospital, she arrived home one day to find him shivering on the steps outside the apartment block in a T-shirt and shorts that was so Ben, so idiotically forgetful of the reverse in seasons, that along with her stabbing joy at seeing someone she knew and loved, propelled her straight into his arms for—she was certain of this at the time—the best hug she'd ever received in her life. He had finished his exams and boarded a plane the same day. It was such a brainless, noble, hideously romantic thing to do, and she was so very happy to see him, that it allowed them to erase the misdemeanours of the past year, to begin again, as adults.

*   *   *

The initial years after college pass quickly for Stevie into the realities of work, the freedom of money, illusions of choice and power, grown-up holidays and nice clothes and restaurants and wine and a car, the costume of adulthood donned willingly, until one day it's no longer a costume but a straitjacket of her own design.

Stevie has been a homeowner for approximately two months and already the allure is gone. Twenty-five years old with a mortgage—why was she ever excited by that? Sure, the day she got the keys from the agent, she walked into the uninhabited apartment in the edgy new build off the north quays and was amazed that it belonged to her, but since then she's spent her free time outside work haggling for furniture, organising utilities, arguing over hidden management fees and, most vexing of all, in constant battle with Ben about why he can't move in.

She has been clear: she loves him; for now she likes renting to her friend. The annoying thing is that Ben is happy in his current flatshare with fellow unemployed actors, brothers-in-arms, and he's only pressing her on the issue because she didn't ask him in the first place. It's just how her boyfriend works, she accepted this long ago. Endearing, in a way, his desire to be wanted, to be seen.

This evening the tension is focused elsewhere. After driving to Swords and back for a couch that looked nothing like its online photo, Stevie is extremely late for the Leinster game in Ballsbridge. Initially light in tone, Ben's texts have turned reproachful: doesn't she know how important tonight is? Their first proper meeting with Dylan's girlfriend, Rachel Harte. Stevie knows. Stevie says she's sorry. Stevie says she's nearly there.

She gets out of the taxi with barely ten minutes left on the clock, Ulster a point ahead on the scoreboard. Under the stadium lights the pitch is a wintery yellow, the players' breaths fogging in the cold March air. Quickly she scans for Dylan, delighted to see him on the wing, waiting for play to resume. The ref's whistle rings clear into the night. As she climbs the stand to her row, squeezing past seat after seat of courteous older men, she sees Ben at the far end, regaling a petite blonde who is laughing gamely. Stevie feels grateful for her boyfriend's humour, his social skills with people old and new. When they're out she never has to do the work for both of them.

'Dylan's playing!' Stevie says by way of a greeting.

'Came on a few minutes ago,' Ben says.

'I'm so glad,' Rachel says. 'He'll be so pleased to get on. Hi, by the way. I'm—'

'Rachel!' Stevie holds out her hand but lets it drop unshaken as a roar goes up from the stand: the ball intercepted, Leinster have it, outhalf passes long to the left and Dylan catches it with a precision Stevie hasn't seen since his injury. Off he races, getting almost to the twenty-two, before he runs straight into the Ulster fullback.

'Jesus!' Rachel puts her head in her hands.

'It will be OK,' Ben assures her.

'He's grand,' Stevie says. 'He's on his feet.'

A man behind them says that Dylan should have known to offload, he had a clear two *v* one on the far side.

Rachel looks up. 'I just find it hard,' she says to Stevie. 'To see him mangled like that. You know?'

Stevie nods and smiles.

'I can barely watch,' Rachel says of the scramble currently underway on the ground, which Stevie finds to be dramatic. This woman has been with Dylan for nearly a year now. Surely she has gotten used to it. She is different from her pictures on Facebook, not as good-looking in reality, still very striking, but in her wool coat, pink scarf and matching hat, she appears prim, guarded, a little overdone. This is only the second time Stevie has seen her in person, and of the first, all she can really remember is the outlandish dress and the way Rachel was blatantly using her body to sell overpriced shots of vodka muck. They were supposed to meet up properly as a foursome long before now, but between Dylan's other life with his Leinster buddies, Stevie's busyness with the apartment, and in truth, her reluctance to meet this woman, which is to say, to acknowledge or sanction the relationship as distinct from Dylan's other more transient liaisons, they have not done so till now.

The final minutes of the game consist of tired, protracted play, a missed penalty, a Leinster scrum that provokes a low, collective *heave* from the crowd, fun to join in and draw out the vowels—*heeeeve*—which has the seemingly miraculous effect of energising the pack to move forward a few metres, until the ball pops out and is stylishly flicked right by the scrumhalf to his number ten, a dummy, a step inside, then left, and left again, into the capable hands of Dylan, who is away down the pitch with rapid determination.

From her elevated position in the stand, Stevie can see the line he needs to take, the line the old Dylan would have instinctively taken. Instead he heads for the corner and is about to be tackled into touch when at the last moment he realises his error, somehow passes it back inside. Two phases later and the outhalf sets up for the drop goal, shunting the ball high between the posts with seconds to go and it's all over with three piercing toots—Leinster for the win.

Rachel is ecstatic, jumping up and down in high-heeled boots that clack against the concrete. Ben puts an arm around them both. Stevie joins in the cheering but her eyes are on Dylan, his perfunctory clapping as he leaves the pitch, the fake smile that shows he's forgotten his part in the result, has already gone down the wormhole of his mistakes.

Afterwards in the clubhouse Stevie sits on a stool, chatting to the wives and girlfriends. In this group of thin women with huge handbags she feels for a second like she's doubled in size, but everyone is nice to her, friendly in a southside way, bright with manners.

Dylan joins them with his friend Jim, the flanker. Jim puts his arm around one of the women, Alice, who congratulates him on man of the match with a kiss on the cheek.

'Well deserved,' Dylan agrees. 'Hi,' he says to Stevie.

'You did great,' she says.

'Yeah, man,' says Jim. 'You did a lot.'

'Not a lot you can do in thirteen minutes.'

'You gave Seanie the drop goal,' Jim says.

'Ah,' says Dylan, 'I did and I didn't.'

More players join and Stevie is introduced to the ones she doesn't know. A pleasure to see how popular Dylan is, how well respected, each one congratulating him on his few minutes on the pitch. It is almost excessive, steeped in their common understanding of what he's been through.

Sean, the lock, hears she's a physio and comes over to ask her views on surgery for his shoulder joint.

'What does the consultant think?' she says.

He towers over her, his softly spoken Dublin accent at odds with his build. 'You know what they're like,' he says. 'Mad for the knife.'

'If you can avoid it, I probably would,' she says. 'But I'm in the rehab hospital in Dún Laoghaire at the moment, and it's incredible the gains people can make after surgery. Look at this lad.' She points at Dylan.

'Lazarus,' Sean says, clapping him on the back.

Dylan smiles at Stevie then shyly looks away. 'Where's Rach?' he says to Alice.

They follow Alice's finger to the bar, where Ben and Rachel are in vibrant conversation with another woman, an actress married to the number eight.

'Full charm offensive,' Dylan jokes to Stevie.

'He'll be on the telly by the end of the night,' she says, and everyone laughs.

As they drift back to rugby talk, Stevie keeps an eye on Ben, who is clearly flirting with the women in a way that is just innate to him, like his personality at birth came out set to suave. It doesn't bother her except that she is slightly bothered by the fact she isn't bothered. And she knows she should be over there with him, making the effort. When they first came in she declined, without thinking, Rachel's offer of a cocktail in favour of beer, not realising it was a 2-for-1 female bonding deal. On the next round she tried to recover, proposing she get them for herself and Rachel, but by then it was too late, Rachel had moved on to G&Ts. This was not the only problem. Stevie found it hard to watch the way Rachel behaved around the other women, fawning over their clothes, laughing at stories that weren't particularly funny. She felt sorry for her that she was so unsure of her place among them.

Jim goes to get a round in now and Stevie offers to sort herself. 'Don't be mad,' he says. 'Any friend of Dyl's is a friend of ours.'

Sean accompanies him to the bar. The women resume their chats.

Dylan turns towards Stevie. 'So,' he says, nodding at the counter. 'What do you think of Rach?'

'She's great,' Stevie says.

His face takes on a sudden, heartrending lightness, a pure smile, all the perfect teeth present and accounted for.

'Seriously,' he says. 'You mean that?'

'Yes,' Stevie says with feeling. 'I do.'

JANUARY

For the first time in her life, Rachel didn't mind the new year winter mornings. Sitting at the kitchen table, she stared out the window at the thinning darkness and felt at home. There was something reassuring about the way it lifted from the sky each day to reveal the familiar terrain, when so much of her current existence had the shaded quality of a dream. Though the night of the play was months ago, her confrontation with Stevie had seeped into the cracks of her self, dampened her sense of what was real and true, leaving her unsure of her place in the world.

The early starts helped her feel ahead of herself, like she was cheating time. Today she had risen at six and now much of the prep for Leah's party was done. Sausage rolls in neat lines on baking trays, sheet cake cooling on the counter, streamers pinned in colourful half-moons along the wall. She could rest for a bit, before her daughter woke and came bounding down the stairs to this most exciting of days, the day she had been brought into the world five years earlier, when Rachel had lain prostrate on a bed for hours, roaring for an anaesthetist who never came, pushing her first child into the world in a manic burst of gore and effort while her husband stood beside her gripping her hand as tightly as a man going over a cliff.

What would it be like this time round? She wondered if he would even be there; tried to picture the alternative. Alone in the fearful delivery room with no hand to hold. It was a sad image, but she would manage, she had uncommon reserves and something greater than herself to live for. And she would be drugged, gloriously drugged, she would not step over the threshold of The Coombe until they assured her there was a doctor in the vicinity with a long needle ready to be injected into her spine.

Nearly fifteen weeks now—and Dylan still hadn't noticed. This was the extent of the disengagement, his brutal disloyalty. That no one else had figured out her news did not excuse him. She'd wanted to tell him so many times, but somehow the situation they were in, that he had put them in, prevented it. Living together under this roof like two distant but conscientious flat-mates who happened to share a child. She put a hand on her stomach. The material of his old Leinster jersey was pleasantly coarse and she rubbed her palm over and back across the bump. How had he not wondered at her renewed interest in his grubby cast-offs? How had he not seen?

The cold morning sun came in through the window in a stretch of silvery light that made the far end of the table seem frosted. She looked over at the sheet cake. Too early yet for piping. Mentally she listed the remaining tasks until she grew weary of the effort ahead. When the sun reached the patch of grain on the rim of the table she would get up and begin again.

Somewhere in the house she caught the faraway sound of an alarm clock, though it could be next door, her senses were so alert, a factor of the pregnancy, or the thousands of nerve endings that had awakened the night of the play. The baby growing inside her as she'd finally found the courage to square up to Stevie Jones. There was no going back now. Rachel was all antennae these days; she missed nothing. It made the prospect of a party both tempting and terrifying. She thought of the many messages she'd received from Ben in recent weeks, his new keenness to meet up when they rarely had anything to do with each other outside the confines of the foursome. She knew he suspected something too. What would happen if he kicked off today? Imagine her guests witnessing a meltdown. Imagine her mother, the pleasure it would give her to see the dysfunction in Rachel's life. Ten adults, fifteen kids and one crippled stick of dynamite was not the way to throw a party.

More and more she wished she could fast forward her life, the next five months and all the worry. *Think positive*, the doctors said, a useless phrase that held within it a note of blame, a hint of future failure and who would be responsible. She couldn't think this pregnancy to life. If that worked she would have thousands of children by now. At least she was out of the danger zone. That was something to hold onto. Still precarious enough to be called in for regular scans, for which she had prepared an array of excuses she never had to use because Dylan never asked. She made sure the appointments were during work hours when Stevie was at the physio clinic. She wasn't stupid, she wouldn't make it easy for them.

There was extraordinary pain in the betrayal, even if she had no hard evidence yet, just her instinct it had started and was likely unfolding in one big blur before her eyes without the specifics needed to tackle it. Rachel had lost control, she had given the reins to her husband and a woman—it was OK to say this now—whom she despised. There seemed to be no solution. Calling out the affair would somehow make it more permissible, might allow him then to leave. And she was stymied too, she thought bitterly, by her fear of the past, the solitary splinter she'd pressed deep into her skin and managed to keep there without festering for years. Her conversation with Stevie outside the theatre was as far as she could go. Anything beyond was full of risk and Rachel, from a very young age, had always been risk-averse.

The sudden patter of feet down the stairs, *Mummy* on repeat, in stereo. Rachel grabbed a roll of tinfoil from the pantry, covered the cake in time.

'Mummy!' Leah burst into the kitchen with the impressive whirlwind presence she'd inherited from Helen. 'It's my birthday!' Her bed-warm body clung to Rachel, the crown of her head pressing against the bump. Something registered in Leah too, her hand reached up to confirm, and she uttered a word, very quietly, she said, 'Hard.'

Rachel removed the hand, kept hold of it, tried to spin her daughter under her arm in one of their dance moves. 'Whose birthday is it?' she smiled. 'Tell me.'

'*My* birthday. Yesterday I was four. Today I'm five years old,' she said, still considering Rachel's stomach.

There was nothing for it but to give her a present. Swiftly she marched her into the living room where the stack of glittery parcels teetered on the coffee table.

'Mummy! So many presents.'

Yes, Rachel thought, as she watched her daughter rip open her birthday gifts while her father remained upstairs, it was as blatant a display of shop-bought happiness as she had ever seen in her life.

*   *   *

On the morning of the child's fifth birthday, Ben was out for blood. Hobbling around the apartment in two jumpers, a stripy grandfather shirt and tartan green pyjama bottoms tucked into his socks, he refused to turn on the heater. Stevie could do it herself when she got up. Usually he relented in the cold winter months after Christmas, allowing full power for the short, gloomy days, but on this second Saturday of the new year he wasn't yet ready to relinquish control over the heating system, which seemed at this point in their life together to be the very last thing within his dominion. He looked protectively at the scorch-marked storage heater on the wall. Mine, he thought, *mine*.

Bringing his tea over to the couch, he elevated the cumbersome black boot onto the thick orthopaedic cushion Stevie had bought specifically for this purpose. The guilt cushion, as he liked to think of it. He took a sip of the drink and reminded himself he was almost there, only had to wear the boot for another few weeks, then he'd be ready to unleash himself on the world. Ben was unsure who he would kill first, just that the three of them would be gruesomely deceased, and maybe Rachel too, because it seemed unfair to leave her behind to deal with the mess. Who would look after the child, he wondered. Well, that was not his concern.

The night of the abortive opening they had gone to the emergency department at The Mater, the four of them sitting for hours in a taciturn line as his body ignited in pain after the gargantuan effort of ignoring it for the duration of the play. Correction: duration of the scene. That was all he had lasted. All he was worth. When a doctor had finally, multiple scans later, confirmed a grade three strain of his Achilles, a near-rupture, when she'd expressed her shock at his ability to stand, let alone walk, he had shaken his head because she had it so wrong, she did not understand: a real man, and it was his father's voice he heard, a real man would have seen things through to the end.

The past few months had been a bitter slog out of that hole of self-reproach and failure, a harder recovery than the tendon itself. Time and chondroitin supplements didn't fix a person's soul. They didn't fix the constant metastasising unease he felt now that he had nothing to do: no job, no auditions, no exercise, no interest in socialising, in being seen by the outside world. Initially he blamed himself for his misfortunes, but after the fog lifted, after he'd run out of prescription painkillers, his sadness turned to anger, like flipping a coin, and he began to think about his life in broader terms, long before the injury. Where had it all gone wrong? And who exactly was to blame? Assisted by the great lucidity of rage, an accounting of sorts took place, and now, following weeks of meticulous data-entry, Ben had a handle on the books. In his head was a very legible spreadsheet of betrayal, with a shocking number of entries in glaring red.

Bloodiest, which was to say, most damning: the day of the play, the specifics of which spoke for themselves. Dylan and Stevie had spent the morning together swimming, they'd sat apart from the others in the theatre, had even disappeared off together during the interminable stint in A&E. After Rachel left to relieve the babysitter, Ben must have fallen asleep because he woke up alone, stretched across the four seats, one side of his face slick with dribble. He was about to phone Stevie when she and Dylan came strolling down the corridor with paper cups and identical sympathy smiles. True, that he didn't think much of this at the time, that he remembered the detail about the lack of steam from said cups weeks later, but since then it had accrued huge significance, it seemed to hold the answers to the mystery of his life.

Then there was Rachel. Before she'd gone home from the hospital she was tense and alert, shifting in her chair each time the automatic doors opened with another mess of a human to add to the queue. She'd snapped at Dylan about the parking app, ignored Stevie's query on the babysitter. She had hardly spoken the whole time she was there. Ben put this down to her irritation that his injury had hijacked their big night out, but then he remembered (exhibit a) that Rachel wasn't drinking and (b) although she could be ruthless if you bored her, the woman wasn't narcissistic, she was not the sort of person to begrudge a man an emergency. No, something else had been going on that night, Ben was certain.

In the intervening weeks his suspicions deepened. The fact that he and Stevie no longer had sex changed from an issue of mutual lethargy into a death knell. Why had they stopped? When had this happened? It had been so long he couldn't even pin it to a month. All that remained was one persistent, tragic image of Stevie laughing at him keeping his socks on for the duration of the deed. There followed a period of furious masturbation, a throwback to his teenage years, until he caught sight of his adult face in the bathroom mirror one afternoon—contorted features, hectic glow—frantically trying to get a third one in before Stevie returned from work. He went back to his biweekly efforts in the shower after that. He had proven his point, had won all the medals for virility in the big penis debate inside his head.

Ben had other problems, other leads to worry about this morning. Rachel hadn't returned his calls since the night of the play. She'd sent one cursory text wishing him well and beyond that had ignored his overtures to meet. It was not unlike how she'd behaved in the run-up to her wedding: keen to avoid him, happier, always, with the rugby crowd. Thinking about that time only angered him further. Rachel knew something, and she knew he knew that she knew. The party today was going to be a great unravelling of all those knowings. Rachel wouldn't be able to avoid him. She would be trapped in her fancy redbrick, hemmed in by her guests. Ben had already pinpointed the enormous utility room as the perfect location for the interrogation, but if she tried to hide among the partygoers, if she tried to use her child as a shield, he wasn't above doing the whole thing in public. Twenty years of drama training meant he was more than capable of causing a scene. It was up to Rachel if she wanted an audience. Either way, Ben had decided that today would bring an end to the unbearable wondering, to the fakery of daily life.

Hearing Stevie stir in the bedroom he was reminded of the other clear tell of the past few months: the change in her behaviour and routines. The rehab sessions with Dylan had stopped. When Ben came home from the hospital, they were instantly, obtrusively over. Without a word, as if they had never existed. Instead Stevie worked all the time and when she wasn't working, she came home to take care of Ben. Every night she flopped into bed and slept like the dead while he seethed in the dark beside her. Though there were reasons for her long hours at the clinic—two colleagues on maternity leave—he still felt deception in his bones. For one thing, she never complained. She seemed to accept all her new clients with grace and goodwill. Similarly at home, she tended to his needs, his moods, with heinous equanimity. She did the shopping, laundry, pharmacy runs, batch-cooked their meals for the week. No matter how ungrateful he appeared, she refused to argue with him. Refused to engage. A force field around her he was unable to penetrate.

Ben could barely stand her right now, yet at the same time he lived in terror of losing her, she was all he had ever known.

The rush of the kitchen tap interrupted his thoughts. His tea had gone cold in the mug, a greasy skin close to solidifying.

'Morning,' Stevie said from the kitchenette.

'Is it still morning?'

'Have you had breakfast?'

'I can make toast.'

'It's good to have skills. How's the ankle today?'

'Sore.'

'Pain is unavoidable,' she said breezily. 'Suffering optional.'

When she turned her back to fill up the kettle he gave her the finger.

After a few minutes she brought two mugs into the living room, put one within his reach. He watched the wisping steam rise off the liquid and wanted to knock over the mug. The feeling he'd been nurturing for weeks was starting to take shape, and that shape was violence.

Stevie took the far couch, her silk dressing gown gaping as she bent forward for her tea and enquired, as she did every morning, if he had done his exercises. He replied tersely and she asked nothing more. From across the room he pretended to ignore her while staying attuned to her every move. Lounging on the couch, doing a fine impersonation of herself, she who had declared the very first time he met her, all those years ago, that she would rather *die* than get up on stage, here she was, in the torturous amphitheatre of life, treating them both to an award-worthy performance of a caring, faithful partner. The great dissembler. Applause, applause.

Sensing his discontent, she busied herself with the free magazine that had been in the apartment for months, the one with the article on upcoming productions that listed *Betrayal* as a *must-see* but only named his co-stars, as if the journalist had some inkling of what was to come. He remembered Caroline's anger at his exclusion and wondered if she still considered him a client after the way he'd treated her following his inglorious departure. He suspected not. They hadn't spoken in weeks. He was ashamed at the language he'd used in their final call.

'What time do you want to go today?' Stevie said.

'Early.'

'Good idea, we can bail early too.'

There was a ping from her phone in the bedroom. He watched her deliberately not react to the sound.

'Why?' he said. 'I'd like a proper night out.'

'Kid's birthday will be over by six.'

'Not if we don't leave. We could even stay.'

'Overnight?'

'Yes.'

'At Dylan's?'

'Dylan *and* Rachel's.'

'Of course.'

'I'm sure they wouldn't mind,' he said.

'But why?'

'Why not? It's not like we have children to worry about, eh?'

She looked over the back of the couch. 'No,' she said, returning. 'Doesn't appear to be any down there.'

His face stayed inert as her little laugh rose and died.

'We'd save on a taxi if we stayed,' he said.

'It's only Terenure. Anyway, I might drive.'

'Why would you do that?'

'Headache,' she said, unconvincingly.

'Oh really. Would you care for some tablets?'

'No thanks.'

'But surely you need tablets if you've a headache? You shouldn't choose to be in agony.' He saw her flinch and felt like he had won something.

'Leave off, Ben,' she said, 'will you? I'm barely awake.'

He watched her finish her tea while his own went cold once more.

'What did you get Leah?' he said.

'What?'

'Leah, for her birthday.'

Stevie's hand went to her mouth. 'I meant to get something yesterday.'

'That's not good. Not good at all.' Nobly, he pointed to his boot. 'I could make it as far as the chemist. There was a game of Twister in the window last week.'

'It won't be good enough for Rachel.'

'Screw Rachel,' he said, more viciously than intended.

Her head jerked in his direction but she did not investigate further. This new Stevie didn't engage in anything remotely contentious. The urge to punish her intensified. 'Why didn't you bring me coffee?' he said.

'Thought you were having tea.'

'I mean that night.'

'What night?'

'At the hospital.'

She looked out the window at the clouds moving quickly over the city's grey contours. 'What are you talking about?'

'You and Dylan disappeared. You were gone for ages.' This he had no proof of, just the innate sense it might be true.

'We just went to get coffee,' she said, rising. 'I'll head to the toy shop on Parnell Street. What about a giant stuffed animal?'

'So why didn't you bring me one?' he persisted.

'I didn't think you'd want one.'

'Because you know me so well?'

'Yes,' she said.

'Really?'

'Of course I do.'

'Isn't it far more likely that we're total strangers?'

'What?'

'I mean,' he said, 'the human race.'

They stared at each other. A spark in her eyes, challenge or fear. At least it was something. She wasn't gone completely. In any other situation he would blow things open right around now—that had always been his job in the relationship, to delve into the wreck—but he refused to do it for her this time. As she retreated into the kitchen with her mug, he wanted to take the cushion from under his boot and throttle something. He wondered what would kill a man first, the simmering aggression or the artifice. He couldn't wait to get to the party. All these long months recuperating and now that he was nearly better, he couldn't wait to take a hammer to his life.

*   *   *

In the warehouse shop at the end of Parnell Street, a bright orange concourse gave way to aisles of unending choice and colour. Stevie traversed them, overwhelmed by the variety of toys. In the fourth aisle she took down a piebald giraffe from a menagerie of stuffed animals before deciding it was too big and showy for a child's party, too much of an announcement, when all she wanted was to get in and out as quietly as possible. But the smaller ones looked token and uncaring. In the end she went for a dolphin with a sheeny silver pelt.

At the registers a mother with a baby in snug bondage to her chest tried to pay while placating a toddler clumsily smacking the counter in an effort to access her toy. 'You'll hurt yourself,' the mother said. 'Be careful.' Stevie admired her patience, the way she often secretly admired women in public who were marshalling unruly children. How did they get all those bitsy clothes on? It was a puzzle, solved every morning by parents everywhere. She thought she might, at some future point, learn the answers herself but instead of that future coming closer, it now seemed further away than ever. Stevie wasn't sure what she had been waiting for all this time, just that it hadn't arrived. Or it showed up a few days a year, during particularly heavy cycles, like a travelling salesman back to hawk his wares. This did not seem remotely enough.

The assistant called her to the till, scanned the toy and put it headfirst into a shopping bag, the arc of the tail protruding. Stevie thanked her and paid. On the way back to the car complete strangers smiled at her, a little boy asked to look inside her bag, and for a brief few minutes she forgot herself, forgot she was a terrible person.

Driving home down the quays she wondered if it would be feasible to carry a large toy animal around with her on a daily basis. She could keep a stuffed panda in a backpack, a chimpanzee in the clinic, anything that might help to shake the feelings of yuck that shadowed her throughout the waking day. Yet she found herself unable to stop what she was doing, to stop participating in the despicable, savagely engaging second life that was laced through her real life like gold filaments through hay.

That night at the hospital—how many times had she replayed it since? At half twelve in the morning, with Rachel gone and Ben asleep, Dylan glanced left in her direction, all that was needed for the pair of them to stand without a word, walk carefully along the rows of sick and injured people, continue in silence down the sterile corridors until they had taken enough lefts and rights and at least one block of stairs to find themselves in a part of the building that was darkly quiet, just the sound of monitors in a sleeping ward, the glowing emergency exit sign, and a lone arrow pointing to the morgue.

Dylan had pushed her against the wall with a force that propelled their body parts into action. Such blatant urgency to the kissing, he held her arms over her head at one point, as if they were in the way. Every inventive move he tried was matched by one of her own. His hands went under her top, in her pants, it all seemed to happen so quickly, but when they broke apart at the sound of approaching voices, at least half an hour had passed and her jawbone ached. The two nurses barely acknowledged them, which was just as well as Stevie was seriously giddy—what else could you do with Dylan's perfunctory nod and guilty smile, with his lopsided curls and the top buttons of his long dress shirt undone. From the way he looked at her she imagined similar dishevelment. A gratifying rawness to the soft skin around her mouth. The blazer down over her shoulders. Her steamrolled mind. The brain, she had learnt years ago in college, didn't register stability, only change. That night it felt as if she gave it enough for several lifetimes.

On the way back to the waiting area she nudged him over to the coffee machine, watched as he figured it out, as the reality of their actions dawned on him as they had already dawned on her: no, she was not partial to a coffee at quarter past one in the morning. They needed to bring the drinks back. Already the smut, the concealment, had begun. Of course the machine was broken, no hot water available. When they returned with two empty decoy cups, Ben was awake and gothically pale. In a plaintive voice he said, 'Where did you go?' But he had fallen asleep again shortly afterwards and they'd stayed there watching him in silence till they were called, afraid to speak, to look at each other, to see their own desperate longing reflected in the other's eyes.

Stevie was so lost in her heated brain that she almost missed the turn for home. A sharp right to catch the electric gates for the underground car park; gift bag toppled forward, the dolphin tail falling into the space between the front seats. Glancing at its pillowy plumpness she felt like going back to bed. Today was going to be extremely difficult. She knew she would be under surveillance, from at least one source. Her plan was to stay sober, on guard, obviously no pills. She had stopped taking them. Hours of research, all the latest studies, before she chose a structured withdrawal option, initially limiting herself to twice a week, once, then every two weeks. Right now she couldn't remember the last day she'd taken one, which would have been unthinkable a few months ago. The pills didn't help her any more, she had no interest in the haze. Her mind craved clarity and direction. Whatever road she chose at this junction, she didn't want to look back years from now and say she couldn't read the signs.

There was also the small problem of Rachel. Since the night of the play, the woman had turned militant. Stevie and Dylan had barely seen each other. It felt too dangerous to text or email, neither of them was ready to commit their actions to print; a reluctance to brand themselves. Which left few options: phone calls to the clinic from a Dublin number she didn't recognise, one where he hung up mid-sentence, the odd lunch break in the upstairs room of an old man pub on Baggot Street, delicious lost minutes in an alley, a taxi cab, and the most recent, a brisk, unhinged meeting in Merrion Square on a rainy midweek morning where they'd huddled under a sycamore and struggled to put their feelings into words. Walking the wet footpath back to work she'd wished they were in college again, in the world of the young with its myriad possibilities. Instead all she had was the image, the feel of him, which kept returning to her over and over again, like the jolt of a dreamer waking briefly from a dream.

Her adult self had bouts of staggering guilt—even though they were yet to have sex. It was mind-boggling to her now, as she sat alone in the car park with the engine off. Titillating, maddening. Absurd. She was nearly forty and behaving like a teenager. Why didn't they just book a hotel room? Get it over with. Do the deed. They were both afraid of the point of no return, understanding, without ever openly stating it, that this wasn't an affair, but the rest of their lives. And so they were subsisting, for now, in suspended reality, caught in a loop of escalating want and frenzied near-release. She wondered if this was part of the draw. The thought disgusted her.

Once more the guilt began, the dread of going back into the apartment to another stilted exchange with Ben. She found these conversations impossible to negotiate. They contained supremely real feelings about imaginary events. What did he actually know? Nothing. Stevie was sure Rachel hadn't spoken to him, hadn't aired her own suspicions, because really, what did Rachel herself know? There was so very little *to* know. Only that the four of them were in turmoil, Stevie was honest enough to admit that. A great paradox of this almost affair, that it contained so little action but resulted in so many thoughts, and that these thoughts themselves amassed a kind of energy, which like all energies couldn't be destroyed but merely converted into something else. Good or bad, that was the question: where would it end?

*   *   *

Dylan was in the hallway, getting ready to leave his house. The air smelled of cleaning products, the stained glass panels on either side of the front door were brilliantly wet, small diamonds of yellow, red and blue, bordered on all sides by a deep, dominant green. He reached for his coat before realising the hanger had none of the usual hats and scarves, even their puffas were removed to make room for guests, as if Rachel equated tidiness to vacancy, to no one living here at all.

His wife's voice, her familiar question, pinned him to the spot.

'Off-licence,' he said.

She appeared at the far end of the hall in his old Leinster shirt and leggings, her hair in curlers. He laughed.

'What?'

'Nothing,' he smiled. 'I just like the look.' Rachel did look good, bizarrely good, now that he had no interest in looking at her. It occurred to him she was in the jersey in order to feel close to him, but he dismissed the idea as soon as he had it. These days he found he could dismiss whatever he liked. Felt no compunction at all, like he had gone out one night and lost his conscience. Back on the pitch again, a young buck, processing the play in his head right as he was doing it. Stevie Jones. His everyday captivity made his secret life with her feel wonderfully free. No fear of others when he was with her, even, on occasion, the mad desire to be seen.

217

'We have all the booze we need,' Rachel said. 'There's only ten adults.'

'Who dropped out?'

'Jim. And Macca.'

'Seriously?'

'Alice rang during the week. Training schedule changed. They're in camp down in Limerick this weekend.'

Dylan said nothing, didn't want her to see his disappointment. He'd only asked his two best rugby mates, and still they couldn't come. More than twenty years of his life to the sport and after three years away from it, he barely heard from them.

Following Rachel down the gleaming chequerboard tiles into the kitchen, he went to the fridge to make sure she was right about the booze. The spiced meat of the sausage rolls came at him as he opened the door. He counted the wine and beer, went to the utility to check the reserves, then texted the lads to wish them luck in training. No hard feelings or whatever. After he sent the messages he felt like a groupie, someone who had never even played. They knew he was looking for work. Everyone knew. He'd sent a blanket email to management at the end of November and was still waiting for a meeting. It was too painful, too worrying to think about. He went back to his messages and fired off a text to Stevie.

'Who are you texting?' Rachel looked up from icing a cake.

'The lads,' he said. 'Just to say no bother about today.'

'Any word on the job front?'

'It's hardly their area.'

'Whose area is it then? You can't keep waiting, Dylan. You've all your badges.'

'What else am I supposed to do?'

Here she left down the piping bag and considered him. 'Get a job,' she said.

'Doing what? You know I didn't finish my degree.'

'Talk to your father, that's all you have to do. He'll get you an interview with the civil service.'

Dylan tried not to grimace. He couldn't ask his father for a job, he wasn't eleven.

She took up the piping bag again, wiped the residue off the table, wrote their daughter's name in beautiful cursive across the cake. Adding an exclamation mark, she stood back to survey her work, then turned the dot into a heart. In his pocket his phone vibrated. 'Who's that?' she said.

Taking it out, he saw with relief the message was from Jim, emojis of a rugby ball and smiley face.

'Jim,' he said, triumphantly turning the screen towards her right as another notification popped up.

'That's from Stevie,' she said. 'Why is she texting you?'

'Maybe they're cancelling too.'

'Open it.'

'Jesus, Rachel. What's with the tone?'

Moving the phone out of her line of vision he pressed into the message.

Hello Dylan, we will be there for two o'clock. We are looking forward to it. I got Leah a furry dolphin. I hope that is OK and she will like it. Best, Stevie.

As his heart began to function again he passed the phone to his wife.

'Who buys a teddy as a present for a five-year-old?' she said. 'And why is she signing her texts?'

'What's wrong with a dolphin? At least they're coming. Who else pulled out?'

'My father,' said Rachel. 'Obviously.'

'Aw. I'm sorry.'

Surprisingly her eyes filled with tears. He went to hug her but she sidestepped him. It was unclear why her father's behaviour bothered her today when she was so inured to his antics over time that she barely referenced him at all. She had stated it plainly at the beginning of their relationship, without sentiment or the need for sympathy: her father was a scrounger and a cheat, someone who showed up at the family home in Drimnagh one Sunday out of four and left once he was fed. Rachel wiped her eyes, straightened her shoulders in a way that reminded him of his daughter.

'Where's Leah?' he said.

'In the toy room. Playing with her princesses and the *Frozen* castle,' Rachel said. 'Not with a bloody dolphin.' She picked up the cake, told him to make room in the fridge.

'Wait,' he said, when it was safely inside. 'Did you open her presents without me?'

'She was excited, I couldn't stop her.'

Dylan looked down at his hands. 'So who is coming today? Is it all women?'

'Your parents, my mother, Ben and Stevie, Suzanne next door, Nina and Marie from the school mothers. Oh,' she said. 'And fifteen kids.'

At that moment the doorbell rang.

'An hour early!' Rachel said.

'Bet you it's my folks.'

'Let me get upstairs first.'

She left the kitchen, slowly he thought, for someone looking to flee. On the back of the jersey his name had faded, his old number peeling in yellow jags. When he heard her on the landing he took a deep breath and braced himself for the door. It rang again loudly on his way down the hall—his father, he was now sure.

As predicted his parents stood there in their weekend finery, his mother a burst of sunset-coloured fabrics, his father in slacks and a shirt.

'Hi,' said Dylan. 'You're early.'

'Is that any way to answer a door?' Sean said.

Dylan stood back to let them in.

His mother shoved four gift bags at him and went off to find the birthday girl.

Alone now, the men stood uneasily in the hallway, chess pieces waiting to be moved, before Dylan remembered this was his house and he had the power. 'Would you like a drink?' he said.

Sean walked towards the living room, turning half-heartedly, in remonstration that Dylan, his own flesh and blood, had forgotten the match. 'O'Byrne Cup,' he said. 'Ten minutes to kick-off. You think I'd miss it?'

'Sure Dublin will hammer them,' Dylan said.

'Not necessarily.'

'They're entitled to, the way they've played all season.'

Sean grunted. 'But isn't that the lesson of sport, lad?'

Dylan struggled to hide his irritation. 'What?'

'No man is entitled to anything.'

The clever eyes bore into his nothing soul. He felt exposed. His father signalled for a beer and set off for the couch. Dylan went into the kitchen to get him the drink, but on hearing the thick, lilting accents of the excitable commentators boom from the living room, the volume at an ear-splitting level as was his father's wont, he walked straight through the kitchen and utility out the back door, closing it softly behind him to rest for a while on the damp step before more people arrived. The need for meditative silence felt akin to his preparation on match days. The fact he was even thinking this showed just how far he'd come. He had stopped the oxygen therapy, reluctantly, a month ago and there had been no backwards slide. Stevie was right. He was strong enough to train normally now. He could go for a run, a cycle, a hike. Hoover the car. Haul a mountain of presents up and down stairs last night when Leah was asleep. Daily chores no longer left him breathless or fatigued. Most of the time he didn't even think about it, which was unbelievable, how easy it was to take for granted a state of well-being that only months ago he was sure he'd never see. His mind drifted to the night of the poker game, when he and Stevie had lingered here in the garden though they knew the others were inside waiting. It seemed that this was the beginning of things and, for the first time in years, he was struck by the sense of his own agency and all that might mean.

*   *   *

Some hours later Dylan found himself back in the hallway, in a worse stalemate than before, actually wishing his father might come and save him. The party was in full swing, all the maniac children were at war in the living room, with most of the adults taking refuge in the kitchen.

'So it's healing up?' he said to Ben.

'You asked me that already.'

'Just checking in.'

'It's practically better,' Ben said.

'That's great.'

'It is great.'

'Two more weeks, you said.'

'I did.'

'Not long to go so. You'll be flying it soon.'

'Is that right?' Ben said.

Dylan couldn't tell if his mood was generally bad or if there was a specific badness driving it. 'Sorry I haven't been around more,' he said.

'You haven't been around at all.'

The 'Let It Go' song came blaring from the living room. At Leah's cry of delight, Dylan smiled.

Ben remained stone-faced, a tinge of green.

'I'm sure I was there since the injury,' Dylan said. 'Didn't I—'

'You did not.'

'The job stuff is taking up all my time.'

'Right,' Ben said after an awkward few beats. 'Any joy?'

Dylan clung to this bit of civility. He began talking about nonsense job hopes, interview preparation and, in major news to himself, his thoughts about returning to university to finish his degree.

'I guess you could do that if you wanted.'

'Rachel thinks I should ask my father, but I dunno, feels wrong.'

'Such probity,' Ben said.

'What does that mean?'

'Look it up.'

Another dreadful lull.

'Will we get a fresh drink?' Dylan chanced a smile. 'Can of Dutch?'

Ben stared flatly at him, said he'd stick to Heineken and walked off to sort himself.

*   *   *

In the kitchen the women were talking about the cost of eating out in Dublin.

'It's madness,' said Helen. 'You'd get three meals in Sallins for the price.'

'Everything's shot up,' said Nina.

'Seriously,' Rachel said. 'We've basically stopped going out.'

'How are people supposed to live?' said Helen.

Stevie nodded along to the talk of gouging, hoping her brain would presently connect to her mouth and she'd be able to contribute with words. She was still holding the gift, which was starting to get uncomfortable. She shifted it against her shoulder, cashmere jumper bunching, exposing her midriff.

'Do you want to leave that down?' Rachel said.

Stevie tightened her grip. The wrapping paper crinkled beneath her fingertips. 'It's not heavy,' she said.

Nina asked what it was.

'Somewhat left field.' Stevie looked at Rachel, who looked at the ceiling. 'A dolphin.'

'How unusual!' said Helen.

'The rest of the presents are in the living room,' Rachel said in a tone so measured Stevie could clearly read the message underneath: Get out of my house, you do not belong here.

'Sure,' Stevie said. 'I'll leave it in.'

'Come right back now,' Helen said. 'You need a drink. Sean! Get Stevie a drink.'

On her way to the presents she had to pass Dylan, who was standing near the table talking to a school mum. Hyperconscious of him since entering the room, she didn't trust herself to look over, just let the burr of his voice wash over her, the

224

quietly cheerful enquiries, the goodwill. Extraordinary, that the simple, innocent shape of him in a room could send her mind tumbling down stairs.

In the sanctuary of the living room, vacant now except for one comatosed toddler curled on the armchair, Stevie took her time rearranging the presents on the couch, partly out of necessity—it really was a big dolphin—and also, she wanted to continue listening to him, so soothing, his voice, his interest in others, this uncommon decency she had always loved. She felt a sudden terrifying responsibility for what they were doing, that she alone held the knife to carve out the shapes of the future.

When she looked up from the pile he was there at the alcove, watching her. His shirt brought out the colour of his eyes—spectacular distraction.

'Hi,' he said.

'Hey.'

'How are you?'

'OK,' she smiled. 'How are you?'

'Good,' he said. 'I'm good now.'

She felt sleepy, it was something to do with his smile, or a general somnolence had descended on the room, the proof of which could be heard in the rasping breaths of the child.

'Dylan!' Rachel's shout was like an explosion.

Stevie turned to examine the presents.

'Dylan! Get the door.'

'Bye,' he said.

She faced him once again, and from her wrist gave a sad wave.

*　　　*　　　*

'Sorry!' said Rachel. 'I didn't think anyone was in here.'

She had just opened the downstairs loo to Stevie washing her hands. The tap was on full blast and little splashes of water were bouncing off the sink onto the black wicker handstand and the trio of prints from Montparnasse.

Stevie turned off the water, reached for a towel.

'Yeah, sorry,' she said. 'I'm here.'

'Would you not lock the door?'

'It was locked. I'm finished now.'

'I'll go upstairs,' Rachel said.

'Honestly,' Stevie held up her hands, 'I'm all done.'

Rachel was already away.

Every sentence, every single word she had to exchange with the woman was as costly to her as blood. She pounded up the stairs thinking, what sort of a person unlocked the door of the toilet *before* she washed her hands? Gross, that's what Stevie Jones was, just totally gross.

*   *   *

Dylan put in some time with his mother-in-law.

'Noreen,' he said. 'Delighted you could make it.' She was in a short sparkly dress, a Christmassy thing. 'Are you well?'

'Everything seems in order.' Noreen gestured to the table laden with treats.

'All Rachel,' he said.

'I don't doubt it,' she said. 'Who's your one over there?' She nodded at their neighbour Suzanne, who was chatting to Stevie by the island.

Dylan was happy to have an excuse to look at her again, even these brief snatches. Glossy wave of hair, black V-neck jumper, plain gold chain. Her collarbones. His fingers touching them.

'Hello?' Noreen said.

'Suzanne's our neighbour. Two doors down. Owns three of the monsters inside.'

They turned towards the living room where the children had retired from their escapades in the garden and were now in a collective trance on the carpet in front of the kaleidoscopic colours of the flatscreen.

'And the other one?' Noreen said.

'What?'

Her attention was back on the women.

'That's Stevie,' he said. 'You know Stevie?'

'I do now,' Noreen said.

Dylan started to edge away from her. 'Can I get you another drink?'

'When are we doing the cake?' The abrupt sharpness of her voice exposed her vulnerability, how she was here alone, as always. He felt bad for trying to get away.

'It will be a while yet, I'm afraid. The children's entertainer still has to arrive.'

'The what?'

'All the rage.'

'They'll grow up without imaginations,' Noreen said. 'You wait and see.'

'I think she does crafts with them.'

Noreen shifted to a new mode of attack. 'How's the job hunt going?'

'Not great.'

'Where are you looking?'

'Around.'

Across the way Stevie laughed a proper Stevie laugh, head thrown back. He didn't mean to become distracted by it, couldn't help himself, his attraction to her had the furrowed neural pathways of an addiction.

'Right,' he heard his mother-in-law say.

He smiled benevolently at her. 'What was that?'

Noreen squinted at him, then took herself off to the living room to hang out with the kids.

*   *   *

Opening his fourth can, Ben drifted away from the adult conversations in the kitchen and went to watch the children's entertainer, who had taken up one half of the double sitting room with her prancing pantomime routine. Her red wig was lopsided, the chalky make-up fading on her face, the clown suit looked like one of those cheap supermarket affairs and the cylindrical balloon she was currently inflating was close to bursting, any fool could see, another failed attempt to add to the scraps of shrivelled rubber on the windowsill. It was pathetic. It was amateur hour. It was probably paying two hundred quid for an afternoon's work and he wondered if he should get in on the act. The spellbound faces of the children sitting on the ground came to animated life as the balloon burst. Their laughter brought back painful memories. For the first time all week his ankle began to throb. He hated the boot, how tight it felt, heat emanating from within. He shifted his weight onto his good foot, though Stevie had warned him not to. When one side of the body was injured it took very little for the rot to spread. He turned towards the kitchen to seek her out but she was no longer at the breakfast bar with the school mothers. His eyes darted over the room till he found her, standing near the utility with Dylan, drinking cans of Dutch. The way they were set apart seemed marked and intentional, almost worse than contact. An impenetrable aura radiated. Smiling at something now, they thought they were invincible, unique, as if they were the only two people in the history of the world who had ever considered cheating.

Someone coughed behind him.

Rachel's mother was sitting alone on the far end of the brocade couch, moving an unlit cigarette between her fingers in talismanic fashion. In the afternoon light her side profile was similar to her daughter's, the same length to their legs, the strong nose. The same alertness, as she turned her head and said, 'Which one are you again?'

'I'm Ben,' and when this meant nothing to her, 'Stevie's partner.'

'I have you now. The actor lad.'

'That's me,' he said, holding up his can. 'Cheers.'

'Is it broken?' She pointed to the boot.

'Tendon injury.'

'Whatcha make of this circus?' The woman looked towards the children, who were now failing to blow up their own balloons.

'The kids seem to like it.'

'I think the world's gone mad.' She nodded at the pile of abandoned presents on the opposite couch. 'What child needs a life-size dolphin?'

'Ridiculous,' said Ben. 'A terrible gift.'

Rachel's mother regarded him. He wondered if it was too late to ask her name. He'd only met her a handful of times, had one memory of her—an untuneful rendition of 'Patricia the Stripper' at two in the morning in the residents' bar at Dylan's wedding—and he struggled to continue the conversation. She didn't seem to be the sort who would go in for small talk. Proving his point, she looked towards the kitchen now and said, 'Is there trouble in paradise?'

'What?'

'With Mr Jock.'

Ben laughed. This woman was a tonic. He decided to call her Patricia in his head. Perching on the couch, he asked her to elaborate.

'In the marriage,' she said, so simply it caught his breath.

'Dylan's?'

'There's something going on.'

'You think?'

'Indeed I do.' Her eyes narrowed with recognition.

For a second he felt sorry for Rachel. Sorry for himself. Whatever this woman thought she knew was about to get a whole lot more real. For the first time since he arrived he wondered about his plan. Not everything had to be done on a stage, he recalled someone in his family once telling him.

'Have you talked to Rachel?' he said, which was more than he'd been able to do himself.

'Talked to Rachel?' Patricia echoed.

'Who's talking to Rachel?' Suddenly she was there, standing beneath the arched alcove in her shapeless peach dress. 'What's going on, Mam?' she said. 'What are you up to?'

Patricia said nothing, just held the cigarette aloft in her hand like a bored muse.

'Don't even think about it,' Rachel said.

'I wouldn't dare.' Patricia had a harsh blast of a laugh that reminded him of his own mother, a lifelong smoker from that generation who were willing to die for their fags. He felt a sudden affinity with Rachel, as he had in the past. Their backgrounds tallied. They had early knowledge of the adult world and how little it took to break things.

'Is it time for the cake?' Patricia said.

At the mere mention of the word Ben began to sweat. After the candles, this was his plan. *Put out the light, and then put out the light.* The line spun inside his head.

'You're barely here an hour, Mam,' said Rachel. 'We'll have cake soon enough. Can I get you anything? Ben?'

'How about I give you a hand,' Ben said. With the boot he got up awkwardly, liquid spraying from his can onto the carpet. Apologising, he took a tissue from his pocket.

'I wouldn't,' said Rachel.

'It's clean,' he said.

'I'll take care of it,' Patricia said. 'No stress.' As she passed, she touched her daughter gently on the shoulder, which seemed to leave Rachel in a stupor.

Ben took this to be his chance.

'Hear,' he said. 'Can we talk?'

Her eyes gave a verdant flash. 'I'm busy.'

'It will only take a minute.'

'The sausage rolls, I smell burning.'

'We've already eaten them.'

At that she seemed to relent, taking his arm for a moment. 'Ben,' she sighed. 'Not today. Please.'

'What's going on?' he said. 'You know something, Rachel. I know you do. It's not fair.' They looked at the children, gathered in a crescent on the ground. From a makeshift projector connected to her smartphone the entertainer was doing finger puppets on the wall. A baby rabbit grew into an adult rabbit chased away by a fearsome wolf. The children oohed and ahhed. In the middle Leah was entranced, her eyes unnaturally round, head reclining at an angle that was only achievable with the malleable bones of a child.

'Please.' Rachel leant away from him with effort. 'Don't ruin her day.'

'What are you accusing me of?'

'Nothing,' she said. 'I don't know.'

'I'm not the one in the wrong here.'

'You sure about that?' Her body stiffened as she faced him with the dull severity of a guard.

'Yes,' he said. 'I've done nothing wrong.'

'Are you thick?'

'*Excuse* me?'

She gave him an odd, curdled look that peeled back years of their knowing each other, years of knowledge itself, and still he felt it, the certainty of his own righteousness, which he had tended so carefully over months that all it could do now was gorge like a fattened animal on the carcass of his life.

Rachel turned away.

He knew he had to name it. 'Are they,' he put his hand on her arm, 'are Stevie and Dylan having an affair?'

She drew back. 'Leave. Me. Alone.'

Into the dark space that opened like a portal between them ran a child. A child who was no longer transfixed by the finger gymnastics of an amateur clown. A child who didn't look like a cheerful birthday girl. A child whose pallid face had the softening, resigned expression of tears about to be shed.

'Mummy.' Leah grabbed the ends of Rachel's dress. 'What's wrong?'

'Everything's fine.'

Ben watched her take her daughter by the hand and walk away. He began to doubt his plan, this confrontation. He wouldn't do it. Unless there was something more substantial to go on. It wasn't fair, to the child, or to Rachel.

*   *   *

Stevie and Dylan were in the utility room for less than ten seconds when they were suddenly pressed together against the smooth wall. Door closed. Alcohol warm on their breaths. Abnormal gravity pulling them down. She moved away from him, too wrong, the clean space, laundry detergent, antiseptic judgement. A miniature pink dress drying on a rack. But then he put his hand down the front of her trousers and the probe of his fingers against the damp cotton of her underwear made her legs tremble and the sliding sensation began once more.

'I locked it,' he whispered.

She glanced at the door to the kitchen, a sturdy wooden barricade between them and the rest of humanity. Behind it, the sound of people enjoying themselves, which is to say, fooled into believing they had any idea of what real enjoyment entailed. This was the only thing that had ever happened in the world.

'Jesus,' he said softly, kissing her again.

The room disappeared.

Until the door handle rattled with a noise so loud it went beyond the pain threshold of the human ear.

'Jesus,' he said, in a roundly different inflection.

The child's voice calling his name.

'Go,' he said, nodding at the back door. 'Go!'

*   *   *

Rachel fled from her conversation with Ben to the kitchen, Leah trailing despondently after her. The room was abuzz with life, kids on the loose, weaving in and out between the chairs and stools and standing adults, snatching at crisp bowls, popcorn, fizzy drinks, whatever else they could find. Much of the party had drifted to the corner by the picture wall where Helen was holding court. She looked to be entertaining the school mothers and for that Rachel was grateful. Sean was on the periphery, white curls nodding to the flow in a gentlemanly display of interest. She had been lucky in her in-laws, she knew that. They were kind people who showed up when it mattered and brought with them the illusion of safety from the outside world.

'Dirty,' said Leah.

Rachel looked at the two palms presented in the style of a thief caught in the act.

'Yucky marshmallows,' said Rachel.

'Yucky-yum.'

Rachel laughed in spite of herself. 'Come on, let's wash them.' She led her daughter past the utility room whose door was weirdly closed.

'Where's Daddy?' Leah said.

With the fleeting triumph of knowledge gained, Rachel knew who was on the other side of the door. She was sure she'd had an eye on Dylan, on *her*, at all times today, but of course they had been watching her too, waiting for a chance, however brief, to sneak away. The deviousness astounded her. What was she supposed to do, stand around here and watch her husband succumb? A tight band of pain at the top of her rib cage, then the baby kicked. *Succumb*. Such a nasty, truthful word, remove a few letters and you were even closer to it.

'Mummy?' Leah's sticky hand pressed on the brass door handle. 'Daddy!'

Time in a general sense seemed to fracture. The only thing still going was the life growing inside her. From the utility came a thud, the sound of something falling.

'Mummy, it won't open.' Leah's face creased with effort. She put both hands on the brass and swung from it.

'Stop it, Leah.'

'But Mummy, it's not working.' She began to cry.

Rachel pulled her off the handle, all the while listening to the grotesque shuffling noise behind the door. Leah's cry grew louder, drawing the attention of the guests. Rachel was close to tears herself. She blinked a few times. When she refocused her mother was beside her with Leah in her arms.

'You'll hurt your back,' Rachel said uselessly.

'Nonsense,' Noreen said. 'It's your back you should be minding.' She looked discreetly at the bump. Stepping in front of Rachel, she pounded a fist on the utility door. 'Who's in there?' she said. 'Come out now.' Repeated the instruction, with its wicked playground echoes. *Come out, come out, wherever you are.*

The door opened as the sound of another door closed. Rachel caught the shape of her husband emerging from the utility but didn't bother to wait for the whole of him, turning her head towards the horizontal window across the back wall of the kitchen, which held like a strip of negatives the quickly moving image of Stevie striding across the patio for all the world to see. Head down, hair shielding her wanton face.

'Alright, Noreen?' Dylan said.

Her mother gave him a death stare, another memory from childhood—the dark concentration of someone about to pounce.

'Daddy!' Leah sang out and reached across.

In one move he took her high onto his shoulders, into the position Rachel disliked, her daughter taller now, less able to remain steady. He jostled her left and right as he made for the living room. Watching them go, Rachel stood astonished. The guests resumed their conversations. Her mother withdrew too, following Leah, which stung like a second abandonment. Rachel felt something had just been lost; and now, a terrible sadness, encroaching, no, already here—and all along?

That first time she'd met Dylan, in the nightclub so many years ago, first time she'd even heard of him, she remembered one of the other shot girls telling her he was past his prime; a bad injury meant he was no longer 'top tier material'. Rachel had found the comment repugnant, but now she wondered if that girl was right, maybe she'd chosen a faulty model for a husband. Second-hand goods, without warranty.

Feeling the baby kick again she went to get water. At the tap, with her back to everyone, she drank slowly, tried to calm her racing heart. She couldn't believe the cruelty of his behaviour, how obvious he was being. The hypocrisy. All the small betrayals contained within the big one. While his co-conspirator skulked outside, he was in the next room playing the family man. She could hear him joking now with the clown, the children responding with innocent laughter. The thing that killed her, even more than the infidelity itself, was that he was acting as if fate had intervened in his life and compelled him to cheat. Nothing to do with him, no responsibility, it was just the way things were. Rachel needed the day to be over. They would do the cake and she would wind things up.

Finishing her drink, she left the glass in the sink, took the candles from the drawer, went to the table where Ben's angry presence was casting about like a fishhook. He sat at the head chair, staring at the utility. Rachel said his name but it didn't register.

Straining for normal, she went about putting a white candle in each of the corners of the cake and a pink one in the middle.

'We're going to do the cake,' she said loudly.

Still he ignored her, so she said it again.

On the third go, he came to life.

'OK,' he said. 'I'm ready.'

'What?'

There was a vaguely psychotic bent to his features, the dragonish flare of his nostrils, a half-smile that didn't reach his eyes.

'Ben?' she said. 'Are you OK?' She tried to keep her voice even. 'Are we good? Ben?'

A cold burst filled the kitchen as Stevie came through the utility reeking of smoke.

'Oh, we're good,' said Ben. 'We are *terrific*.'

'Hey,' Stevie sidled over to them, 'I hope I didn't miss the cake.'

Rachel couldn't look at her. 'Dylan!' she called towards the front room. 'Cake!'

Over by the picture wall heads turned.

Ben rose from his seat, stretched his hands above his head. As Rachel patted the front pockets of her dress for the matches, she heard him say to Stevie, 'What were you doing in there?' His voice was brash, indiscreet, other conversations swallowed up by its insistence.

'Dylan had a migraine,' Stevie said. 'I was trying to help him. He needed a quiet space.'

Just then Dylan arrived laughing into the kitchen with Leah on his shoulders, two other children pulling at his legs.

'Put her down,' Rachel said sharply.

For the first time all day he looked chastened. He lowered Leah carefully to the ground. Her daughter's head darted between them.

The adults moved to the table as if someone had blown a whistle. Rachel wondered if everyone just knew, but then she remembered the cake, they were coming over to sing. Children spilled in, taking their places shyly behind Leah, whose expectant gaze was on the shiny chocolate icing. Sean hit the dimmer switch on the wall. The room grew hushed and spellbound.

Turning the pockets of her dress inside out Rachel still couldn't find the matches.

'Here,' said Stevie, offering a lighter.

Rachel's arms were welded to her body.

There was a long pause, then a monstrous action where Stevie took it upon herself to crouch over the cake and light the candles. The sleeve of her jumper withdrew with feline grace as sounds of *happy birthday* began, Ben's baritone and Helen's soprano drowning out everyone else, which was just as well—Rachel couldn't get the words out.

Ben's fearsome singing propelled him forward through the crowd, into the centre, he was heading for the table with purpose, almost colliding with a child, who Dylan scooped out of the way in time. Everyone was watching Ben. Even Leah looked up from the cake to stare at him in wonder, this adult man who did not understand the rules of birthdays. At the end of the song Rachel managed a hoarse cheer. Then her daughter, her gorgeous, sensitive little girl, stood on her tiptoes to blow out the wavy lights. Ben gave a single histrionic clap and stood back from the table to glower at Dylan in full view of the party. Something of an accusatory nature was said because Helen's face stretched in shock, but all Rachel could hear was the blood thumping in her eardrums. They were onto *jolly good fellow* when the outlines of the furniture became squiggly, at first a pleasant, distracting sense of motion, then a vertiginous drop as the room fell sideways, at which point she was no longer standing, the cool hardness of the ceramic tiles was rising to meet her.

*   *   *

When Leah was finally asleep, Dylan came downstairs to find Ben and Stevie still there. The kitchen, the whole house, was clean, four large bin bags propped against the wall by the utility door.

'We didn't know where to put them,' said Ben.

'Have you heard from the hospital?' Stevie said.

Dylan sighed. 'You need to leave.'

'Listen—' Stevie stepped towards him and he moved around the island to get away from her.

'Come on,' said Ben. 'Have you heard? Is she OK?'

'Just go,' Dylan said.

'What the hell?'

'I don't know anything. She left her phone here. I don't know a goddamn thing. Why did you have to do it like that? In front of everyone.'

'Seriously, mate?' Ben said. 'I don't think *that's* the question.'

'Don't you?' said Dylan.

'You know well,' Ben snarled.

'We never meant.' Here Dylan managed to glance at Stevie. 'We didn't, did we?'

In the space of an hour their lives had imploded.

She said, 'It wasn't planned—'

'Liar!' said Ben.

'Lower your voice,' Dylan warned. 'I've just got Leah to sleep.'

'Father of the year,' said Ben.

It hit him where it was meant to: reality, a jab in the solar plexus.

'Please,' Dylan said. 'Will you just go?'

But Stevie sank trancelike into a chair, a horrible vacancy in her eyes, the light of so many years extinguished.

In the hallway the phone rang.

'Answer it,' said Ben.

*   *   *

They didn't speak a word until they were out of the hospital, safely in the car and on the road. Then Noreen said gravely, 'Are you going to leave him?' She was driving at twenty kilometres up Cork Street and Rachel wanted to tell her to hurry up. It was dark now, desolately cold, only a handful of cars on the road. Many businesses and apartment blocks still had their Christmas lights up, persistent colours blinking in the night.

'I don't know,' she said.

They went back to silence after that and she was glad of her mother's ability to let things lie, they were similar in that way. She'd once heard someone say that a person got the children they deserved and she wondered now what her baby would be like, if he would be like Leah, or entirely new and different. She hadn't wanted to know the gender, but in the madness of the last few hours one of the nurses in The Coombe had let slip.

After Rachel came round on the kitchen floor, her mother and Helen by her side, a towel under her head and another wet scrap across her brow, she had one thought: the baby. What had happened to the baby? She couldn't remember if she'd said this out loud, though she was sure she had only wanted her mother and in-laws to accompany her to the hospital, that she'd refused outright to let Dylan go too, so everybody knew, if they hadn't already figured it out, that her life, her marriage, was in pieces.

Curiously, this didn't seem to matter now. The baby was OK. Her little boy was OK. Her blood pressure had dropped; everything was fine now. In the cosy darkness of the car Rachel found herself smiling. She reached to turn the heater on high, sat back and closed her eyes.

At the crossroads her mother asked if she wanted to come home for a night or two. 'To rest,' she said.

'No,' said Rachel. 'Thanks.' She wanted to speak to Dylan as soon as possible. For the first time in years, maybe the first time in their marriage, she wasn't encumbered by fear. At the sound of the heartbeat it had lifted, right there in the scanning room with the cold gel all over her stomach. She understood: the splinter had to come out.

'Did you tell him?' Rachel said.

'That you're pregnant?'

'Yes.'

'Of course not,' her mother said. 'But you can bet Helen did. She had the phone already out as they were leaving the ward. They were happy though. Both of them were very happy for you, Rachel. And relieved.'

When they reached the house the curtains were drawn across the big bay window of the living room. Before Rachel unbuckled her seatbelt the front door opened and Dylan ran towards the car, his shape slicing through the misty headlights. He went for the passenger handle, but the car was locked. She pressed the wrong button and the window lowered.

'Are you OK?' he said.

Rachel nodded.

'Is it true?'

She nodded again.

'And is the baby OK too?'

'Yes,' she said. 'Everything's OK.'

'Rachel,' he said. 'I'm so sorry.'

She curled her tired toes inside her shoes and looked down at the footwell.

'It's freezing,' her mother said. 'Get in or get out.'

Rachel bent across, kissed the papery skin of her cheek.

'I'll call you in the morning,' Noreen said.

No sooner were they in the door than Rachel sensed they were not alone, the house held the tension of outsiders. The car lights flashed up the hallway as her mother reversed and drove away. Rachel knew exactly who was here.

'They wouldn't leave,' Dylan said. 'I told them to go.'

'Where's Leah?' she said.

'In bed.'

Rachel looked upstairs to the glowy light.

'She's asleep,' Dylan said.

Rachel walked calmly towards the living room, Dylan following with a doglike servitude she no longer needed or desired.

Stevie was by the window with her coat on. 'We're not staying,' she announced. 'We just wanted to make sure you're OK.' Her voice was thick with shame.

Ben stood up. 'I didn't know. Really, Rachel, I didn't have a clue. I didn't think.' Then the grand confession. 'I wasn't thinking of anyone but myself.'

'Is the baby OK?' Stevie said.

For the first time in months, Rachel didn't want to make her suffer. 'The baby is fine. I'm fine. We're both fine.'

'Can we do anything?' Ben said.

Rachel gave a sharp laugh. 'You can sit down.' It was not how she'd envisaged the conversation, but in a way it felt right. The four of them were in it together.

They looked at each other doubtfully before Stevie obeyed. Ben went beside her on the couch. They sat primly, their backs not touching the cushions.

'Rachel?' Dylan said.

'You too.' She aimed the pistol of her index finger at the last seat on the couch so they were lined up in front of her like schoolchildren. Ben shifted away from Dylan. The three of them watched her keenly as she crossed the room and leant against the mahogany bureau they'd been gifted by Helen and Sean for the anniversary that was marked by wood.

Looking at her husband, Rachel cleared her throat. 'Whatever has been going on between the two of you, and for quite some time, I want you—'

'It's over,' said Dylan.

Stevie said, 'It's nothing. Nothing really happened.'

Ben interlaced his fingers so tightly his knuckles whitened.

'Is that right?' Rachel said, feeling the edges of her anger return at how easily they had given up, at how even in the denials, the renouncing of each other, they seemed to be collaborating. It was a new form of betrayal. Then she remembered what she was about to confess herself and the anger ebbed away. She put her hands flat against the slanted panel of the bureau. 'It doesn't matter,' she said. 'None of it matters. The point is, I don't care any more. It's all built on lies.'

'Rach,' Dylan made like he might get up, 'please.' His remorse was too hard to witness, she didn't want anything to do with it now.

'No, you listen,' she said. 'I don't care what's going on between you. I really don't. I just want it out in the open. You can do what you want. Just stop going around pretending like you have one over on us. Because you absolutely don't.'

Ben's quick eyes fired. Rachel was drawn into their keen intelligence and for an instant everything in the room receded, leaving only the pair of them adrift on stage without their lines, and beyond the dark hole of their wordless being, the audience waiting. Her composure left her. She gave the final bit of her speech in a rush, with none of the poignant fatalism she had intended. 'Long before whatever this is,' the pistol returned, flicking between Dylan and Stevie, 'long before—centuries ago—we had our own secret. Things we never told you.'

It took her husband more than a moment to realise the *we* did not include him. He looked first at Ben, in awed horror, then back at his wife, who nodded grimly.

RACHEL

Eleven women from various places, north Dublin, south Dublin, Bishopstown, Shannon, a village in Fermanagh too small to have a name, one from Bath, another from Clermont, have come together on a wet and windy Saturday in June to celebrate the upcoming nuptials of Rachel Harte. They're in a plush bar on Dawson Street, it's ten o'clock at night and everyone is drinking mojitos in highball glasses through bright pink penis straws. Everyone that is except for Stevie.

As Rachel pretends to listen to her sister's lengthy, looping story about a benign cyst under her arm, which Rachel has already heard in its entirety in pubs numbers two and seven, secretly she is observing Stevie on the outskirts of the tall tables, legs dangling from the stool in boredom, heavy Doc Martens like chunks of liver on her feet. Stevie's face is knowingly sedate, her posture a kind of contempt, and of course she hasn't bothered with the dress code, which politely asked everyone to wear white so that Rachel, in a classy reversal of the norm, would stand out as the bride in her black silk jumpsuit. Obviously Stevie didn't read the email. As usual she considered herself exempt from the rules, so here she is, coolly sipping her pint in a black string dress, confusing the hell out of every group of men that stops to harass them. *Which one's the bride?* they demand to know with the fervour of pack hunters stalking prey.

The rest of the crew are a vision of white, a mix of colleagues, rugby girlfriends, country cousins and a couple of schoolmates she hasn't spoken to in years. Always working, trying to get ahead, Rachel doesn't have a lot of time for friends, a fact that is embarrassingly obvious from the relatively small number of people who have shown up for her today. Furtively she looks at Alice, who is marrying the Leinster flanker in September, and wonders how she managed to get thirty-six women to Carrick-on-Shannon for a two-night bender earlier this year. How are some people just popular? The contrast, the shame of it, is something Rachel has been dreading, and she's dealt with this by making sure everything is coolly perfect—hip Dublin instead of the bog, fancy Thai trumps hotel carvery, one great night over a second-day hangover, an outfit you might actually want to wear again, not a scrap of glittery pink. She put so much effort into these plans that she came close to fooling herself, right until Stevie showed up for the party bus on the quays in a black dress and black biker jacket, at which point all the carefully constructed scaffolding collapsed, plummeting Rachel back to earth.

But she had no time to metabolise the blow, not with a peaked-cap driver on the clock, flat Prosecco and strawberries, blaring nineties tunes, heroic attempts at dancing on a moving vehicle and a trip out to Sandymount strand, which they all waved at from behind the rainy windows of the bus. There was flower arranging, afternoon tea, drinks in the Horseshoe Bar, drinks in any other bar within the limited walking distance permitted by six-inch heels, an excruciating Mr and Mrs quiz despite Rachel's protests, a thinly spread photobook with mostly generic well wishes, a multicourse dinner of spiced chicken and veiny rice-paper rolls, then more drinks, more syrupy cocktails, until here, several lifetimes later, there is, in the drone of Emma's voice and the surrounding conversations, a surprising quiet time where Rachel is starting to feel the full force of the day, this weird, emotional, crazy day that's meant to divide her life into before and after, child and adult, young and old. She misses Dylan. He hasn't responded to her messages, too busy having fun with his teammates in Barcelona.

'It will be OK,' her sister is saying.

Rachel feels the weight of an arm around her shoulder.

A lad in the jester-bright colours of the Mayo kit appears, asks if he can buy them a drink.

Her sister says she'll take eleven cosmopolitans, thanks very much, and the banter continues from there, Rachel struggling to keep pace, just one lucid thought of the person to blame— Stevie—who is no longer sitting on a stool opposite her, all the stools are in fact gone. She looks at her legs stretched out in front of her, the fine silk crinkled, still wet from the rain. 'Why am I on the ground?' she says.

At that she's lifted in the air, over someone's shoulder, and a man, the Mayo lad, is shouting, 'Look what I won!' to encouraging cheers.

'Put her down.' Her sister's voice again, then Alice, popular Alice, guiding her over to a booth where all her friends, her so-called friends, come into view again.

'Sit down there and get this into you.' Her sister passes her an espresso martini. Rachel appreciates the heady shock of it sliding down her throat.

In the distance, at the far side of the dance floor, the bar is a cluttered oblong rimmed with blazing light.

'Is this Coppers?' she says, horrified.

'You're in The Academy, love,' Emma says. 'Relax! It's all going exactly as you planned.'

Rachel, who still hasn't forgiven her for the quiz that revealed Dylan's favourite position in bed, his ideal number of future children, Rachel's pet name for him—all in front of Stevie—grits her teeth now and gives her sister a flagrantly homicidal look that elicits a roar of laughter from Emma and the cousins.

'I don't think she believes you,' says Orla from Fermanagh. 'Trust me, Rach. This isn't Coppers. I *know* Coppers.'

Rachel supposes that she does. With the stabilising effects of the caffeine, her surroundings come into definition. True enough, they're in the heat-soaked pit of Dublin's coolest nightclub. The carnage is general: hundreds on the dance floor, at the bar, queuing for the toilets, still more spilling up the stairs. And the music! Insanely loud, repetitive and wordless, the type of music Rachel doesn't like, she can't think why she chose this sweaty hellhole, before it comes to her, forcefully, that she did it to impress Stevie, who mentioned the venue in her offhand way one night out after a match.

Rachel stands up with purpose. 'Where's Stevie?' she says.

But everyone, even her sister, is busy with their own conversations. The night has taken off, the plodding embarrassment of so much of the day has shifted, without alerting Rachel, to messy intimacy. The great unburdening has begun.

'They *say* it's benign.' Emma is close to tears.

'Bloody Scotland!'

'Swear on your life.'

'Lost the eye.'

'Disciplinary board!'

Newly awake, born again and annoyed at having her resurrection so definitively ignored, Rachel clinks the empty glasses together till she gets their attention. A desolate Mexican wave started by her tearful sister dies out after Alice.

'Anyone seen Stevie?' Rachel asks.

Heads shake, useless suggestions abound, a cousin says, 'Which one's Stevie?'

'The goth,' says Orla.

'Who?'

'The one who didn't get the dress code,' says Alice, loyally, and Rachel experiences a flash of pure love.

Sophie, another rugby girlfriend, says she saw Stevie in the queue for the bathrooms.

'Right,' says Rachel. 'So she's still here?'

'Come on, come on,' Emma rises. 'Let's dance. I mean it, everyone, up.' But no one looks remotely enthused at the prospect of the thronged dance floor with its mass of stomping bodies.

'Urgh,' says Rachel. 'Urgh!'

'Where are you off to now?' her sister asks.

Rachel waves her away, unhooks the velvet rope of their area and walks diligently down the steps to the main floor. As she wades through the stubborn crowd towards the toilets, obsessed now with finding this woman she barely knows, Rachel thinks of Dylan and longs to be home with him in their new, unfurnished house in Terenure. All they have so far is a bed and kitchen table, a couple of stools from the hardware shop, a duvet from Helen. Rachel feels under pressure to pick the right things for the house, as if these inanimate objects will determine their future happiness. And who knew it took four months for a couch anyway? For a bundle of stuffed cushions to be hoisted on some wood. There is so much of the adult world she doesn't understand.

'Alright, buuurd,' says an inebriated northerner, hands reaching for her waist.

Smiling angelically, Rachel elbows him and he fades into the crowd. Exhausting, the vigilance expected of women, the still permissible, still anticipated snatch-and-grab of these supposedly civilised times. Not for the first time today she wants to leg it. But even if she managed to escape, there would be no Dylan waiting for her. She wonders how much fun he's having in Spain. Five of them let loose on the beer in a country where even the ugly women are tanned and beautiful. Because men deserve a proper party, she thinks bitterly, before remembering it was a surprise: Jim sprung it on him after squaring things with the coach. She didn't mind at the time. She wasn't, for example, half as aggrieved as Ben, who is still, by his own account, in the process of organising the proper stag in Youghal.

After trying to casually bypass the line outside the ladies, Rachel pretends not to hear the abuse and holds her head high as she doubles back to the end of the queue. Ordinarily she'd just use the men's but she's on a mission to find Stevie, who seems to matter more right now than the rest of the hen group together. More than Rachel herself. Stevie is so close to Dylan that Rachel feels obliged to befriend her, afraid of the consequences if she doesn't make an effort. Of what, specifically, she is unclear, just a promise of trouble, with the knowledge she's unarmed. The closer she gets to the wedding, the more she fears it will fall apart. Dylan has done nothing to prompt these fears; they are all her own. He's the first man she's ever truly loved, and because love doesn't come easy to her, she feels always on the brink of messing up. One thing is certain, she cannot go back to being the shots girl. Adrenal panic floods her stomach. She places an arm over it to settle herself.

On and on the wait for the toilets, fists pounding doors, shouts to hurry up, threats, cries, greetings, laughter, and the magic cubicle at the end of the row, where girl after girl walk out in succession to eventual gridlock at the sinks. Until finally—finally!—Rachel enters a cubicle of her own, more safehouse than toilet, a bunker where she can hide from the world, lid down on her plastic throne. She spends so much time luxuriating in the privacy, texting Dylan once, twice, another for luck, that she's struggling to remember why she came into the toilets at all when she hears, from the cubicle next door, the low, rich voice on the phone.

'So dull,' Stevie is saying. 'Totally vapid. But I better go back, I'm gone ages. Kill me now, Laura.'

A sister, older or younger, Rachel can't remember.

Stevie laughs at the response. 'At least I'm not dressed like a Victoria's Secret Angel,' she says. And they're off again with the abhorrent laughter.

Stretching her arms so that her hands are flat against the cubicle walls, Rachel presses as hard as she can. The eaves-dropping is too intense, drunkenly fluid proof of what she has long suspected: this woman scorns her lifestyle, and everything it represents.

'Exactly,' Stevie says. 'I should be on the stag! OK, bye, bye. Bye!'

Callous bang of the stall door against the shuddering frame. Rachel stays put. Waits a few minutes. Another, just to be sure. Slots the door open with trembling fingers.

'Hurray!' says a girl at the top of the queue. 'We thought you were dead.'

Rachel smiles weakly, goes to wash her hands, unsteady, the muscles in her legs suddenly feel the long hours in sparkly Jimmy Choos. A tired image greets her in the mirror, like she's done rounds in a physical fight. She splashes water on her face, not caring about the orange drops that fall into the sink, quick dabs to give her strength to return to the wild.

'Rachel! Omigod, hi!'

At a neighbouring sink there's an old colleague from the drinks company. Another half-model, non-model, uselessly attractive shots girl like Rachel.

'Shauna!'

Breaking away from the hug, Rachel feels she has to make excuses for the state of her face. 'It's my hen!' she says.

Shauna, in a green bandage dress and platform heels, shushes her, grabs her hand and sneaks them both into a cubicle, to the outrage of the queue.

'Dylan Turner,' she locks the door, 'you lucky cow.'

Then the powder is out on the cistern, Rachel is whooshing away her cares, the whole nightmare of the phone call shoots up her nose, dissolves in a thousand particles, into her bloodstream, into her brain.

Once more unto the breach, the pounding pit of the night-club swallows her up. She returns to the alcove, joins easily now in the tangled conversations—the coke has revived her. Time goes in all directions, into the past with her mother's refusal to come to the hen, into the future with her fears for the wedding, fears that her father will show, fears that he won't, into the present and the radio silence from Barcelona and the lads and their threesome videos and and where is her bag? Through the chaos, the facts keep changing. Stevie is there. Stevie is missing. Stevie is gone.

At some unknowable hour Rachel is on the dance floor, giving it everything, letting her body make the shapes, it seems to know innately what to do, as if there was a small demented raver living inside her all along, when through the vibrating crowds she sees her sister—definitely Emma, fake tan in tigerish stripes across the corset top—and she's drunk, beyond drunk, arms stretched in front of her, hands flapping over and back, doing the Macarena with gusto, which is to say, wrecking the heads of everyone around her. Rachel goes to stop her but finds herself dragged backwards, the dance floor is a treadmill, ever more resistant as she presses onward, but wait, someone has a hold of her, and that someone—somehow—is Ben.

Clear unadulterated delight at seeing him. His smirking, handsome face is the face of a friend, of togetherness and belonging, the very opposite of how she's been feeling all day.

'Ben!' she shouts and his arms are around her, she's lifted in the air, and it's not until her sore feet are back on the ground and he's still hugging her that she realises he's had quite a few himself. 'You shouldn't be here,' she says. 'It's my hen! No men.'

'Ha,' he says into her ear, a warm buzz, 'haha.'

It transpires that Ben was out with his drama crew and has come to meet Stevie, but he's missed her, she's in a taxi on her way to a house party in Foxrock. 'She said to follow her,' he shouts. 'Invited us all.'

Rachel sincerely doubts that. She pulls him off the dance floor so they can stop roaring at each other. They stand against a pulsing wall of condensation. Thin strobe lights spear electric green in the background.

'So she definitely left?' Rachel says. 'Stevie?'

Ben shrugs. 'Sorry, you know what she's like.'

'Mean,' Rachel says.

Ben agrees, angry she didn't ring him before she got the taxi. 'As if I can afford one on my own. She's just like Dylan—selfish.'

His eyes search her face and she stills them with a swift, penetrating look. 'What did Dylan do?'

'Off to Barcelona with his real mates.'

Rachel gives him a hug. 'Forget them, and Stevie too,' she says, immediately undercutting her own advice. 'Whose party was so important anyway?'

'You know her mate Noel?'

Rachel can't place him, but all of Stevie's Killiney friends are the same. 'The dickhead,' she says.

'Exactly!' Ben beams at her, then asks if she has drugs.

That is the reason they go back to her hotel room at The Clarence.

She clings to this knowledge when she wakes up the following morning, though it does nothing to help the paralysing guilt, the cruel line of dawn light beaming straight at her hungover head from the gap in the ornate curtains. Beside her in the bed Emma is snoring soundly, but long before she got back, Rachel and Ben came here alone.

Like bold teenagers they left the club without telling anyone and got a rickshaw to the hotel. She snuck him past a front desk attendant who had no interest in whether he was there or not, which seemed to make the deceit even funnier, they were crying laughing in the mirrored lift up to the penthouse suite where the remainder of the powder provided a wonderful time of talking, sharing, resenting, lamenting, understanding, being understood, which is to say, included, allowed in on the joke, for once.

One of them, it might even have been her, suggested the minibar at some point and this is where the trouble started, she thinks now, her heart banging so loudly in her chest she is sure it will wake her sister, will be heard in all the other hotel rooms too, the city at large.

The half bottle of champagne looked extraordinarily small in Ben's hands, that was all it seemed to take, how is it possible, the simple thought that his hands were slender and strong, rough knuckles on otherwise elegant fingers, then without words, without premeditation, or anyone even making a move—though surely it was him?—they were kissing. What happened after that Rachel knows, with bleak hungover certainty, she will have to spend every day for the rest of her life forgetting. This is the last time she will allow herself to think about it, as she lies here tongue-parched, head hammering, with her sweaty lower arm blocking the brutal new day from her eyes, how it was quick, unreal and embodied in a good way all the feelings of exclusion she had felt about their little clique, Dylan in Spain, Stevie in Foxrock and Ben right there beside her, taking her in his arms, giving her for the first and only time a piece of history, a piece of them.

JUNE

Six months after the child's fifth birthday, Ben is no longer out for blood. He has nothing left inside him for that type of thing. On his way to meet Dylan in a pub on George's Street, he sits on the top deck of the bus and watches the city he used to call home go by in all its splendid indifference. These days it takes everything he has to get from one place to the next, one day to another, he is concentrating solely on repairing his life as it is right now, because the past has finally caught up with the present, the prologue has ended in tears, and all that remains is the commonly allocated hours of each given day, which hope-fully over time will amount to something like the future.

At late afternoon the pub is just open, a gassy smell of beer kegs, dusty particles drifting over dark wood. Behind the counter a girl polishes a row of glasses. Bare tables everywhere, except for the one in the corner where Dylan stares dreamily at the head of his pint. He looks up as Ben approaches, in that way of old friends attuned to each other's presence.

Even though he's intending not to make this easy, Ben says hello first. A shyness comes over him, as if he's on a date.

'Hi,' says Dylan. 'I'm a bit early.' In his pink shirt he looks lean, fit, and his face radiates health—a man who knows how to take care of himself.

Ben is disconcerted, which is to say, envious. 'I'm only going to have tea,' he mumbles.

Dylan shrugs. 'Fine.'

But when the bar girl appears Ben changes his mind and orders a Guinness. With the pint delivered to the table, she gives them the once over, smiling to herself as she goes. Dylan holds up his pint to cheers and there is nothing to do but match him. Afterwards, Ben shifts awkwardly on the low stool, dragging it closer to the table.

'So how's life?'

'Grand,' Dylan says. 'Good, actually.'

'Yeah?'

'Yeah.'

'What's going on?'

'Rachel's nearly there,' he says. 'They'll take her in if she hasn't gone by the weekend.'

Ben is somewhat thrown by the answer, but perhaps he has no right to be, a new life coming into the world surely counts as news. 'Right,' he says. 'Wow. It's really happening.' He doesn't know what else to say. 'How's the job going?'

'It's not the worst,' Dylan says. 'I've to do a year with passports, then they'll review me. And the people are sound.'

'Passports?'

'Sean picked the one he thought I'd hate the most.' A familiar glint comes into his eyes. Ben will not fall for something as obvious as that. He remains impassive, watching with a certain amount of pleasure the merriment fade from Dylan's face.

'How's the foot?' A nod at Ben's shoe.

'Running still hurts a bit.'

Sounding just like Stevie, Dylan warns him not to rush his recovery.

'Yeah, yeah,' Ben sniffs. 'I'm not a child. I get it.'

The conversation stalls and he begins to regret saying it, or he regrets his decision to come here at all, shifting his focus to the young lad in the foreground, the neat swipes of his mop across the amber floor.

'Listen,' says Dylan. 'How are you? I mean—'

Ben shakes his head, takes another swig of the pint. He's only had eggs for breakfast and his stomach gives a sulphurous groan. 'How's Leah?' he says.

'Excited. She's decided it's a boy.'

'Is it?'

Dylan says he doesn't know.

'Does Rachel know?'

'Rachel knows everything.'

For the first time since Ben sat down the lightness, the bright candour, is gone from Dylan's voice. He presses his fingers to his temples and says, 'Christ.'

'What?'

'Nothing. I mean, come on—this is hard.'

Ben twists his mouth, as if to say, what did you expect?

They go back to silence, watching the door with the acid-etched glass.

'Listen, mate,' says Dylan.

'Mate?'

'Yes,' he says, a touch wearily.

'I don't think we're at "mate" just yet.' Ben tightens his grip on the glass. 'Not at all.' The old competitiveness flares inside him, and with it, a need for control.

'What are you talking about?'

'You know well.'

'OK,' Dylan says. 'Fine.' He leans against the wall, shuts his eyes, tight enough that the paler skin around the sockets shows its surprising laxity.

They are old, Ben thinks, they are too old for this. 'Look,' he says, 'you're here. I'm here.' Dylan opens his eyes and again the roundly optimistic gaze is hard to take, but Ben presses on. 'It's something, that we both showed up today.'

'Maybe we could make it a regular thing?' Dylan says. 'Like a weekly drink.'

Ben finishes his pint and halves the beer mat, halves it again.

'Or monthly?' Dylan says.

Ben flicks a quarter across the table, another and another, the last one up into Dylan's face so that the smile, the row of white, disappears.

'What the hell?'

'I'm wondering,' Ben says, 'what's wrong with you.'

'What?'

'Like, why aren't you angry?'

'Of course I am,' Dylan says, but he doesn't continue.

Ben knows why. If the situation was reversed and he found out Dylan and Stevie had been together one time—nearly a decade ago—he probably wouldn't be that angry either. The two betrayals are not equal. He was stabbed in the eyeball, Dylan merely mauled.

'I was drunk,' Ben says. 'I was locked when it happened. So was Rachel.'

'A month before my wedding. Where you were the best man.'

It is true that Ben found the wedding difficult, particularly his speech, which he faltered through so badly his own mother suggested, later that evening when everyone was knee-deep in bacon sandwiches, that he give up the acting for a job that didn't require public speaking. Annoyed at the memory, he forgoes the apology and hurls another accusation. 'You were my best *friend*, Dylan. You were sober. Adults. This is real life. And you were planning it for months.' Ben reconsiders. 'For years.'

'We weren't!' Dylan says.

The *we* kills Ben. He feels it in every tightening tissue of his body—a reminder of everything he's lost, all the rejections of his near-miss life rolled into one. He hasn't seen the other half of that *we* in months. The fight was one long vitriolic night of attack and counterattack, until they finally fell asleep from the soul-splitting sordidness of it all, and in the morning when he woke, she was gone.

'You ruined my life,' Ben says now, a plainly juvenile statement that gets the reaction he's looking for.

'Ah, would you ever listen to yourself,' says Dylan. 'What do you want? To be the best of the assholes? Congratulations— you're the best.'

Ben is offended, or he feigns offence, hard to differentiate. What he wants is information. A diary of the last six months, every foul day and night that Dylan and Stevie have spent shacked up together. He should never have moved out of the apartment. He waited three days for her to return, survived on a diet of gin-gernuts, black tea and sardines, then he'd packed everything he owned, and some of her favourite things that they owned together, like the car, and drove home to Sallins where the house was in darkness because of course his mother was at a yoga retreat in Cavan, but she had at least thought to leave a key under the bin.

'Ben?'

'What?'

'Will we get another?'

He gives a non-committal grunt, which Dylan understands as a yes, rising and confidently striding to the bar. Punters start to trickle in, older men on their own who take stools at the counter away from each other only to start up conversations across the bar girl's head. She puts on the radio and Ben taps his foot, unwillingly, in time to the music. Though the tendon is healed, the surrounding nerves haven't settled, the trauma lingers. A feeling of injustice consumes him, the sense that he has lost the most out of everyone. He wishes he lived in a different era, some cruel, inequitable former century where Stephanie 'Stevie' Jones would be forced to choose between arsenic, train tracks and the nunnery.

'Those old lads can put it away,' Dylan says on his return. 'Five o'clock and on the whiskey.'

'I could do with one myself,' Ben says, truthfully.

The gesture eases things between them and once Dylan has settled, the eager expression returns. He lifts his pint. 'It's good to see you.'

They clink again. The second pint is nicer, creamier, like all second pints. They get to talking about the world around them, the genocide in Gaza, the housing crisis, the fire in the old hotel in Sallins that the guards suspect was arson. They are well into the third drink before they feel able to return to the existential question of themselves. Again Ben wants information, as if reality will protect him from the worst of his imagination, but he is unable to ask for it directly. Instead he tells Dylan his own news, hoping for an exchange.

'I won't be able to do this weekly,' he says, lifting his glass.

'I guess it's a lot to ask.'

'It's not that,' Ben says. 'I'm going away. Moving to London.'

'Seriously?'

'End of the month. Caroline took me back, she said it wasn't even a strop compared to some of the things she's seen. She got me in as understudy for the Royal Court run. I might get a few nights. It seems that Walter appreciates my talent now that I'm gone.'

Dylan shakes his head in wonder. 'Brilliant,' he says.

'Is it? I can't judge anything.'

'It's what you've always wanted. What you deserve.'

'Thanks,' says Ben, while some other part of him is thinking, thanks—*thanks*? Thanks for destroying my life just because yours got hard.

'It's great news altogether,' says Dylan.

'A new start, anyway.'

'Where will you live?'

'Wales, by the look of the rents.'

'That bad?'

'Sebastian has a couch if I'm stuck.' Ben finally smiles. 'For a hundred a week.'

'Ah,' says Dylan. 'The English are born landlords.'

They laugh and when it's finished there is such obvious longing, a mournful gap between them, that they both sit for a minute, not knowing what to do.

'Another?' Ben says.

Dylan declines. 'I'd love to but,' he taps his forehead, 'I get a migraine if I push it. Or if I'm stressed, a bit tired even. The doctors say it might always be like that.'

'Living in fear.'

'Sure look, it's better than I was.'

Ben checks his phone. 'I'm going to stay for one more.'

'Fair,' says Dylan.

'You're sure?'

Dylan hovers off the stool to get the jacket he's been sitting on. 'I have to get home, I'll be killed.'

One final silence, the bleep of the card machine at the bar is piercingly loud. Ben knows it's now or never. 'How is she?' he says.

'At her wits' end.'

'Why?'

'She just wants it to be over.'

'What do you mean?' Ben says.

'She's so close now. And after all the worry.'

'What are you talking about?' Ben says.

Dylan stops fiddling with his jacket zip. 'Rachel. I told you at the start. She's about to pop.'

'Are you not—' Ben says. And very slowly, after a painful gulp of a breath, 'Are you not with Stevie?'

*   *   *

In the beautician's on Sundrive Road, Rachel's bump is so big it takes two of the petite Asian women to hoist her onto the pedicure chair, and once she's positioned on the sturdy recliner, parked up like a blimp, marooned, she closes her eyes and gives herself up to the care of others, lets them remove her shoes and socks and place her swollen feet in the basin of warm, bubbling water.

'Temperature OK?' the technician says.

Rachel nods. 'Thank you.'

The gobbling water makes her think of the only holiday she ever went on with her father, a week in Magaluf when she was ten or eleven, the first time she was abroad, his drunken laughter as he sat in a chair on the promenade and let dozens of tiny fish eat the skin off his feet.

When the woman starts with the pumice Rachel closes her eyes for a snooze, but the chiming conversations of two teenagers at the manicure station keep her in the room. She listens to the intricacies of a scandalous break-up at the Omniplex in Rathmines, where an unfortunate girl called Emily waited an hour for her boyfriend, only to see him walk out of an earlier showing of the very same movie they were meant to see *together* with his hand in the back pocket of another girl's jeans. Cue peals of laughter, threats of cancelling and bodily harm, then an abandonment of the topic entirely in favour of a debate on the benefits of gel nails.

But Rachel continues to think of Emily, the faceless girl—the girl of every generation, every bad relationship—who has been maligned, cheated on, publicly humiliated because her boyfriend chose not to see her as a person. So full of his own image there was no room for anyone else. Because how else could you hurt someone so fundamentally, except by thinking them a lesser person? Less important than oneself. It is, she thinks, an issue of hierarchy, and the lies we tell ourselves about how much we matter.

'Shellac or regular?' the technician says.

Rachel blinks as the key chain of colours is dangled somewhere south of the bump. She intended to go for permanent polish but knows her dream of a classy motherhood will soon disappear into a lengthy calendarless period of feeds, nappies and sleep deprivation, which means the likelihood of getting back to the salon to have the polish removed will happen sometime around year two. An image of a corpse with coiled, yellow talons.

'Regular.'

'Usual?' The technician holds up Gotcha Pink.

'No,' says Rachel, 'not today.' She flicks through the palette, chooses a goldy one.

'Steel Gaze,' the lady says. 'Good on pale skin.' Which is nice of her: Rachel's poor feet have the hue of trotters in these final few weeks.

As the teenagers pay and leave the salon, she hits recline on the chair, puts on the gentle massage, which is as gentle as a hammering fist along the bony protrusions of her spine. She settles instead for a heated seat, closes her eyes once more, unused to this feeling of calm inside her, all the more astonishing because she brought it about herself. The thing she was most afraid of has saved her. Her whole troublesome past erased. There is a madness in that which is best not to think about, too close to an epiphany, and Rachel doesn't go in for all that. It is enough to say she saved her family by being brave. Firstly by admitting her secret shame, but latterly, and most importantly, by allowing her husband to walk.

The night of the birthday party seems almost funny to her now, a scene from one of Ben's plays, which she can recall with the enthusiasm of someone who enjoyed the show. It *was* kind of enjoyable, in a strange way, the unburdening, like an emetic for the soul. After she confessed, she wondered why she had bothered to carry it for so long. She used to think there was something noble in it, shielding her husband from the worst parts of herself, but really it was fear, the most destructive of emotions, the great justifier of so many awful things.

The three stooges sat on the couch that night as she unjustified herself, the men rendered silent by the news, Ben just staring in disbelief at a spot on the wall behind her, Dylan with his head in his hands. Then Stevie, out of nowhere, started laughing, sharp, convulsing folds that made her bend forward and hold her stomach. In the otherwise solemn atmosphere it was like watching someone lose their mind. 'Alright, alright,'

Ben eventually found his voice. 'We get it,' he said bitterly. 'It's hilarious. That's how little you care about us. Me cheating on you doesn't matter at all.' This shut her up, until Dylan said, 'I really don't believe it,' and she was gone again. When Rachel had enough of the spectacle she told her to be quiet, Leah was asleep upstairs. The mention of her daughter's name, the thought of any child perhaps, restored the gravity of the situation. Stevie sat up straight. 'I can't believe it,' Dylan said again, and this time no one laughed. Ben, meanwhile, had evidently been preparing his defence (or had it ready to go for years) because in response to Dylan's bafflement he unleashed, in meticulous order, the reasonings, allowances, mitigations, vindications of the night in question, which wasn't even a night in a traditional temporal sense, just a few moments stitched together by an inebriated imp. Then the fight between the men began and Rachel and Stevie faded into insignificance, ceding their own betrayals to the alpha-betrayal of a friendship almost forty years in the making. It was venomous, wounding, deeply riveting stuff. A fusillade of cool bands and school plays and teenage girlfriends. Accusations of misery, parsimony, father envy, the last of which caused Ben to throw back his head and howl. That night there was so much blame. Everyone was the cause of everyone else's mistakes, until, finally, Rachel called time on the denunciations, kicking Ben and Stevie out to continue the war back on their own turf. No one walked them out, no one saw them off, a mistake as it happened, because Ben used the opportunity to slam the front door with all of his gangly might. Dylan cursed, rose from the couch and shot out of the room, he went after his friend with such a palpable thirst for violence that Rachel thought he might kill him. She caught up with them in the driveway, ordered her husband back into the house. The last she saw of the other two before she shut the door was short little Stevie attempting to pull Ben further up the street in the hostile lamplight, an outlandish struggle that seemed to represent their collective battle to act as normal people in normal relationships all these many years.

'Swap foot,' the technician says.

Rachel obeys, then checks her phone to see if there's a message from her mother, who has brought Leah to the park to watch the cyclists in the velodrome. Nothing but a text from Dylan, asking her to bring him home a bacon sandwich from the café with the hatch. Only a few pints, he swore in drunken disclosure as he was getting into bed last night, but he did not come home till after closing and though the spare bedroom was empty when she checked it this morning, the patchy attempt at making the bed and the big sooty footprint on the cream rug is classic Ben. So they have made up, she thinks, these men who are able to forgive each other while keeping for their women a hot kernel of rage deep within whose embers will diminish over time but never fully extinguish.

That much was apparent the morning after the big reveal, when Rachel sent her daughter to the neighbours and waited impatiently in the kitchen for her husband to show his face. At five to eleven on the cuckoo clock, after much banging upstairs, he came into the room with his kitbag jammed beyond the point of closing. A solitary shirtsleeve hung over the edge of the bag and the top of his electric toothbrush protruded from the pocket. In that instant she regretted her confession, all the stultifying fear came clouding in and her impulse was to bargain, to plead with him to stay. But the way he casually dropped his bag on the ground, stared at her with eyes of recalcitrant blue, as if to say, *get down on your knees and beg me,* strengthened her resolve.

'You're off?' she said, returning to her coffee. He continued to glower at her. After a few sips she looked up again. The insolence remained, though it had frozen somewhat, a glacial loveliness as the cogs began to turn. When he finally spoke his voice was soft and forlorn. 'Is that all you have to say to me?' he asked. Here she was careful. She had stayed awake for most of the night thinking of how this would go, and she told him, honestly, that she felt it was best if he moved out, he needed to see what life was like without her. 'Scratch the itch,' she said, because it seemed fittingly unclean. 'And please, Dylan, don't come back if you've any doubt.' He looked like he might crumple down on top of his possessions but he soon gathered himself, adopting nonchalance as he picked up his bag, took a few steps towards the door, before reality landed and he spun around. 'You won't keep me from Leah,' he said. 'Or the baby.' She managed not to show how much this hurt her until he was gone, the lonely purr of his car in the driveway, until it was gone too, at which point she put her head on the kitchen table and cried wholeheartedly for all they had lost.

'Pressure OK?' the technician says.

The massage part of the pedicure is usually her favourite but today she finds it too intimate. Withdrawing her foot she says, 'Can we just get on to the polish?' A sense of urgency has taken hold of her, as if she's left Leah alone somewhere. She calls her mother who doesn't answer.

Noreen picks up the second time but seems distracted, a moaning wind between them on the line.

'Mam, is everything OK? I won't be long now.'

'We're fine.'

'Where are you?'

'Still at the park.'

In the background Rachel can hear her daughter talking to someone about the stabilisers on her bike.

'Is that Leah?' she says.

Her mother says nothing.

'Mam?'

'Yes, all OK. We've bumped into someone on our travels.'

'Who?'

'Stevie. Say hello, Stevie.'

There is a pause, before the low voice in the background.

'What?' Rachel says. 'Why is Stevie there?'

'I told you,' her mother says. 'We just met her in the park.'

Rachel feels as if she's on camera. Helplessly she looks around the salon, to the occupied workers and clients on their phones, down at the technician assiduously applying the polish.

'Mam,' she says. 'I'll meet you and Leah at the café across the road. Alone. OK?'

'There's no rush.'

As she hangs up Rachel has a mad vision of Stevie kidnapping her daughter, bundling her into a car packed with enormous stuffed animals.

'Nearly done,' the technician says. 'You like the colour?'

Rachel does not. Should have gone for her usual. 'Yes,' she says. 'It's lovely.'

'When are you due?'

'Literally any day.'

'Not here,' the lady says. 'Not in the chair!'

The laughter is grounding. Rachel reminds herself that life is good, things have worked out in her favour. She has won. Giving the woman a large tip, she flip-flops out of the salon on a high.

At the café her mother and Leah are standing near the take-away hatch. Rachel greets them without mentioning the phone call. They go in for a treat while they wait for Dylan's sandwich. Two iced buns, a brownie for Leah, the mucky sort of cake she likes. Rachel watches her stick her fingers into the gloop, the chocolate moustache a given, thinks what a marvel she is, this child, whose happiness Rachel will do her best, always, to ensure.

'Messer,' Noreen says.

Leah giggles, bangs the table, crumbs go flying.

'Any more of that and granny will have to eat it.'

They engage in a mock theft that goes on for some time. When they're finished and Leah is back playing with the brownie, her mother says, 'Stevie wanted me to pass on her regards to you and the baby.'

Rachel had decided not to ask. Disappointing that her mother didn't take the hint. 'Did she now,' she says.

'Yes.'

'What was she doing there?' Rachel says.

'Running, I think.'

Rachel knows straight away, with genetic certainty, that her mother is lying. 'But it's miles from where she lives.'

'Is it?'

'You know it is. Was she on her own?'

'Yes.'

'Then it makes no sense.' Rachel looks at her mother. 'Just tell me.'

'She rang me last week, out of the blue. Wanted to meet you, asked for my help.'

'How did she have your number? Did you *give* her your number?'

'There's this mysterious ancient tome called the phone book.'

'Hilarious. What did she want?'

'She didn't think you'd take a call from her, and she didn't want to show up at the house.'

'She was right,' Rachel says. 'I'm over it. But that's it, we're done. It's one of the perks of this mess. I never have to see her again.'

'Is that realistic?'

'Why not? Herself and Ben are finished.'

'OK,' Noreen says. 'But is it fair?'

'Since when did you mind about fair? I don't remember anything being fair when I was growing up. Just you shouting your heads off at each other all the time.'

'Careful,' her mother says.

'What? It's true.'

Leah's attention shifts in her direction. Rachel knows she should stop, but her mother's collusion with the enemy has opened some neglected chamber of her heart. 'You took your troubles out on us,' she says.

As Noreen turns her gaze on her granddaughter, there is a moment that stretches incomprehensibly over generations, the three of them caught in a chain of looking, yearning, a show of need, Rachel thinks, the need to know how things go wrong.

Her mother refocuses with a sigh. 'Yes,' she says. 'I did.'

It is a satisfying statement, without qualification or excuse. Rachel feels her defences give way.

'Which is why,' her mother says, 'you should try and sort things with Stevie as best you can. Hear her out. Because I can tell you one thing, Rachel—the ghosts don't stay in the box for long.'

'What ghosts?' Leah says fearfully, and the women laugh and tell her to finish her brownie, the adults are talking nonsense, everything is fine.

*   *   *

It was like a jigsaw where the correct shapes were cut to fit the mould, appearing as if they would slot into position, until she went to put them together and it became clear the dimensions were imperceptibly off. Down to a fine wooden shaving, the breadth of a hair. In the end the only thing to do was to walk away, save whatever was left of herself. So that's what Stevie did, she blew up the life that blew up her life, and now she just has to keep going.

In the travel agency in Stephen's Green shopping centre she waits on a bench for a desk to become available, inhaling the synthetic sweetness of the ice cream concession across the way. Another customer joins her, asks about the wait. She tells him half an hour, ignores his disbelieving face. There is only one agent working, a sign of the times. Stevie could easily have booked online, but coming here is an attempt at legitimacy, for the trip, or herself, she'll take whatever she can get.

All the decor in the room—furniture, walls, even the ceiling—is yellow or blue, a seascape transported to a rainy July afternoon in Dublin's city centre. A couple with two small children are currently at the desk, sitting on squat stools, listening attentively to the agent. Stevie drums her fingers against the shiny brochure she was given on arrival, trying not to stare. The way the father holds his daughter on his knee speaks painfully of comfort and care, things Stevie is no longer permitted, she has chosen to leave that life behind. Single for the first time as an adult, the terrific, shattering freedom in that.

The man beside her is an impatient type who believes he can control the speed of the queue with his intermittent huffing. At the third puff she puts in her headphones, hits the first playlist she can find, the Chill list, which starts with the Flaming Lips album Dylan loves, the one he put on the Friday night he turned up on her doorstep with his worn old kitbag. After ten days in a hotel, he felt ready to begin his new life. The shock of him outside her apartment block, his face tilted downward except for the quick, roving eyes, like a dog doing its business in public, nothing to be ashamed of really, and yet. They sat up drinking till half past three because both of them knew—perhaps had always known—that now there was nothing stopping them, it all seemed far too real.

Of course they got into bed at some point, they fumbled about in the shadows, a deep exhaustion creeping over her at the fraternal chumminess she was desperately, quite literally, trying to override. Stevie was all bells and whistles and reverse positions in those solidly dark winter hours, before the relieving light of daybreak made it acceptable to lie down in defeat. Except she could not sleep with him in the bed beside her. As the very material figure of him breathed softly a few inches away, she couldn't shut down her mind. On the inside of her eyelids were a thousand flashed-up images of lives derailed, the thoughts accumulating with a flickering speed that caused the veins in her neck to throb. She wondered what Dylan had been thinking before he fell asleep, if he had felt it too, the ghastly absence of desire, the way their movements had the jerking quality of unoiled parts. Where was the fluid rush of their previous encounters? She felt cheated, parched, as if she had been sucked dry. He was no longer the man who had pulled her hair in a bathroom cubicle, just a stranger on a busy street who bore a vague resemblance.

With only the cool green digits of the radio alarm clock for company, a terrible loneliness entered her. She thought to get up and take a tablet, but she had flushed them months before, confident she no longer needed them. Afraid of disturbing Dylan, she lay rigid in the bed. No idea what type of sleeper he was, just the irrational notion he would be angry if she woke him—an agitated man far from home. She stayed there for over an hour, listening to his breath. When the clock neared eight she got up, crossed the hall to the icy spare that still smelled unmistakably of Ben.

Later that day she woke to find Dylan in the living room with three types of pastries and a latte waiting for her. She said a shy good morning, sat down at the table even as she could see he was lowering his legs to accommodate her on the couch. Though she hadn't drunk lattes since college, she downed the concoction in a few milky swallows, heard someone who sounded like her distant cousin from the nineteenth century offer profuse gratitude for his kindness. Then she stuffed a croissant into her mouth so she wouldn't be able to speak. While she chewed, Dylan took up the conversation, reading out the headlines of the sports supplement he had grasped over his knees in a way that seemed oddly prim and feminine, utterly unlike the man she thought she knew. Even his voice was different: strained, countrified. As he gave the highlights of a GAA match, he sounded more like his father than himself. She continued to chew, wondering how the tepid coffee had made her feel so hot inside, an intense, fizzy sensation rolling up her body. 'The heat is on!' she said, realising. 'It's been on all night. The place has never been so warm.' Dylan didn't seem to think it unusually hot and they exchanged more words about winter and insulation and temperatures generally and whether gas boilers were more efficient than air-to-water pumps. When she couldn't bear another word, she took up her phone. She had slept late, it was one o'clock. She was estimating how long it would be before she could plausibly sleep again when Dylan said he was going for a shower. He got up sluggishly, came over to where she was sitting, kissed her softly on the lips, then went off about his business as if they had always lived together in their roasting desert apartment of creamy beverages and laminated treats.

So it continued for weeks. Abysmal sex, unbearable goodwill, horrific intimacy. There was nothing she could do. Whoever shot and killed the fox had to keep the fur—even if they were now appalled by its presence. Stevie did her best to move past this. She suppressed her misgivings, returned his affection, tried to tap into the depth of feeling, regard and mutual understanding that had defined their friendship for years. For a while it grew easier, they got into a routine. She felt herself get used to the role she was playing, which was not so very different from her pretence with Ben in those months before they broke up. She had hated the deception. It had turned her into a person who needed to be constantly moving or asleep. A person afraid of her own damn mind, of her spirit, which she had never fully known or believed in yet had somehow managed to destroy. Now she found herself back in the vortex, except this time it was worse. At least Ben had suspected her. Dylan seemed maddeningly oblivious; he was so lost in the fantasy of what they could be, he was unable to see what they were.

Things eventually came to a head in the most awful manner. Even now, several months later, she finds the specifics hard to think about. So public and shocking, as if she stunned him with a cattle prod halfway down Grafton Street. His pale face, the awful feeling he was going to cry—until he opened his mouth and let her have it. People slowed down to watch them, drawn into their sorry world the way birds are drawn to power lines. Afterwards, when it was over and she was walking home alone, she wondered if anyone had recognised him, this one-time famous rugby star reduced to a street brawler in a free show. And she understood, finally, that the reason she and Dylan hadn't gotten together when they were young was not because a child nearly died on a beach, or because she went to Australia, or that Ben followed her there, it was, quite simply, never meant to be. Or it was meant to be in a different life, one that had nothing to do with reality. A bleak thought, that a person needed more than one lifetime to truly grow up. Her life, all their lives, so significant and small.

'Ready for you,' the agent calls out.

Stevie is alone on the bench, the huffer gone, worn out by his own nonsense. He reminded her in part of Ben, without the sardonic self-awareness. Waiting for the agent to prepare a clipboard and forms, it occurs to her that she will never get to see what older Ben is like. No, she will only catch him in glimpses, in third-hand gossip, in the media if he eventually makes it, which she thinks on the whole he has the tenacity and talent to do. A part of her really misses him. For so long her emotions flowed through him, through his big personality and even bigger ambitions, and now that he's gone, she has to figure out feeling for herself.

And what of Dylan—Dylan Turner? Very little to say, no desire to think of him, as if he has been purged from her, nothing remains but a lingering aftertaste of regrettable excess. A sad story whose pinnacle was, maybe, right at the beginning, at the moment of connection, of confession, sitting beside each other in the dark.

'Ignore the section at the end.' The girl, who looks barely out of school, hands her the clipboard. 'That's for us.'

Stevie fills in her information, returns the form.

'You missed your date of birth.'

Writing it down, Stevie senses the young woman is trying to figure her out.

'It's a solo trip?' she says.

'Yes.'

'Cool. How long?'

'I don't really know. But at least six months.'

She has budgeted for up to a year. Now that rent in the city is more than her mortgage repayments, the apartment is no longer a burden. Another improvement: she did not, in the lonely, remorseful weeks after Dylan left, succumb to her yearning for benzodiazepine. She did what most people do—she waited. Turns out Stevie wasn't anxious, she did not have anxiety; she was simply in the wrong life, and unable for a time to recognise this. Quite a protracted time, to be fair, stretching into decades, but today she feels strongly that there is no such thing as wasted time, just being alive, and trying, and trying again. If that doesn't work, there is always, as the GP advised her—when yes, yes, OK, she went looking for more pills—the less addictive, socially respectable option of antidepressants.

'So where exactly?' the girl asks.

'South America, and flying as little as possible.'

'It's winter there,' the girl says.

'I know,' says Stevie. 'I just fancy it.' An idea of herself skiing across the snowy plains of Argentina. Travelling by bus, boat or bike.

'OK—this changes everything!'

Watching the girl close a dozen windows on the computer, all the possible tomorrows vanishing with quick clicks, Stevie regrets that it's taken her this long to travel. She used to say it was the apartment that kept her in Dublin, but her parents could have helped her if she asked them. The truth is she stayed because Ben wanted to stay in case the role of his dreams fell out of the sky into their laps. The waiting for it to happen became their life, which goes some way to explaining why it failed in the end to feel right, why walking away looked more like love than remaining. As the unhappiness she's lived through, that she has put others through, threatens to land, she focuses on the wall of fake sky behind the girl's head.

'I know the route already,' Stevie says.

The girl interrupts her every so often with a suggestion or addendum, but when it becomes clear how much effort has gone into the planning, which is to say, how much headspace it was necessary to fill with those thick doorstops of travel guides, she acquiesces and starts to make notes. They go through various flight options, before agreeing on an open-ended ticket to Rio de Janeiro via Orlando.

'Want to stop at Disney World first?' the girl says.

'Not a chance.'

'I guess it's more of a family thing.'

'Yes,' says Stevie. 'For sure.' There is a passing beat of terror so intense that once it's over she finds she can easily convince herself it didn't happen.

The girl takes a while to book the various hostels, campsites and the odd hotel Stevie's treating herself to on days she imagines she'll need it: arrivals, her birthday, Christmas. It's nearing six by the time she leaves the agency, buoyed up by the dubious sort of self-esteem that comes from spending nearly a third of her salary in one go.

Town has the pumped-up quality of Thursday evening, the rain now cleared, a lively bent to the groups of young workers, harried shoppers and inveterate buskers, the crowd of onlookers jostling for space in a cramped circle around a man on a unicycle. Crossing the tram lines over to Stephen's Green, she finds a quiet stretch by the pavilion where the evening sun splits the pond on a diagonal. She takes the solitary end of an occupied bench, watches the ducks vie with each other for the dappled light. The couple on the bench get up shortly afterwards, the girl slipping daintily off her boyfriend's legs. Stevie feels bad when they walk off, as if she has intruded, though it is equally possible, from the way they're focusing on each other instead of the path, that they didn't notice her at all. She feels suddenly tired, afraid of her age, the digits she wrote down so flippantly for the travel agent that now feel frighteningly close to forty, because they are. Is this her midlife crisis, her red convertible? Enter doubt, not as a manageable abstract, but in the tangible form of bunk beds, overnight bus trips and the drunken antics of gap year students. Sincerely, between herself and the ducks, she doesn't know if she will last the pace. If she will learn, finally, thousands of miles from home, the right way to inhabit her life. Taking out her phone to go through the itinerary once more, she spots an unread message, opens it and laughs so loudly a couple of nearby pigeons are scared into juddering flight.

From Rachel:

Heard you're off to see the world, good luck with that. It's full on here at the moment—a boy, John!—but maybe when you're back, if you do come back, we could have a chat. PS stop stalking my mother

It is so very Rachel, meticulous, funny and brusque, that Stevie feels as if the woman has sat down beside her. She hesitates before replying, wonders if she should start with an apology for all that's gone on, but in the end she settles for the truth.

Rachel, she types, *I would love that.*

*   *   *

Returning from lunch Dylan lets his colleagues go ahead of him into the brown building whose upper-floor windows have been open since morning, the dark frames fanned over the street. He leans against the warm frontage, facing away from the sun to call Rachel, leaves a short message to confirm he'll be home after work. Though he has been back in the house for months, her anxiety over his movements has yet to ease. The arrival of the baby actually made the situation worse for a while, the unexpected depression she experienced after giving birth, which was no doubt linked to his disgraceful behaviour during her pregnancy. That they are through the worst of it now, the bond between mother and son late but fervent, doesn't lessen the guilt. He knows his betrayal has taken something from his family that can never be recovered, he has chipped away at the foundation of a monumental structure and even if everything remains upright for the rest of their lives, there will always be fear in the mortar. When he thinks too much about this, the fear turns to dread—thoughts of his daughter becoming a teenager, asking questions, finding things out.

Through the rotating door into reception, Dylan passes large promotional posters featuring images of smiling people off on their holidays with shiny new passports. Waiting for the lift, he glances left into the hall at the queue of exasperated faces and says a silent thank you for his back office job.

On the second floor, a colleague looks up from his computer.

'Warm out there,' Dylan says.

'September summer. I'm clocking off soon, like half the office.'

Dylan considers the sparsely populated desks. 'Sounds like a plan,' he says, though he hasn't yet figured out the intricacies of flexitime.

Back at his desk he doesn't like the thought of his work piling up, still at heart the athlete who prefers to tackle things straight on. Secretly he is giving the job everything he has in the hope they'll move him into sports after a year.

Logging on, he returns to the spreadsheet he was compiling before lunch. His eyes drift through the column lines. Left leg starts to twitch. Five o'clock suddenly seems far away. His colleague's restlessness has infected him; the vacant chairs around the office are an affront. Even the open windows, which offered breezy relief this morning, now seem linked to escape, voices of freedom rising from the street below.

Beside his computer there's a photo Rachel framed for him on his first day: a handsome family who shows no sign of the torment of the last few years. He never thought he would see himself like this again—healthy, almost wholesome, father to two happy children. Dylan knows he's lucky. Lately he has forgotten the statistics, like a soldier blanking out the war, but millions of people around the world are still afflicted, and some of them may never recover. Earlier in the week he watched an online video of a famous singer with symptoms that sounded just like his own in the bad days and he realised, an obvious thing really, that nobody, no matter who they are in life, gets to escape from pain.

Looking at John's alert little face, he smiles. The love landed the moment he held him, as if the child had always existed. Throughout Rachel's depression Dylan did the grunt work and night shifts, managing to keep it up through the start of the new job, in a way that seems superhuman compared to what he was capable of a year ago. Already he has plans for John's rugby career, he has mapped it all, his three-month-old winger for Ireland who will achieve the things his father couldn't. With these fantasies comes a belated appreciation of his own father, and sorrow for the many irretrievable times Dylan refused Sean's advice down through the years, too dimly stubborn to see it for what it was, not an attempt to control him, but to love.

He gives up on the spreadsheet, clicks into his email, one from a woman in front office marked urgent, asking him to rush through an application for a twenty-year-old from Waterford who is *wailing the place down* in the hall below because she forgot to check her passport before a backpacking trip with friends. He thinks immediately of Stevie, wonders where in the world she might be. Before leaving she sent a text informing him of her plans, to which he did not reply. He was angry at her. He is still angry. He resents that she underestimated him after their years of knowing each other. She couldn't just speak her mind and tell him how she felt. It showed a profound disrespect towards him, towards herself, that she was willing to pretend, to live like a hostage in her own home, expecting him to wield the gun.

On another, undoubtedly shallower level, he feels as if he was used. Made to look a fool, to his family and friends, to the rugby crew who know who he is and care about such things. Risking his marriage for a woman who didn't want him. And for what? After the hurt and recrimination and shame, this is the question he's left with, the question at the end of all affairs.

To be clear, he tells her now, which is to say, he imagines telling her: he was not going to propose.

That final afternoon they spent together, after the retrospectively uneasy pints in Neary's and the aimless walk down Clarendon Street, *she* was the one to turn onto the famous lane of jewellery shops, though it was in the wrong direction for their bikes. *She* was the one agog at the glistening windows of jewels white, blue and green. *She* was the one to smile up at him, an image imprinted in his memory because of the grave expressions that followed. He was just taking her lead, had yet to process what the sparkling displays signified—when it suddenly hit him. He didn't want to hurt her feelings so he gave one small, deplorable smile that she took as encouragement, or entreaty. And then it all came tumbling out of her in one guilty burst, the fake nice life they had been living, the extent of how wrong it felt. For her.

What he wishes to have said in return—that of course he felt the physical awkwardness too, the weak, wavering desire, the irreparable gap between youth and adulthood, but he was giving it a red hot go because that is what they committed to—is several registers away from the words that came out of his mouth, the headlines of which he recalls with painful clarity as *wrong*, *ruined* and, most regrettably of all, *prick tease*.

He was not going to propose, he reassures himself now, finishing off the last of his water, crushing the cup into a ball. He had no intention of it. For one thing, he was still in his head, and in practice, married to Rachel. Stevie wasn't the only one capable of delusion. All four of them had at one time or another thought themselves free to try on different lives as if they were entitled to more than an ordinary share of happiness, as easy as picking up another coat in a cloakroom.

After submitting the backpacker's application, he closes the folders on his computer to the department's default backdrop, a map of the world overlaid with a hologram of the Irish passport, its stately harp. By the time Stevie comes back from her travels, they will hopefully all have moved on. Clear to him at last that their long friendship is over, but if that is the sole casualty of this almost massacre, he would do well to accept it. With only a mild sense of inequity, he thinks of his plans to see Ben at the end of the month, the fringe festival in Hackney he has agreed to go to in a trade-off for a Sunday match. Although his mother is coming to help Rachel with the kids, Dylan will be sure to ring home regularly. Right now he can't imagine being away from them for one weekend, let alone his whole life.

Changing into trainers and retrieving his helmet from under the desk, he packs his bag, gliding by two women still busy at work.

Quick goodbye to his mate, then he continues cheerfully across the floor to the lobby, declines the offer of a lift about to close, rounds the corner to the blindingly bright stairwell, takes the steps a few at a time, easily first down to the ground to tip a hand to the security guard and bounce out the door.

At the bike stands there is a black cat curled up in the sunshine in the basket of a woman's cruiser. Before he unlocks his new racer, he takes a picture for Leah, sends the image to Rachel, and anticipating their reactions, forgets about the helmet in his bag.

On Mount Street, with minimal traffic, he scoots across the road, pedals quickly down to the canal whose still water looks lifeless in the heat. Here the weekend mayhem reveals itself in long lines of cars. A tour bus towers awkwardly over the deadlock, the effortful hiss of its break releasing to crawl another few inches. He joins a disordered clump of cyclists at the junction, one of whom is a man in his fifties who nods shyly at him in recognition, causing Dylan to smile. It hasn't happened in a while. As the old wound of legacy gives an itch, he marvels at how little it matters now, ridiculous in a way, the worry he used to have over what future unknown generations would make of his successes and failures. He can't remember why he cared so much. Maybe it was just the human condition, to spend the first half of your life trying to be someone and the second realising you always were. His legacy is his children, they are what will remain of him when he's gone. If the last year has taught him anything it is the meaning of enough. To be a good father, husband, to support his family in whatever ways he can for the short time he has here on earth, this is enough. Stepping outside his life has allowed him to see its fragility.

The lights finally change and the driver at the front blows his horn at a cyclist blocking his way, almost knocking the man off his bike. Dylan capitalises on the dispute to make an illegal right turn onto the cycle lane along the canal. A chorus of beeping ensues. He doesn't look around, he does not acknowledge his error or the angry people he leaves in his wake, just puts the head down, his feet hard on the pedals and lets his mind blank with nothing but speed, the wonderful feel of it over the hot, splitting tarmac as he defiantly makes his way home.

Acknowledgements

Thank you to Laura Macaulay and Juliet Garcia for the hugely insightful edits that helped to shape the book. To the team at Pushkin, and to Jo Walker for her gorgeous cover. Thanks as always to Sallyanne Sweeney. To the Arts Council of Ireland for their vital support. To the staff and students at Dublin City University, where I had a wonderful year as writer-in-residence: thank you for the generous welcome and the time afforded me to write. A special thanks to Marcella Bannon and Dr Darran McCann. To Gabriel Fulcher for the rugby notes. To Danny Erskine at The Abbey for answering my questions. To Nicole Matthews and Shaun McHugh for the cover chats. Thanks also to Aingeala Flannery, Kathy Givens, Barry John Kinsella, Lisa Madsen, Henrietta McKervey, Sean Reilly and Mikey Stafford. To Joseph O'Connor for his support of emerging writers, what a legend. Sheila Purdy, thank you so much for everything.